MAX'S body seized up. He tried to swim, but his arms were locked.

A wave hit him full in the face. As he coughed out seawater, his arms began to thrash wildly.

Don't fight it. Left to its own devices, a human body floats. Especially a human body with a life vest.

Fact.

Panic is one of the main causes of death in the water.

Fact.

Exposure is the loss of body heat, which can kill a person who stays in cold water too long.

Fact.

Max lifted his head. He took a couple of gasping breaths. A wave hit him on the exhalation, but he did not panic. He allowed it to wash over him.

ALSO BY PETER LERANGIS

MAX TILT: FIRE THE DEPTHS

MAX TILT: 80 DAYS OR DIE

THE SEVEN WONDERS SERIES

THE LOST GIRLS TRILOGY

THE DRAMA CLUB SERIES

THE SPY X SERIES

THE ABRACADABRA SERIES

THE ANTARCTICA SERIES

THE WATCHERS SERIES

39 CLUES: THE SWORD THIEF

39 CLUES: THE VIPER'S NEST

39 CLUES: VESPERS RISING
(WITH RICK RIORDAN, GORDAN KORMAN, AND JUDE WATSON)

39 CLUES: CAHILLS VS. VESPERS: THE DEAD OF NIGHT

HARPER
An Imprint of HarperCollins*Publishers*

Max Tilt: Enter the Core
 For information address HarperCollins Children's Books, a division of HarperCollins Publishers, 195 Broadway, New York, NY 10007.
www.harpercollinschildrens.com

Library of Congress Control Number: 2018964878
ISBN 978-0-06-244107-2

Typography by Andrea Vandergrift
19 20 21 22 23 PC/BRR 10 9 8 7 6 5 4 3 2 1
❖
First paperback edition, 2019

To the wonderful librarians and booksellers throughout the U.S. and the world, for all they do to get good stories into the hands of kids: not only reading and recommending books, but hosting authors in stores and libraries, organizing conferences and book festivals, bringing us into schools, and promoting literature as the portal to a future of bright, compassionate thinkers and leaders.

PROLOGUE

BITSY Bentham hadn't planned on biting a bus driver.

The thing was, thievery made her nervous. There was so much to think about. Choosing a fake name, for instance, should have been devilishly easy. But the ones that came to mind sounded just wrong—*Pinky LaRue, Becky Pancake, Ann Anson.* She was distracted by her backpack, which smelled like the farts of a sick old dog. The five vials inside were *sealed*, so they should have been odorless. Worse still, the bus hadn't yet left the parking lot in Savile, Ohio, and all she had to eat was a stale scone and a cup of lukewarm tea. So her hands were full when a gray-uniformed arm reached for her pack and a voice in the aisle said, "Before we start, young lady, why don't I put this heavy thing on the overhead rack for you!"

Under the circumstances, teeth were her only option.

"Heeempf!" For a big walrus of a man, the driver had an oddly dainty scream. As he yanked his arm away, Bitsy's mouth was left with the taste of stale coffee, laundry detergent, and old polyester.

"So sorry," she managed to say. "You scared me. Erm . . . I'd like to keep the backpack on the seat if it's all the same. I'm . . . very attached." She flashed her sweetest, most embarrassed smile.

"Right . . . no problem . . . uh, ticket, please?" The man took a deep breath, straightening himself out as Bitsy reached into her pocket. "So I'm guessing you're from Australia?"

Whatever sympathy she felt for him vanished in a puff. What was it about Americans, always trying to guess at accents, always wanting to invade a person's privacy? Bitsy stopped herself from snapping the obvious answer—*No, English, you fool!* But secrecy was paramount.

With a smile, she held out her ticket and replied in her best New England accent, "I'm a stoo-dent at Haaaaahvard."

The attempt was terrible. Her statement was a lie, and it sounded like a lie. This was another thing Bitsy would have to work on, her acting.

Fortunately it didn't seem to matter. The man chuckled and nodded. "Well, stay right on. It's a long trip." He rubbed his arm where she'd bitten him. "What do you study there . . . at Harvard? Cannibalism? Heh heh heh."

Bitsy gritted her teeth. "Grrrr."

The driver flinched, then smiled weakly and waddled to his seat.

At long last the bus began to pull out. Bitsy looked over the parking lot. Mr. Tilt's car was long gone. By now he'd be trawling the streets in a confused tizzy over "losing" Bitsy. He'd feel like it was his fault. Soon he'd return to the house. It wouldn't be long before he, or his wife, or their son, Max, or their niece Alex would run upstairs to check the safe.

It gave her heart a tug to think of their faces when they realized the vials were gone. They had traveled the world to find these ingredients, which together made the greatest healing power the world had ever known. They had trusted her.

But business was business. An opportunity like this had to be exploited properly. A world of customers was waiting, and someone had to serve them. Something this important could not be left in the hands of a goofy American kid and his eccentric Canadian cousin.

Bitsy felt for the two phones in her pocket. She'd shut

hers off, of course. No one would be able to track her on that, and soon she would destroy it.

The other was a disposable one, a so-called *burner.* How lovely that the bus station was located in a part of town where these things were sold. A gloomy little gadget shop where no questions were asked and money was pushed under bulletproof glass.

As the bus turned onto the highway, she set her breakfast on the tray table. The grubby little phone could still access the local NPR station's website on its browser. She was dying to hear this morning's news report again, which would be posted by now.

News about Papa.

She had overheard the report live, on the Tilts' radio station that morning, before the escape. But what fun it would be to hear it clearly.

Inserting her earbuds, she moved the indicator toward the end of the broadcast: "And in one last breaking item this morning . . . some news about the disgraced American industrialist Spencer Niemand, last seen trying to steal a treasure from two young Ohio descendants of Jules Verne . . ."

As she listened intently, Bitsy couldn't help grinning.

No, not Bitsy anymore. Elizabeth. Why bother with

fake names, when you have a perfectly good one that nobody knows? From here on, she would use the name she'd been born with. She would be *Elizabeth Niemand.*

Papa would be happy. She hadn't seen him in such a long time.

"MAX, *are you all right? Talk to me!"*

For Max Tilt, nearly being hit by a car was a rotten way to start the day. Especially a car being driven by his dad. Who was now pushing his way out the door, looking very upset.

Dad was the kind of guy who wouldn't even run over a grasshopper if he could help it, let alone his own son. So Max knew it wasn't Dad's fault. Which meant it must have been Max's. And that was upsetting, because he couldn't remember the last few minutes.

One moment Max was in his living room, the next he was here—in the road outside his house, spitting gravel. These things sometimes happened, and Max wasn't always sure how. Right now he was only sure of three things: (1) The left side of his face stung. (2) He smelled burning rubber from the tires, which were only a few inches away. (3) He also smelled dark chocolate, but that was because Max always smelled dark chocolate when he was relieved.

Dad knelt beside him, cradling a strong hand around the back of Max's neck. Max couldn't help noticing how distorted his father's face looked, grim and tight like somebody was pulling the skin from behind. This was scary, because it was exactly the same expression he'd had when Max's mom was diagnosed with cancer. So Max asked the first question that popped into his mind. "Is Mom OK?"

Dad cocked his head. "Mom? Yes, she's fine, but—"

"The serum worked, right?" Max pressed. "It wasn't some crazy dream?"

"Yes. I mean no. No dream!" Dad sputtered. "But *you*—are *you* hurt? You ran right in front of me, Max! What happened?"

It was a good question. Little fragments of memories slipped into Max's brain, like knives ripping through a tent to reveal a thunderstorm. "The safe . . ." he said. "She broke into it and took everything. Bitsy. She stole the vials."

"Oh, Max . . ." His dad held him close to his chest, but Max pulled away.

"Then she went shopping with you, and you let her disappear," Max went on, struggling to his feet. The aroma of chocolate was fading now, giving way to the smell of cat pee, which meant anger.

Four people were heading toward him. His cousin Alex was fastest, her thick curly hair flopping in the wind. Behind her was Max's best friend, Smriti, from across the street, her face like a giant exclamation point. Third was Max's mom. And last was his robotics partner, Evelyn Lopez, who still needed a cane to walk.

Alex got to him first, taking him by the shoulder. "Dude, is this a thing with you—running into the street when you get upset? You have to control this."

Control.

Max shook loose and looked away. He didn't want to meet her eyes. He knew this wasn't about him running into the street. This was about *control*—about having it and then losing it.

He and Alex had just lost it, big time.

What good was it to have traveled all over the world and risked your lives, to have found ingredients for the most miraculous serum in the world, something that would help every single human being—when you let someone steal it from under your noses? *Poof*—gone!

Running to the passenger door of his dad's car, Max

yanked it open. "Why are we standing here? I'm fine. Come on!"

"Where are we supposed to go?" asked his mom, whose slower walking pace had finally caught her up to Alex and Smriti.

"To get Bitsy, duh!" Max blurted.

"Bitsy's been gone a while, Max," Smriti pointed out. "She could be anywhere."

"We'll go to the airport!" Max said. "We'll go to the train station! The . . . the news media!"

Alex came eye to eye with him. "OK, I get it. You know me. I want to jump on this too. But face facts, Max, she's too smart to do anything obvious. And going to the news media means exposing our discovery. So I'm accessing my inner Max here. I'm thinking we need a strategy. The only way we'll get her is to outthink her. What do you always tell me when we're faced with a really complicated problem?"

Max's heart was banging away. He forced himself to look into Alex's big green eyes. "Break it down," he murmured. "Into parts."

"We know she's gone," Alex said. "We also know she's sneaky. She told your dad she was the daughter of Spencer Niemand. This does not surprise me. I think she has his evil-mastermind genes."

Max thought back to their confrontation with Gloria Bentham, Bitsy's mom. *It's Bitsy I don't trust*, she'd said—about her own daughter! "Her mom tried to warn us," Max said. "We ignored her. We thought *she* was the traitor! We got her locked up."

"Pending a hearing," Max's mom reminded him.

"Can you talk to her?" Smriti suggested. "She might have some idea where Bitsy went."

"One step ahead of you." Alex held up her phone. "When we heard Bitsy was gone, the first thing Evelyn said was, 'Call the prison.' So I did. They said we can visit Gloria at four if we want."

Now Evelyn and her mom were approaching. A day earlier, Evelyn had been in a wheelchair. Her body had been growing stiff with the effects of a disease called scleroderma. Mom had been unconscious and riddled with cancer. Now they were both standing upright. They were on their way to health, because of the serum. And now the serum was gone.

Max glanced at his watch. "That's *seven hours* from now! We can't just go now? Tell them to change our reservation?"

"It's a jail, Max, not a restaurant," Alex said. "They have strict hours."

"But—but Bitsy could be halfway around the world by then!" Max protested.

Smriti was trying hard to understand. "Wait . . . Bitsy stole your stuff? Why?"

"Maybe if we knew that, we'd have some clue how to track her," Alex suggested.

They were interrupted by the tooting of a car horn, someone trying to get by.

"Can we move this conversation out of the street?" Mom asked, taking Max's arm. As she led him to the sidewalk, Dad got back into the car and began steering it slowly into the driveway.

"Maybe she's going to make a deal with some chemical factory," Max murmured, nearly tripping over the curb, "and make gazillions of dollars selling the cure."

Alex shrugged. "Or sell the vials on the black market and make a quick killing."

"Whatever it is, she needs to find people who will believe her," Smriti remarked. "People she can trust to keep her secret. Those are two things in your favor. I mean, really—*Hey, I have a magic cure for cancer made from weird waters from around the world.* Who's not going to just laugh at her? So it'll take time for her to do this. And while she's doing it, she'll need to keep those vials safe."

"So we may have a chance to get her before she does anything stupid or greedy," Alex said. "Time is on our side."

"Can I ask a question?" Evelyn said. "Why do you need the serum anymore? I'm feeling amazing. I haven't been able to stand in two months and now I can. I can feel my body repairing itself. And your mom looks awesome."

Mom smiled at her. Mom's face was thinner, her eyes sunken, but she was a million times healthier than she was a few days ago.

"She looked awesome after the first round of treatments too," Max said. "From the Mayo Clinic. We had all this money from the treasure we found, and we thought we had bought her the best care in the world. But then . . ."

Skunk, the smell of sadness, was twirling its way faintly up his nostrils. So he didn't say *relapse*. Sometimes certain words made things worse. That one would have caused the stink to be unbearable.

"You're afraid," Evelyn said, "that it might wear off. Or that we'll need follow-up doses. So much of this is unknown."

Max saw Mrs. Lopez put her arm around her daughter, and it made him mad and afraid and sad, all at the same time. "You could actually drop dead," he said. "At a moment's notice."

"Max . . ." Alex hissed.

"Let's go inside," Mom said. "I'm expecting visitors. Some friends want to come over and celebrate my health. You guys can hang until you're ready to go meet Gloria Bentham. Alex is right. Be thorough and be patient. Deal?"

"Deal," said Alex.

"Deal," said Smriti.

"Me three," said Evelyn.

"Max?" Mom said.

"Easy for all of you to say," Max grumbled. "*You* don't have to smell cat pee for seven hours."

The living room was full of Mom's friends. Rufus Peeble, the quiet neighbor with shredded-wheat hair, was secretly squeezing the chocolates in the box he'd brought. Mom's author friend Stephanie Pappas was signing her new book with a flourish, like it was the Declaration of Independence. Evelyn was sketching out the plans for a robot that she and Max were working on, before a small group of fascinated adults. Every couple of minutes a new visitor came with gifts or flowers.

Max sat on a chair in the corner, fiddling with a shiny metallic Rubik's Cube. He couldn't stop staring at Mom. When she burped, Max raced to get her some seltzer. When she coughed, he rubbed her back. When she sneezed, he nearly jumped to the ceiling.

That was when Alex finally broke away and approached him. "Dude, are you *trying* to creep everyone out," she whispered, "or does this behavior just come naturally?"

"Mercaptan," Max replied.

Alex cocked her head. "Say what?"

"I'm feeling anxious," Max said. "And when I'm anxious I smell mercaptan. It's a chemical that gives off that rotten-eggy odor when you turn on a stove. They add it to the methane for safety, because methane is odorless."

"Thank you, Mr. Factoid." Alex pushed back her thick black hair, and it seemed to flash a million colors in the chandelier light. "Your mom's starting to worry about you, Max. Usually you try to make conversation for about three nanoseconds, then go into your room to make impossible inventions. I think she'd be happy if you stopped staring at her and acted like yourself. This is a celebration, not an audition for Zombie Children of Ohio."

"Are you being sarcastic? I'm not good at sarcasm."

Alex let out a breath. "Sorry. I'm anxious too, just like you. I close my eyes and see Bitsy laughing at us. I open my eyes and I imagine everyone in this room thinking we're wimps for letting her steal the vials." She glanced toward the wall, at the dark old portrait of their great-great-great-grandfather, the famous science-fiction writer Jules Verne. "I even think he's mad at us."

"Wow," Max said. "And you're not even on the spectrum."

The portrait seemed to be staring at them, over the heads of everyone in the room. With his thick gray beard and heavy wool coat, Verne seemed on the verge of jumping out.

"Do you think his eyes are moving?" Max whispered.

Alex stood and moved deeper into the living room. Spotting her, Rufus offered a half-squashed chocolate, but Alex ignored him. She kept her eyes on the painting and edged back to Max. "Creepy. Know what else? He has a twin. On the gift table."

She pointed toward a pile of presents, at the top of which was a glossy hardcover book called *Journey to the Center of a Genius: The Life and Times of Jules Verne*. And on its cover was the exact image of the portrait on the wall.

No. Not exact.

Max lifted the book from the table. He stared at it closely, then at the painting on the wall. "Actually, they aren't twins."

"You are so literal," Alex said. "What I mean is, it's the same painting."

"Nope." Max held out the book closer to Alex. "What do you see at the lower right-hand edge of this book cover?"

"A very thick wool jacket that should have a sweat stain on it but doesn't?" Alex said.

"Exactly." Max turned to the portrait on the wall, gesturing toward the same spot. "And what do you see there, in the same place?"

Alex leaned closer to the painting. Over Verne's jacket was a signature. It was in black ink against the muted browns of the jacket fabric, but both of them could read it.

LEVI HEK
AZZA

"What the heck?" Alex said.

"*Levi* Hek," Max corrected her.

"No, I mean what-the-heck, as in why is this one

signed and the other one not?" Alex asked.

Max shrugged. He noticed that Mom was staring at the portrait too now, along with a thin woman with owlish glasses and unruly silver hair pulled into a ponytail. "That," the woman said, "is a very astute question, my dear."

"Who are you?" Max asked.

The old woman looked shocked by the question, which seemed perfectly logical to Max. With a smile, his mom said, "Professor Grigson teaches nineteenth-century art and literature. She brought this lovely book. What do you think, professor? Why is one signed and the other not?"

"Odd . . ." The woman's eyes darted from the book to the wall. "I certainly do not recognize the name. The portrait on the book cover is the original from a museum. This one on your wall is clearly a print. So perhaps Mr. Azza is a cheeky collector—a budding graffiti artist. Ah well. You know, these chocolates . . . they appear to have been involved in an accident. . . ."

As the two women turned away, chitchatting about random things, Max thumbed the name LEVI HEK AZZA into his phone. It probably meant nothing, but you never knew.

Jules Verne worked in mysterious ways.

As he typed in the last letters, Alex grabbed him by the arm. With her other arm, she flashed the face of her watch.

3:45.

"It's time," she said, "to go to jail."

2

THE visitor area of the Greater Southeastern Ohio Correction Facility smelled like a locker room that hadn't been cleaned in a week. "Fragrant," Alex said.

"Glad I'm not the only one who noticed," Max replied.

They sat on blue plastic chairs at one side of a long counter, separated from the other side by a Plexiglas barrier. Each of them wore a lanyard with a plastic ID card marked VISITOR, and Max fingered his nervously. It was greasy and frayed at the edges. A bored-looking prison guard led Gloria Bentham into the other room through a thick metal door. Gloria walked with a straight back and raised eyebrows, inspecting the room as if she owned it. Even without makeup and carefully styled hair, she projected authority. "Thank you, my dear Florence," she said to the guard.

"It's Flo," the guard grumbled.

As Gloria sat across from Max and Alex, the guard retreated closer to the wall. She faced them with folded arms and a slight scowl, as if she had much more important things to do. "Charming place, isn't it?" Gloria said.

Alex took a deep breath. "First of all, Mrs. Bentham, we're sorry."

To their surprise, Gloria Bentham smiled and waved the comment away. "Well, if I were you, I would have done the same thing. I . . . er, took something from you, and in your ignorance you had every reason to hate me for that. But I must defend my actions—"

"We know we were wrong," Alex said.

"You were trying to protect the vials," Max added. "You warned us about Bitsy."

"Yes, well, she can be a charmer," Gloria replied with a sigh. "Look, I understand. You spent time with her. She had gained your trust. And so had that unctuous will-o'-the-wisp, Nigel."

"We know who she is now," Alex said. "Spencer Niemand's daughter. I mean, not that it means anything. Sometimes bad people have good children. But Niemand nearly killed us, so we're not big fans."

"Besides, Bitsy betrayed us," Max said.

Gloria massaged her forehead. "Spencer wanted nothing to do with her after the divorce. I tried so hard to raise her right. Bitsy was smart, so much sweeter and more compassionate than her papa. I had hope for her. But as she became a teen, I began discovering texts, emails, notes, all to her father. Spencer was obsessed with Jules Verne's lost treasure, and Bitsy was sucked into the excitement. She needed his attention. She wanted so badly to be on his good side." With a sigh, she folded her arms and leaned forward. "So. Let me guess. She stole the *Isis hippuris.* She knew the ancient waters wouldn't work without that precious piece of deep-sea coral."

"Even worse," Max said. "She stole it plus all the vials of magic water."

Gloria stared at him a long moment, then threw her head back with a barking laugh. It was so loud and sudden that Flo the guard, who had fallen asleep on her feet, let out a sharp "Yeep!" and stepped closer.

Max and Alex stared awkwardly as Gloria's raucous burst morphed into what sounded like a sob. When she lowered her head, her eyes were moist. "I feared this would happen. Well, darlings, this puts us in a pretty predicament. Now we are on the same side, aren't we?"

"That's why we're here," Alex said. "We were hoping you could help us figure out where she would go."

Gloria thought for a moment, then lowered her voice to a whisper. "The walls have big ears here. And so do the guards. We must speak quickly and quietly. I do not want to remain in this place. My hearing comes up in a few days. Is this really necessary for an innocent woman? My life would be made a lot easier if you would drop your charges."

"How can we trust you?" Max asked. "What if you lie to us?"

Gloria nodded. "Fair point. I did lie to you. Lying erodes trust, and trust must be earned. But if I have information that will help you, it's only fair to require something in return."

Max looked at Alex. He wanted to trust Gloria Bentham, but it was hard to think of her as one of the good guys.

Alex held up an index finger to Gloria, then slid her chair back, pulling Max with her. "We can't just let her go," Max said. "What if she double-crosses us? She's creepy. She smells like ammonia."

"You're right, but she's trapped," Alex reminded him. "We have the upper hand. She has no incentive to lie."

"Unless it can get her out of jail!" Max said.

"Exactly," Alex said. "So we can dangle that possibility and negotiate. Leave this to me."

As Max nodded hesitantly, Alex rolled back to Gloria. "Mrs. Bentham," she said.

"Call me Gloria, please," Gloria Bentham said, cocking her head curiously.

"Whatever. Let's take this one step at a time. You tell us your information first. We will take that information and see where it leads us. If it helps us get the vials back, we will drop the charges."

"My dear, this involves chasing and finding someone," Gloria Bentham said. "That could take a long time."

Alex looked at Max. Neither knew what to say, so they both shrugged. "We'll . . . ask for a retrial?" Alex offered. "Or something?"

Gloria nodded sadly and lowered her head. When she lifted it again, her lips were set firmly. She gestured the cousins closer to the glass. "I suppose I deserve this. And honestly, I do not want to see Spencer get away with one more scheme. Now listen closely. My daughter is quite clever, but I don't believe she has the gumption or the wherewithal to do much with the vials. Which leads me to believe she is trying to impress her father."

"I could have told you that," Max said.

"Do not underestimate my ex-husband," Gloria continued. "He foresaw that Verne based novels on his real-life adventures. Spencer had maps and secret notes that had been left to Verne's editor who died on the *Titanic*."

Alex nodded. "Pierre-Jules Pretzel."

"Hetzel," Max corrected her.

"Spencer insisted those notes were not complete," Gloria said. "He suspected Hetzel had more information. He was obsessed with the idea that Verne had buried secrets in other books, not only *Twenty Thousand Leagues Under the Sea*."

"He's right about that," Max said. "The search for the serum ingredients turned into *Around the World in 80 Days*."

Gloria nodded. "You outran him on that one. I would not be surprised if he believes that your discovery—the completed serum—is now connected to some other crazy science-fiction story."

"But Spencer Niemand is in Greenland!" Alex

exclaimed. "Do you think Bitsy's headed toward—?"

Gloria Bentham silenced her with a raised hand, glancing toward Flo the guard, who was lumbering closer. "Big ears . . ." Gloria whispered.

"OK, come on, Your Majesty," Flo said with a big yawn, "time's up."

Max stared curiously at the guard. "Her ears aren't that big."

Flo stopped short. "Huh?"

"Gloria, tell us where Bitsy's going!" Alex hissed.

But the guard's hand was on Gloria's shoulder. Standing slowly, Gloria said with a wary smile, "On your way out, buy yourselves a copy of the *Savile Gazette*. All proceeds are donated to prison reform."

"Wait!" Max cried out. "Can't we have just another minute—"

"Yeah—next time you visit," Flo snapped.

"There are some fascinating articles on the front page!" Gloria sang, as Flo ushered her through the door.

As the door slammed shut, Max banged on the Plexiglas. *"No! Wait!"*

On their side of the divider, another guard rushed toward them. Alex pulled Max away from the barrier before he could be grabbed. "Max, it's OK," she said.

"It's a start. We need to set up another appointment, that's all."

"When? Tomorrow? We don't have the time!" Max shook loose. Circling around the guard, he bounded out of the room.

Alex followed him down a worn linoleum-floored corridor toward a crowded waiting room. **NO SMOKING** signs were posted on three walls, but the place smelled of cigarettes and sadness. As Max headed for the door, Alex held him back by the arm. "Dude, we have to officially sign out."

Max turned. He removed the lanyard from his neck and handed it to her. As she returned it to a clerk behind a gray metal desk, Max caught a glimpse of the newspapers for sale. He lifted a copy of the *Savile Gazette* and scanned all the usual boring stuff—news about taxes and store closings and meetings.

There are some fascinating articles on the front page. That's what Gloria Bentham had said.

His eyes rested on a small section marked International News at the bottom left side. And he let out a squeal so loud that three sleeping people woke up.

Alex scooted over to him. "What? Are you OK?"

"She *was* trying to tell us something," Max said.

He turned the newspaper toward her and pointed to a small headline:

CONVICTED AMERICAN INDUSTRIALIST EXTRADITED FROM GREENLAND TO MASSACHUSETTS PRISON

"What the . . . ?" Alex said.

"I think the word is 'Bingo,'" Max replied.

BITSY knew her papa hated sweets. So it didn't make much sense to bring him a chocolate cheesecake at the Bilgewater State Penitentiary. But she held one in her lap anyway, in a neat white box wrapped with string.

Papa would forgive her. She was sure of that. It was the thought that counted.

The thought of escape.

She'd found the bakery just outside the Niemand Enterprises plant in Waltham, Massachusetts. The box was what she needed. She'd tied it with a string that was given to her inside the plant, by a young techie named Jared. At first she'd remarked the string looked flimsy. So Jared, with a goofy smile, had held it over his head with two hands like dental floss. Screaming *hyeeaah*, he'd brought it down hard on the solid teak arm of a designer bench. As two broken pieces crashed to the floor, split like a stick of butter, Jared proudly assured her it would work on steel. It was made of . . . carbene, carbole, something like that.

Holding the box carefully, Bitsy stepped out of the taxi. She had phoned ahead, so it took only a few moments to get clearance at the prison gate. The guard gave her a bored smile and gestured to an old walkway. "Follow the yellow brick road," he grumbled.

The walkway was cracked and weed choked, leading to a tan-brick building with barred windows. Patches of parched soil flanked the path on either side. Bitsy imagined they were lawns at one time, but now the dirt looked like cracked cement, flecked by grass tendrils that emerged like the withered hands of trapped prisoners. Men with rifles peered down from the rooftop. She did not wave at them.

Although two guards stood just inside the entrance door, she had to open it herself with her free hand. "Thanks for your help," she murmured.

As she walked to the reception desk, she eyed a sign on the wall behind it that announced **VISITORS TO BURGWASSER SUBJECT TO SEARCH, PLEASE OPEN C AGES**. That last word was supposed to be *PACKAGES*, but some joker had managed to scrape away the *PA* and the *K*.

The guard rapped her knuckles on the desk. "Package. Open it."

Bitsy placed the box on the desk, then gestured to the sign. "Is the name really Burgwasser? Everyone refers to it as—"

"Bilgewater. Yeah, that's just a joke, honey," the guard said in a thick Massachusetts accent. "You must be related to the guy with the silver hair. You talk like him."

Bitsy untied the box, letting the string fall to the side. As the guard looked inside, Bitsy tensed. "I . . . er, talk like my mother too. She's also in prison, you know."

"Lucky you." The guard sniffed the cake, took out a plastic knife and cut it into six slices, then ran it through an X-ray scanner. "Sorry, prison rules. You're clear. But you'll have to eat it with your hands, no utensils allowed. Take this directly to the first door on your right. One of the officers will accompany you."

She handed Bitsy the box, laying the unraveled string on top.

Yes.

In a moment she was escorted into a cold little room. She sat at the end of a long bench that was sagging with the weight of grim-faced visitors. Peeling walls, flickering fluorescent lights that buzzed like dentist's drills, a plastic barrier with small windows for hand-holding and gift exchange—this was a far cry from the plush prison where Papa once spent a week for a little misunderstanding about taxes.

She recoiled at the sight of a guard who was practically shoving her father through the prisoner entrance. The uniformed man had a face like a basset hound, a six-foot-five package of too-solid flesh clad in a mud-brown uniform. "That her?" he growled.

Spencer Niemand's face brightened at the sight of his daughter. "Ah, dear Bitsy, may I introduce you to Mr. Schultz? He and I were just having the most lively discussion about quantum physics."

"It's Schmultz," the guard mumbled.

Bitsy stifled a sob in her throat. Behind Papa's beaming smile, his face was drawn and leathery and sad. The dashing silver stripe down the center of his black hair had gone completely white, and it seemed to have widened like a worn footpath. She'd last seen him—when? a year ago?—but he appeared to be a decade older.

As he sat, Bitsy slid the boxed cheesecake toward the closed window. The string lay piled on the top. It looked limp and harmless.

Spencer Niemand stared at the string just a split

second longer than anyone would normally do.

He knew.

With a yawn, Schmultz yanked open the sliding window and Bitsy pushed the box through.

Niemand smiled. "You look well, Elizabeth," he said.

"Happy birthday, Papa," Bitsy replied.

"It's your birthday?" Schmultz asked.

"Don't drool, my good man, you can have a piece too," Niemand said. "You'll have to eat it with your hands like a caveman, but I'm sure you won't mind."

Niemand held out the box with his right hand. With his left, he carefully placed the string on his bench.

THE taxi driver floored the accelerator, and Max felt his face flatten like an astronaut launched into space.

"What are you doing?" Alex shouted, looking up from her phone. "You're going to kill us!"

The driver yanked the steering wheel left and right, to a concert of blaring horns from each side. *"In Boston,"* he shouted back, *"we call it* driving*!"*

Being rich had its advantages. After finding the treasure left by Jules Verne, Max's and Alex's lives had changed big time. They could buy any clothes and eat in any restaurants they wanted to. They could hire private planes and cars. But no amount of money could prevent Max from wanting to puke in the backseat of a zigzagging

Lexus on the Southeast Expressway.

"What's your name?" Alex demanded.

"Mario!" the driver replied.

"Figures," Max said.

"Want me to slow down?" Mario asked.

"Yes!" Alex replied.

"No!" Max shouted.

Time was crucial. Max gripped to the armrest, watching the GPS. The prison was only ten miles and two exits away.

Alex clutched Max's arm, her fingers tightening with every swerve in the traffic. "We need to get there alive," Alex said.

"I'll need both my arms," Max said. "It feels like you're trying to detach one of them."

"Sorry." Alex sat back, pocketing her phone. "I just texted my friend Rod at Harvard. He's the smartest person I know. He once interned for Spencer Niemand. Now he wants to go into criminal law, and he says he'll help us if we need it."

"So, kiddos, who are you seeing at Bilgewater?" Mario asked, as he veered around two SUVs and a silver minivan festooned with bicycles. "Mind if I ask? Anyone famous? White-collar criminal? Ponzi schemer?"

"Burgwasser," Max corrected him.

"Don't know that name. Friend of yours?" Mario asked.

"It's the factual name of the prison," Max said. "*Bilgewater* is the nickname. *Bilge* is the bottom of a boat. When bilgewater collects, it gets slimy and gross. So the name is sarcastic."

"He likes facts," Alex explained.

"My kind of guy." Mario took a right-hand exit and zoomed toward a knot of cars lined up at a red light at the end of the ramp. "Who-o-o-oa . . . hang on . . ."

He stomped on the brakes. The car began to fishtail. The back of a Range Rover loomed closer. Max closed his eyes as the car squealed to a stop.

When he opened them again, a shocked, angry Yorkie was yapping at them through the back window of the Range Rover.

"My bad," Mario said. "Guess it must be a big day at Bilgewater."

"Is it always this crowded?" Max asked.

Mario shrugged. "Dunno. Honestly, most of my customers don't come here."

Yap! Yap! Yap-yap-yap-yap-yap-yap-yap! yapped the Yorkie.

"My thoughts exactly," Alex said.

Max peered through the window at the road to the right. He could see distant flashing red lights. The traffic was bumper-to-bumper all the way to a big tan-brick building about a quarter mile away. "That's the prison," he said. "And it looks like some kind of police action is blocking the traffic."

"No worries," Mario said, looking over his shoulder. "I'll put it in reverse, climb the grassy hill, get back on the highway, take the next exit, and cut through the—"

"No!" Max and Alex cried out together. Before Mario could protest, they unhooked their belts and bolted out of the car.

A dirt path followed along the road, with cement patches that hinted of a former sidewalk. People stared through the windows of small houses, and a homeless woman with a wool cap and a bandaged face staggered toward them, holding a bottle and an empty cup. *"Change? Spare some change?"* she shouted in a guttural voice, lurching into Max's path.

Trying to avoid her, Max jogged from side to side, but the old woman mirrored him. As they slammed into each other, the woman wrapped him in a kind of bear hug. "Shall we dance, old boy?" she said.

Max caught a whiff of fish. "Sorry!" he said, bouncing away

With a grumble, the woman turned her back and staggered up the road as if nothing had happened.

"Come on, Max!" Alex shouted, pulling Max toward the commotion. They elbowed their way through a crowd of people who'd left their cars to stare.

Max had no idea what they were staring at.

They stopped at the line of cars outside the prison. A man and two women with video equipment marked WBGT-TV were just inside the gate. One of the reporters was talking into a mic with a serious look. "Police are examining leads," he said in an announcerish voice, "and the mayor has urged all in the neighborhood to stay inside houses and report any suspicious-looking people. More news at six."

"What happened?" Alex demanded to the closest cop.

"The prison is in lockdown," the cop replied.

"Why?" Alex asked.

"There was an escape," said someone in the crowd.

People began speaking all at once:

"Dug a tunnel with his fingers . . ."

"Bit a guard in the neck . . ."

"A convicted mass murderer . . ."

"Snuck out in a pile of laundry . . ."

Alex looked helplessly at Max. He pulled out his phone and began accessing the social media feed of WBGT. Clicking through a post that said BREAKING NEWS, he read carefully.

"It was an escape. . . ." he murmured, then read aloud, "'The breakout method has not been disclosed, and officials have not released any names, but he is believed to be a white male, age fifty to fifty-five. He is assumed dangerous, and local residents are encouraged to call 911 with any leads.'"

Alex ran toward a group of officials gathering by the TV interviewer, but a policeman stood in her way.

"We have an appointment!" Alex cried out.

"Sorry, not today," he said.

"The person who escaped—do you know anything about him?" Alex asked.

The policeman shook his head. "They have to search the prisoners to be sure."

"How are the residents going to know who to look for?" Max asked.

Not far from him in the crowd, a thin, white-haired woman spoke up: "This has happened before, honey. All of us in the neighborhood look out for one another. We recognize unfamiliar faces. These cons always try to disguise themselves. Last year, one of them wore clothes he found in a dumpster."

"The rotten zucchini stuck to the back of his shirt gave him away," said the man standing next to her, erupting with a big laugh. "Then there was the guy who pretended not to know English. He was wearing a T-shirt and Mickey Mouse undershorts. Like the residents in a prison town wouldn't suspect he ditched his uniform for that getup! Hoo boy, you see every kind of crazy disguise here."

Max began smelling fish again. And he thought back to the old woman he'd collided with.

Shall we dance, old boy?

By now Alex was moving on, talking to more people, trying to get the attention of the officials. Alex and Max looked back up the road from where they'd just come. Littering the cracked walkway was a crumpled-up dollar bill and three Skor bar wrappers.

He shoved his hands into his pocket to get his phone. *"Alex!"*

She elbowed her way back through the crowd. "What happened?"

"I smelled fish. I only smell fish when I feel afraid.

And I only feel afraid when something is very, very wrong." Max pulled his hands from his pockets. "My wallet . . . my money . . . they're gone . . ."

"The homeless woman robbed you?" Alex asked.

"That homeless woman," Max said, "was Spencer Niemand."

5

APPROXIMATELY twenty-nine miles northwest of Bilgewater State Penitentiary was a colony of brick buildings arranged neatly among luscious green lawns. In the Brick Hollow Residences for the Well-Lived, white-haired men and women sat on porches, watching the arcs of hissing sprinklers. Orderlies in crisp white coats pushed residents in wheelchairs along curved paths. In a place where people went to finish out their lives, no one was in much of a hurry, and the loudest voices belonged to the birds.

Which made the speed and the noise of the long black car unusual, as it peeled into the entrance driveway.

Inside the entrance, a woman wearing a pin-striped

suit and a scowl glanced out the window. "I believe your visitors are here, sir!" she announced sharply. "Martin? Did you hear me?"

In a cozy waiting area warmed by a gas-powered fireplace, an ancient man opened his eyes. His head was as smooth as polished pearl, his movements slow. As he turned to the window, the thick lines of his face suggested a feral animal staring through granite crags. "Thank you, Ms. Hughes," he rasped.

These "visitors" had called only a few hours earlier, with an offer of money too high to believe. The amount would more than take care of his ailing wife; his children, who had taken over the family business; and his grandchildren and great-grandchildren. For this, all he needed to do was turn over the papers of his own grandfather. He recalled a fight over them, between Grandpapa and Uncle Oliver. The contents were valuable, but he no longer remembered why.

So much was lost to memory these days.

He fingered the keys to his storage room, then dropped them into his pocket. First, he would talk to these people. His gut instincts would take care of the rest.

Two figures exited the car, one small and lively, the other tall and powerful-looking. Both wore stylish black coats and black wide-brimmed caps, and they seemed to be in a great hurry. The old man hadn't had visitors in such a long time, and he felt a flicker of excitement. Could they be long-lost nieces and nephews? Grandchildren of dear old friends?

He grabbed the handles of his walker and stood. Slowly he shuffled toward the front door, where Ms. Hughes was greeting the two strangers.

They came straight for the old man. His eyesight was nearly gone, but there was something familiar about the taller one's posture and the tilt of his head.

Briefly, as if out of polite habit, the tall man removed his hat. He seemed to think twice about this and placed it immediately back upon his head. But even with diminished vision, in that brief moment the old man could see a full head of jet-black hair—and the path of white down the center, like the Milky Way. He recognized the strange visitor.

It's Uncle Oliver.

Oliver Niemand.

The old man felt the breath catch in his throat. It couldn't be. Oliver was long gone. This had to be a son. Even a grandson.

"Hetzel," the visitor said.

Dear Lord, even the voice was the same. A Niemand voice.

"Mr. Hetzel?" came Ms. Hughes's voice. "Are you all right?"

Before the old man could reply, his grip weakened. He felt himself slip, slip, slipping to the carpet.

ALEX was the first Canadian Max had ever met. The second was her friend Rod Rosas, who had bolted toilet seats to his college dorm room wall. Inside each was a photo of a smiling face.

"The red-haired dude in the pink-padded seat—in the left eye," he said, leaning back in a black wooden chair emblazoned with a Harvard crest.

He flung a plastic dart toward the image of a man pasted to the wall inside a pink toilet seat. The dart embedded itself in the man's right cheek.

"You missed," Alex said. "He's laughing at you."

"He's my physics professor, he doesn't know how to laugh," Rod said.

"This is not helping us!" Max paced the floor, kicking

aside a sweatshirt. The floor was piled with papers, gadgets, empty plastic cups, clothing that was already collecting dust, and a few half-eaten candy bars still in their wrappers. "You said Rod was the smartest guy in your high school. You said he could help us figure out where Stinky went. All he does is play darts."

"Stinky" was the nickname given to Spencer Niemand by his submarine pilot, jolly old Basile Grimsby. He had sacrificed himself to save Max's and Alex's lives, and Max liked to keep his memory alive.

"Throwing darts helps me think," Rod said, as one of his tosses thudded against a toilet seat and clattered to the ground. "I'm still processing that Jules Verne was your great-great-great-grandfather. And the idea that those awesome novels weren't fiction."

"Totally real," Max said. "Verne was trapped in a submarine with an evil captain just like in *Twenty Thousand Leagues Under the Sea*. At the end of that voyage, he hid the treasure. Same with *Around the World in 80 Days*—he went around the globe finding five secret ingredients for a formula."

"We met Bitsy in London, at Basile's funeral," Alex said. "She helped us find another clue, and then she traveled all over the world with us—Greece, Siberia, Nepal, Mexico, Antarctica. We trusted her, and she robbed us."

"Her stepmom, who's in prison in Ohio, says Bitsy might have taken the stuff to her dad, Spencer Niemand, who's in prison in Massachusetts," Max said.

"What an accomplished family." Rod threw another dart, but it thwacked into the door. "Niemand Enterprises has a plant in Waltham, I think. One of my MIT friends interned there. They develop some cool high-tech materials. Like a superadhesive glue that changes the biochemistry of the skin when you touch it. A thin filament that can lift a granite boulder. A targeted explosive that shoots from a ring without injuring the wearer. Mostly military, not authorized for commercial use, top secret to everyone except employees. And maybe some VIPs."

Rod raised an eyebrow, and Max knew just what he meant. "So if, like, the daughter of the founder paid a visit," Max said, "she might be able to sneak out something illegal. Something that could do damage to a prison cell!"

"You are a genius!" Alex added.

Max smiled. "A lot of people say that."

"I meant Rod, not you," Alex shot back.

"Middle toilet, SpongeBob, in his bow tie!" Rod said, finally landing a dart exactly where he said he would. "So where did father and daughter go?"

"We have no clue," Max said. "Maybe they went

someplace to mass manufacture it. Maybe they think they'll get rich selling a secret cure."

"Gloria Bentham—Niemand's ex-wife—thinks he has some plan based on one of Verne's other books," Alex said.

"Seems far-fetched to me," Rod replied, turning away from the toilet seats, "unless one of Verne's books was called *Making Twenty Thousand Gallons of Miracle Serum in Eighty Minutes*!"

Max shrugged. "Anything's possible. We found the first treasure clue in my attic. Then we found other clues in the places we went to, like a scavenger hunt that traced the route of *Twenty Thousand Leagues.* At the end of it all, we found another clue at the bottom of the treasure. That one led us to a discovery inspired by *Around the World*."

"OK, but even if it were hypothetically true—even if Niemand is like, *bwa-ha-ha, now I shall follow Jules Verne's plans for the miracle serum instead of doing the only thing that matters to me, which is making a fortune*—what book would it be?" Rod asked.

"Good question," Alex said.

"Are you sure you found everything Verne hid in the attic?" Rod threw another dart. This one flew into the oval of a dark wooden toilet at the bottom right. "At the start, you guys ran out of there to find the treasure.

Then you got caught up in the second search, saving your mom's life. Everything's been hurry, hurry, hurry. You might be missing something."

Max moved closer to the target. The dart had landed between the eyes of an old black-and-white photo of . . . Jules Verne!

"That wasn't nice," Alex said.

Rod giggled. "I was wondering when you guys would notice him."

Max couldn't look away from the photo. Verne was doing it again, staring at him. Staring *into* him. Beckoning Max with his hundred-fifty-year-old eyes. Max moved closer. Verne seemed to be on the verge of telling a joke. His face had youth and mischief. It was a totally different person than the boring, serious-looking guy he and Alex had found in the . . .

"The oil painting!" Max blurted out.

Alex stared at him blankly.

"Excuse me?" Rod said.

"There's a portrait of Jules Verne on our living room wall," Max replied. "Alex and I found it in the attic. It's signed by the artist. Verne's biography has the same painting on the cover, but the signature isn't there."

"Um, maybe it's *not* actually the same painting?" Rod said.

"It is," Alex said. "One of my aunt's friends figured ours was a copy of the original, and a collector put his name on it."

Rod scrunched up his brow. "Really? That's like vandalizing it. Why would a collector do that?"

It was a good question. And it got Max's mind racing.

"Unless it wasn't a collector!" he blurted out.

He pulled out his phone and navigated quickly to the photo of the painting. Zooming in with his thumb and forefinger, he showed Rod the signature:

LEVI HEK
AZZA

"Levi Hek Azza . . ." Rod pulled out his own phone and did a search. "Nada. Not in Wikipedia. Not anywhere."

"If he existed in the nineteenth century, there would be *something* about him," Alex said.

"Unless," Max piped up, "Levi Hek Azza isn't a real person."

"I don't see where you're going with this," Rod said.

"The painting was in the attic, near the chest where we found the first note," Max said. "So maybe Rod was right. We didn't look hard enough. This one was staring us right in the face. It's got to be a code. Verne loved codes."

"Gotta be an anagram!" Rod accessed a site on his phone and tapped in the name.

Max looked over his shoulder at the results:

No anagrams found.

"Whoa, so much for that idea," Rod murmured. "It's rare you find nothing."

"Verne liked to do substitution codes," Alex said. "You know, each letter is really a different one, like maybe . . . it's really the second letter after it, something like that."

"Or each vowel is the vowel before it, and each consonant is the one three consonants to the left," Max said.

"My head is spinning," Rod replied.

Max stared at the screen. "OK, let's think. Break it down. Verne always provided some way into the solution."

"Some kind of key?" Rod asked.

"Right. If you're supposed to go three letters to the left, he'd include a minus three, for example," Alex said. "One time he gave us the shape of a wheel. You had to put letters at each end of the spokes and substitute one for the other."

"But this is just a name!" Rod said. "No numbers, no wheels."

"True," Alex agreed.

"No," Max said. "Not true! False. Look at the way the name is arranged. The first name and middle name at the top—Levi Hek. The last name at the bottom—Azza. Why?"

Alex looked at Rod. They both shrugged.

"*Azza* is separate. Maybe it's our key? Just winging it here," Alex said.

"Bingo," Max replied. "*A* and *Z* are the first and last letters of the alphabet. You can look at *Azza* as *AZ* followed by *ZA*. So maybe that's a key. Verne is telling us to go from *A* to *Z*, and *Z* to *A*."

"So you substitute letters in a backward alphabet—*A* for *Z*, *B* for *Y*, *C* for *X*, and so on?" Rod asked.

"Yup, like this." Max grabbed a pen and a sheet of paper from Max's desk and began scribbling:

"So if AZZA is the key," Rod said. "Then all we have to do is decode the rest of it—LEVI HEK?"

Max was already at work:

"OK, maybe that's wrong," Max said.

"No, Max, you got it!" Alex said. "SVP is an abbreviation for *s'il vous plaît*, French for 'please.' We have to turn the painting over to see the back!"

"Wait, one word in English, the other in French?" Rod said. "That makes no sense. He was French."

"Maybe *over* was more convenient," Alex shot back. "It translates nicely to 'Levi.' The French would probably be *tourner*. Maybe that would translate to gobbledygook. Anyway, Verne did a lot of business with English speakers, like the Reform Club in London. He spoke it well."

Max quickly put in a video call to his home number. After a few seconds, Dad appeared, his face tight with concern. "Is everything all right?"

"Niemand escaped," Max said.

"What?" Now Mom was squeezing into the frame.

"We think Bitsy helped him," Alex said. "So they're together, with the serum. But maybe you can help us. The name on the bottom of the Jules Verne portrait is a code. It translates to 'over please.' There's something we need to see on the back of the painting. Can you turn it over?"

Max's dad looked doubtful, but he went back to the wall and pulled down the painting. Maneuvering it into position, he turned the back of it to the screen.

The backing was a mottled yellowish brown. "Nothing here, Max," Dad said.

"Maybe it faded," Alex suggested.

"Hello, Mr. and Mrs. Tilt, I'm Alex's friend Rod from Canada." Rod was peering closely at the screen. "OK, you are looking at the portrait's *backing*. When the painting is mounted into a frame, they put protective layers behind it. Sheets of paper and cardboard and stuff. I'm thinking *over* means the other side of the actual painting. So you'll have to take it out of the frame."

Dad examined the frame. "Looks like we'll have to pry it off with a screwdriver." He disappeared for a few moments, and it took him and Mom a few more moments to separate the frame from the painting. Finally Mom held up the portrait. Old Jules Verne looked more fragile now, on a wavy canvas free of its frame, glass, and backing. Max's parents were behind it, snooping at the other side.

"There's something here," Mom said. She and Dad turned the painting around toward the phone. Max, Alex, and Rod nearly banged their heads together looking at it. The canvas was speckled with small raised dots, like pimples.

"Is that mildew?" Alex murmured.

"They're more like little bubbles," Mom replied, running her finger over them. "I guess the canvas didn't age very well. But check out what's on the very top."

She moved the phone upward until they could see a word written in bold capital letters:

YIZROOV

"Yizroov?" Alex repeated.

"Gesundheit," Rod said.

"Ha," Max said. "I didn't think you had a sense of humor."

"I'm wicked funny," Rod replied.

"Modest, too," Alex added.

As Max scribbled down the word YIZROOV on a sheet of paper, Alex looked over his shoulder. "What do you think, Sherlock?"

Max shrugged. "I just see one word. Nothing else. If it were a different code, he'd give something extra, like a new key. So I'm hoping that means we're supposed to use the same reverse-alphabet code as the one we used for Levi Hek."

"*Y* becomes *B* . . ." Rod murmured. "*I* becomes—"

Glancing back and forth to his alphabet key, Max substituted letter by letter. When he was done, they all stared at the result, stunned:

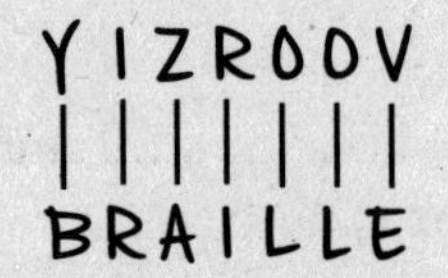

"Those dots?" Max said to his mom. "We need to read them. Yesterday."

7

"IT'S kind of worn out," Rod said.

"It's solvable," Max pointed out.

"It's French." Alex groaned.

The first Braille screenshot glowed from Rod's iPad:

"How can you tell it's French without translating it?" Max said.

The sun was setting, and outside Rod's dorm room

window, groups of kids were throwing Frisbees. Alex looked up wearily from Rod's laptop, where she was doing online Braille research. "You can tell by the first character—see those two dots that are stacked like a colon? In English Braille, it means decimal point. In French Braille, it's a way of saying that the next letter is a capital. And Jules Verne definitely begins his sentences with capital letters. Because that's the kind of guy he is."

"Definitely," Rod said. "But I'm looking at the Braille alphabet, and it looks like that first character is a *K*. One dot over the other."

"You have to imagine that each character is in a grid," Alex said. "I'll show you. This program lets me toggle the imaginary grid. It puts boxes around each dot, so you can see how they're positioned in relation to one another."

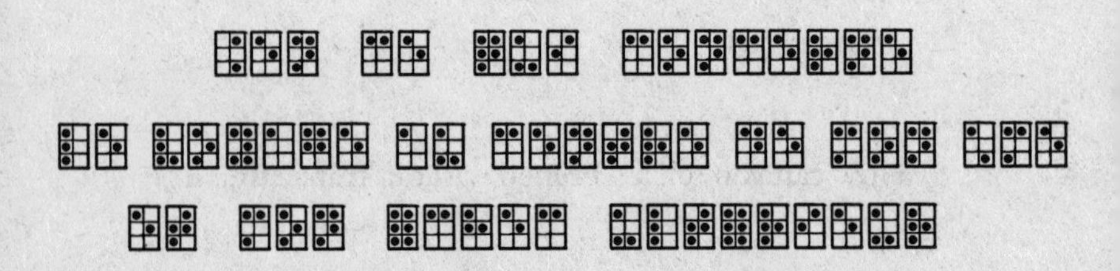

"So look at the first character in that message," Alex continued, her fingers clicking on the keys. "The boxes show you where the two dots are positioned. Now check out the *K* in the French Braille alphabet."

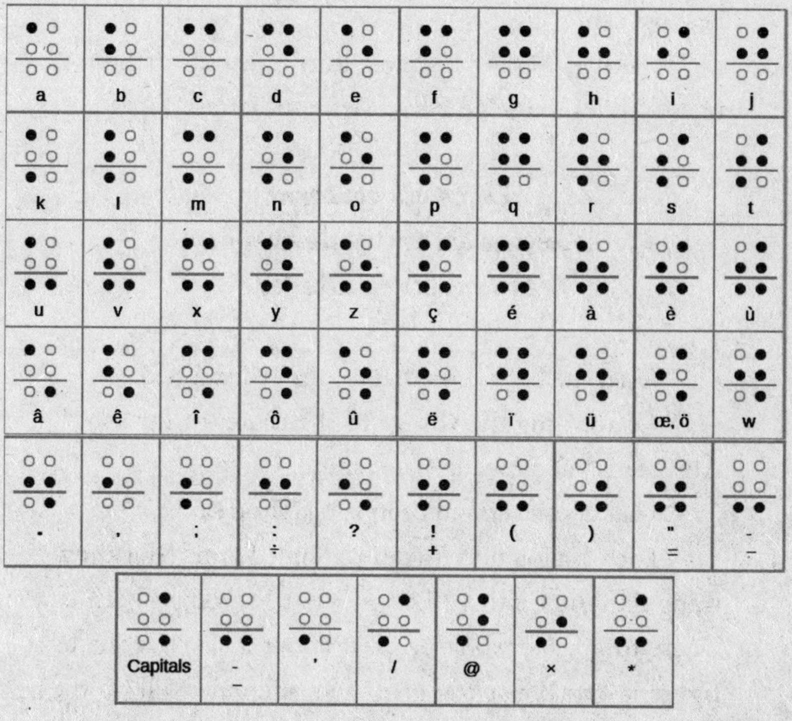

a	b	c	d	e	f	g	h	i	j
k	l	m	n	o	p	q	r	s	t
u	v	x	y	z	ç	é	à	è	ù
â	ê	î	ô	û	ë	ï	ü	œ, ö	w
.	,	;	: ÷	?	! +	(	)	" =	- –

Capitals	- –	'	/	@	×	*

"The *K* is two dots, but the dots are stacked on the *left*. In Verne's message, the two dots are stacked on the right—and that's sort of like a code. It indicates 'the following letter is a capital.' Is that right?" Max said.

"Exactly," Alex said. "So, the top part of the message is pretty clear. But it gets worse as you descend. Parts of it have flaked off and decayed. So we'll do the best we can."

Together, Max, Alex, and Rod transcribed the top lines of Jules Verne's message, letter by letter:

En ce qui concerne
le voyage au centre de mon âme
et mon échec ultérieur

"What the heck does that mean?" Max asked.

"'Concerning the voyage to the center of my soul,'" Alex read, "'and my ultimate failure.'"

"That doesn't sound promising," Rod said.

"There's a lot more," Alex reminded him. "If it's anything like the first two books, Verne is going to tell us where to go. He won't be clear about it. He'll make us figure it out. But if you give me some quiet, I'll do the best I can. It's really degraded."

Max began pacing. It was not easy to smell cat pee and mint at the same time, but that's what happened when he was both scared and excited. "Do you think Bitsy knows about this message?" he asked. "Or Spencer Niemand?"

"If they do," Alex said, "we're in trouble."

"Guys, there had to be a reason this Bitsy sprang her dad from jail," Rod said. "Would she have done that if they *didn't* know where to go?"

"No, no, and no," Max said. "How could they possibly know? We're the ones with the portrait. It's been in the attic for ages. So that means we're also the only ones with the info."

Alex looked up from her work. "Unless they got the info from another source?"

"Or maybe they're coming after you for *your* info," Rod suggested.

"If that were true, then why would Bitsy have stolen from us?" Max asked. "We trusted her. She could have just hung with us until we all figured out what to do."

"With Niemand, anything is possible," Alex said. "I'm worried she'll do whatever crazy, irrational thing Niemand tells her to do." She sighed and looked out the dorm window. "Rod, promise to keep everything we do here a secret. And if you see any old guys with skunk-striped hair, and a blonde girl with a British accent . . ."

"I'll report them to the Harvard campus police," Rod said.

"Somehow," Alex said, "that does not comfort me. Now everyone be quiet and let me work. This could take all night."

THE statue of John Harvard, at the center of Harvard Yard, turned toward Max and grinned. Fire drooled from the left corner of its mouth, and a group of tourists ran to try to catch it. "Don't mind me, Maxxxxxxx," the statue said, "just eavesdropping on all your silly secret plans. Don't let me stop you."

"Wait," Max said, fighting back the smell of fish. "You can't do that. You're not alive."

"Ohhhh?" The statue's bronze skin was growing lighter, creaking like a rusty hinge as the statue turned. Its bronze hair was turning black, except for a streak down the middle that was silver-white.

"That was great fun in Greenland, Max, old boy . . ." the statue hissed. As it rose, its chair exploded into stone fragments. A group of tourists in front shrieked with joy, taking selfies. "But you thwarted my brilliant plan. I needed your help. We would establish underwater cities. We would save the population after the coasts are flooded. I would have set you up with a good life. A position in my government. Now I believe you owe me something. . . ."

"A-A-Alex?" Max squeaked.

The statue leaped off the pedestal, planting its feet on two tourist heads, and crouched. *"Give me that translation no-o-o-o-owww!"*

"*N-N-Nooooo!*"

Max felt a thud. He awoke on a dusty wood floor with an old sock over his forehead and crushed Doritos under his shoulder. As his eyes blinked open, he could see the lawns of Harvard Yard through the window, washed to bright yellow green in the rising sun.

He bolted up, sending the sock flying. The John Harvard statue was sitting in its place, one foot shining gold where tourists had rubbed it. The threats were a dream.

A dream.

As he caught his breath, Max spotted Alex slumped over in her chair. Rod lay openmouthed on an old sofa, arms and legs akimbo. They looked dead. The entire night had gone by, and they were still in Cambridge, Massachusetts.

"If you're alive, wake up!" Max shouted, running over to the desk. "We weren't supposed to sleep! Every minute counts."

Groaning, Alex slowly lifted her head. "Easy for you to say. Sorry, dude, translation is hard. This took a long time."

Rod let out a couple of snorts and a fart, startling himself awake. "Need more coffee?" he blurted.

"We finished, Rod," Alex said. "About two hours ago. Max is looking over our work."

Max was staring at the translation:

Concerning
the voyage to the center of my soul
and my ultimate failure

THE LOST TREASURES
A MEMOIR
By Jules Verne

—PART III —

With thanks to the printing facility of my editor
Pierre-Jules Hetzel,
who retains the original copy

Dearest reader, to encode this final plea, Hetzel and I humbly employ the system of my dear friend Louis Braille, whose ——— w——— gives vision to the sightless. If you are reading this, yet have not found Part I of *The Lost Treasures*, then sadly ———— urge (you?)———————————— this account will have no meaning.

If you have indeed read Book I and found the buried bounty, my deep(est?) congratulations. May you use your wealth for the betterment of humanity. That, my friend, is where ———— ———— journey begins. The most difficult yet.

For hidden in that bounty, of course, was the beginning of *The Lost Treasures Part II.* This message is for the intrepid soul who has attained all five ingredients extracted from the rarest waters of the world, ———————— (proper?) proportions with the sea coral *Isis hippuris.*

But if you have constructed the serum, then you stand here trembling, knowing the glorious power ————— —————————. Perhaps you also know the horror.

My nephew and I envisioned a healed, prosperous, peaceful

humanity. A prosperity ________ since the Garden of Eden. But we found the serum to be short-lived and ________. To that end, we discovered the work of the ________ (philosopher?) S________usse____, who insisted that only by ________ ____ the serum into a large body of properly salinated water would it propagate ________________ this most unusual property.

We had our chance to change the course of ________ ________________ cruel and horrific. What we unleashed must be ________ (overcome?). *The Lost Treasures* will not be complete until this mission is accomplished. I hope to write it before I die. But if ________ the task is yours.

It began, quite inauspiciously, as I was researching a novel that the ancient *hiéro* (?)________________ voyage volcano________________ land whose nomenclature, like its opposite, Greenland, belies the topography________________ theories attributed to ____

____

____

____

____

____

____leading us into

————————— smoldering —————————

——S AE LL.

We —————————————— difficult to notate

—————————————— descent

3ICE

I GIVE UPPPPPP!
ALEX VERNE

——————————

—————————— hope and

Jules Verne

"Is this it?" Max said. "I see a lot of blank lines, and squiggles at the bottom. How does this help us?"

"Curb your enthusiasm," Rod said.

"It's the best I can do," Alex said. "Parts of the message are worn smooth."

"Dude, it's all about the serum," Rod said. "He did something with it. There was this whole elaborate plan."

Alex rubbed her eyes. "Which is nice to know, I guess. I mean, if we had the serum, we could try to follow the clues. But we don't. Bitsy does. Max has a point. This information is useless to us."

"Well . . . maybe not . . ." Max said, his eyes darting all over the page. "Look what this says . . . 'Hetzel, who retains the original copy' . . . So this isn't the only one. There's another out there."

"Well, there *was* another," Alex said.

"How do you know it doesn't still exist?" Max said. "OK, remember when Niemand first captured us in his sub? He went through this whole PowerPoint thing. It was about his great-great-grandfather, remember?"

Alex nodded. "Right. Oliver Niemand . . . or Oscar. He was a collector. And at some auction, he bought artwork from the estate of Jules Verne's editor—the guy Gloria Bentham mentioned, who died on the *Titanic.* So old Oliver or Oscar brings the artwork home, and voilà, hidden inside the frame he finds some of Jules Verne's secret plans! Verne had given it to his editor for safe-keeping."

"The editor's name—the guy who died in the *Titanic*—was Hetzel!" Max stood and began to spin around with excitement. "So if Verne's original copy went to Hetzel, maybe it still exists!"

Gloria Bentham's words came back to Max:

Spencer insisted those notes were not complete. He suspected Hetzel had more information. He was obsessed with the idea that Verne had buried secrets in other books, not only Twenty Thousand Leagues Under the Sea. . . . *I would not be surprised if he believes that your discovery—the completed serum—is now connected to some other crazy science-fiction story.*

"Niemand knew there were more clues," Max said. "He suspected Verne's novels were real. And he also suspected Hetzel had clues to other information. That's what Gloria Bentham told us."

Rod nodded, listening closely. "So if Bitsy springs her dad from jail, maybe that's what they go looking for. Those other clues."

"You think Niemand and Bitsy are going auction-house hopping for more of Hetzel's stuff?" Alex asked.

"Maybe," Rod said. "But after all these years . . .

what's the likelihood it hasn't all been auctioned off?"

"Unless they're not at an auction house . . ." Max's thumbs were already flying on the screen of his phone. "Maybe a *real* house. A house with an attic. Like where we found our hidden messages. Like a house belonging to some descendant of Hetzel!"

Rod snorted. "So what's your plan—contacting everyone in the world named Hetzel and asking them if Niemand stopped by?"

"Do you have any better ideas?" Alex asked.

Max's search turned up a few social media accounts, which seemed like a good start. But his eyes fixed on one link, a new item only an hour old, which he'd almost missed:

Massachusetts Nursing Home Resident Suffers Heart Attack, Is Robbed

[AP] The Brick Hollow Residences for the Well-Lived is prepared for the sudden illnesses of its elderly residents, but not when they are accompanied by a theft of personal property, as in the strange, sad case of ninety-one-year-old Martin **Hetzel** . . .

"Oh. Oh. Oh wow. Mercaptan attack," Max said.

"What?" Rod said.

"That's anxiety," Alex replied, pulling Rod around so that they could both read over Max's shoulders.

"Martin was a bit of a loner," said Rosalie Hughes, vice president of facilities, "so we're always happy when he has visitors, but we couldn't help noticing how agitated he was." She went on to describe a young woman who spoke in a European accent and a ruddy-faced older man, "both wearing wide-brimmed hats indoors, which we found unusual," Hughes said.

Shortly after meeting them, Hetzel collapsed. In the confusion that followed, no one thought much about the two visitors. And it wasn't until hours later that anyone noticed the open door on storage locker #23, belonging to Martin Hetzel, with a key hanging from its hole and a box of personal papers missing . . .

NIEMAND knew.

Max was sure of it. While the crafty old guy was in prison, his daughter was working behind the scenes. Maybe she was the one who tracked down Martin Hetzel's location. She might have done that research while she was a guest at Max's house. Right under their noses.

The intensity of the cat pee smell made Max throw open all Rod's windows. Outside, an a cappella singing group was drawing a small crowd, but Max barely noticed, staring at the text of Jules Verne's message.

If Bitsy and her father were following these instructions, Max and Alex would have to go after them.

"Agghh, do we have to listen to that singing?" Rod moaned, his hands over his ears.

Ignoring him, Max read aloud from the text. "'Land whose nomenclature . . . belies the topography . . .' What does Verne mean by that?"

"Come help us, Rod," Alex said.

"Sorry, I hate a cappella." Rod sidled over. "Well, *belies* is like 'contradicts.' *Nomenclature* is the name of something. So he's talking about a place with a name that means the opposite."

Alex nodded. "Like the country he mentions. Greenland, which is not green, but snowy and cold and icy. What other place in the world is like that?"

"Greece!" Max said. "It's not greasy. It's really dry."

Rod howled with laughter, and Alex elbowed him. "You think of something better, smarty-pants. Or I'll tell that singing group you want to join them."

"What about the title?" Max said, pointing to the top of the text. "Verne calls it a 'voyage to the center of my soul.'"

"So?" Rod asked.

"So that may be a hint," Max replied. "Because when you think about it, *voyage* is another word for . . . ?"

He looked at Alex, who darted over to him and glanced over his shoulder. "Journey?" she said.

"Exactly," Max replied. "It's staring us right in the

face—*journey to the center of my soul.* Which sounds just like . . . ?"

"*Journey to the Center of the Earth!*" Rod said.

"You rock, Max!" Alex exclaimed.

"I thought of it," Rod protested.

"I wish I'd read that book," Max said. "I never did."

"I did, when I was about ten," Alex said. "It's about this young dude and his professor uncle who go into a volcano way up north—Greenland, maybe? Norway? Anyway, the professor thinks they can find a place where you can travel all around the world *below* the continents, in some secret underwater passage. Along the way, they discover lakes, coasts, sources of light, and some . . . surprises. I don't want to spoil anything."

"I get that you guys could travel *Twenty Thousand Leagues Under the Sea*," Rod said. "And you could go *Around the World in 80 Days.* Those are plausible. Human scale. But hello? *Journey to the Center of the Earth*? It's like a bazillion degrees down there."

"Fahrenheit or Celsius?" Max asked.

"It doesn't matter!" Rod replied. "It's impossible. The Earth has a molten core. You'll be toast. Literally."

"The professor guy in the novel, Liedenbrock, says there is no molten core," Alex said. "His theory is that the Earth actually traps coolness. Anyway, it doesn't matter because they don't really go *all* the way to the center. So the title is kind of misleading."

"I guess *Journey Pretty Far Down into the Earth* wouldn't have the same effect," Max said. Now he was accessing a world map, zooming in to the Arctic Circle so that Greenland was on the left and the Scandinavian countries on the right. "OK, look, Greenland is totally white on the map. It's inside the polar ice cap. But to the east, Sweden, Norway, and Finland aren't. Between them you can see the Gulf Stream flowing up from the south, joining with the currents of the North Atlantic Drift, warming the eastern countries."

"And the one smack in the middle," Rod said, "is Iceland! Which is actually pretty green. Unlike Greenland, which is icy. Just like he said in the message. Opposites."

Alex was researching on her phone too. "Bingo. Confirmed, *Journey to the Center of the Earth* does take place in Iceland. The name of the volcano is . . ." She pointed on her phone screen to the name Snaefellsjökull, also known as Snaefell. "It's a real place too. Not fictional. Anyone want to take a crack at pronouncing it?"

"I think Snuffle will work," Max said.

"It's a volcano, not a Muppet," Rod said.

Max took Alex's phone and toggled back to the translation. "I think Verne was writing about that exact place. Look."

He turned the phone sideways and zoomed out to reveal a section of Verne's note:

———————————————leading us into
——————————smoldering——————————
——S AE LL.
We——————————————difficult to notate
——————————descent

"*S, A, E, L, L* . . . those are all letters in Snuffle—I mean, Snaefell," Max said.

"Which means he did go there," Alex said. "But why? What does it have to do with the serum?"

"There's only one way to find out." Max grabbed his backpack from the floor. "And that's to catch Stinky and Daughter while they're on their way down there. Is there an international airport in Iceland?"

"Yup, in the capital, Reykjavík," Rod said. "But wait. You're not—?"

"This is a job for Brandon the Pilot!" Max declared.

"Already texting him," Alex said, thumbs pecking at her phone.

"I'll find out information about how to get to the volcano from the capital," Max said, taking his phone from his pack.

"You guys," said Rod, sinking back onto the sofa, "are out of your minds."

Hello im max. Jules verne was
my great-great-great-grandfather.
Just fyi

Hello from the Icelandic Museum of
Unusual Phenomena
That is very interesting!!!
What an ancestor to have!
I am Kristin Zax-Ericksson.
How may I help you?

Whoa. This is cool that u answer on
ur soc media account so fast.
I wasn't expecting that

Hahaha there's not so much to do here right now, I guess.

My cousin alex & I are on our way to Reykjavik which I am glad I have autocorrect bc it is very hard to spell ☺ anyway I was reading about your museum is it true u have a jules verne wing?

Yes we do! It will be an honor to meet you! Do you need a guide?

Yes!!!!!!

I'll consider it my honor and pleasure.

Thanks oh also have u seen a girl with an English accent & an old guy w hair that looks like a skunk?

Can't say I have, sorry. But I'll keep an eye out.
When will you be arriving?
I will be happy to pick you up at Keflavik.
That's our airport.

I'll check with brandon the pilot
& let u know

Looking at his phone, Max walked directly into Alex's back. She fell forward, catching herself on the steel rails of a rolling staircase. "Walk much?"

"Yes, every day!" Max had to shout to be heard over the sound of a nearby landing jet. He slipped past Alex and took the rail. "I call the copilot seat. Technically, I own the jet."

Alex yanked him back. "Technically, your parents do, and no, you're thirteen. To be in the copilot's seat, you need to be older than eighteen. It's a rule. Ask Brandon."

"That makes no sense!" Max said. "Rod let me sit in the front of his car, all the way up to the airport. Statistically, driving is much more dangerous than flying. Especially driving in Boston. Besides, when *you* sit there you never even try to copilot!"

But Alex was already taking the steps two at a time. As she jumped into the seat, she stuck out her tongue at Max and buckled herself in. Max reluctantly scrambled into the back.

Brandon the Pilot had flown the Tilt family plane ever since they'd bought it with the treasure money. Max didn't know his last name, but he was sure Alex did. Alex seemed very interested in everything about Brandon.

"Weather reports aren't great in Reykjavík, guys," Brandon announced. "Thick cloud cover. High winds and rain. I had to twist arms to get clearance."

"You're good at that," Alex said.

"And you're good at getting yourself to sit next to him," Max said.

"Max!" Alex said.

"Guys—what I'm trying to say is, are you sure you don't want to wait a couple of days?" Brandon asked.

"No!" said Alex and Max at the same time.

With a lopsided smile, Brandon turned the ignition key. "OK, it's your funeral."

Alex slapped him on the shoulder. "You're terrible."

"If he's terrible, then why did you giggle?" Max asked.

"Ignore him," Alex said to Brandon.

As Max buckled in, he caught a glimpse of his phone screen. "Oh. Almost forgot. When are we getting to Iceland? Kristin wants to know. I found her online. We've been texting."

"Kristin?" Alex turned, with a raised eyebrow. "You're using some junior dating site?"

"Our guide in Reykjavík," Max said. "She says she'll give us a private tour of Snuffle. Her museum has a whole Jules Verne wing, so I figure she knows a lot. I should answer her before we lose cell service."

"Sweet," Brandon said. "We'll be five and a half hours, maybe six, depending on headwinds. Problem is, if the weather's too windy, they may reroute us to Norway or Scotland."

"I'll tell her," Max said, typing a reply into the phone.

Brandon adjusted his headphones. "OK, guys, we have a lane, so prepare for takeoff. You're going to need to power off, dude, so finish up."

"Done."

Max shut his phone as the jet began rolling toward the runway. Out the window he could see a commercial jet taking off overhead, soaring toward the glass towers of the Boston skyline. For a moment Max wondered if Bitsy was on the jet, and he caught the sharp stink of fish.

Stop that, he told himself.

He took a deep breath and sat back. The plane was rolling, picking up speed. He watched Brandon's hand slowly pulling back the throttle lever.

It took a few nanoseconds to realize that two hands were on the throttle. Brandon's on top, and Alex's underneath.

"Ew," Max said. "Just . . . ew."

Alex spun around. "Brandon is teaching me! Hey, you were the one who said I should learn how to copilot."

Max leaned back, rolling his eyes up to the ceiling. As the wheels lifted off the ground, he felt as if he were stuck in a cloud of ozone, the sweet-strange smell that happens after a rainstorm.

Ozone meant impatience.

He couldn't wait to power his phone back on. It was going to be a long flight.

The ending of *Journey to the Center of the Earth* hit Max like a punch to the gut.

Or maybe that was his seat belt.

He looked up from his phone. Alex and Brandon the Pilot were no longer touching, or holding hands, or whatever they'd been doing while Max was reading. Now Brandon was flipping switches, throwing levers, and muttering sharply into the mic of his headgear.

Max wanted to talk about the book, but the plane jolted again. A sudden flash of lightning washed the cabin in bluish white. Outside all he could see was a churn of gray, spitting water against the windows. *"What's happening?"* he shouted.

"Storm," Brandon said. "Plus, some volcanic activity."

"We're there already?" Max asked.

Brandon snickered. "Must have been a good book. We've been in the air a long time."

"Did Snuffle explode?" Alex asked.

"No," Brandon replied. "Another one. Not too near, but upwind. The island is full of volcanoes. They warned us that something was brewing. The darkness isn't just cloud cover, it's also ash."

Alex was gripping Brandon's arm now. "Can you lift us out of it?"

"I'll try."

Brandon pulled the throttle slowly, and Max felt himself tipping backward. As the jet rose, it shook side to side like a helpless mouse swatted between the paws of a cat. "I'm going to lose my cheeseburger," Max moaned.

"This isn't going to work," Brandon said. "Not enough fuel. They're telling us to come in now anyway."

"Can you see anything?" Max asked.

"I don't need to," Brandon replied. "We have radar, and they'll guide me. Hang on. This will be over soon."

"I don't like the way that sounds," Alex said.

Brandon shoved the throttle forward. The jet tilted downward and began shaking violently, as if they'd crested a hill only to slide down a bumpy road. Brandon's outline blurred, and Alex's wild mass of hair looked like a storm cloud. Even Max's words seemed to be rattling as he shouted, *"Wha-a-a-at's g-g-going on?"*

"We're good!" Brandon shouted.

Now the engine made a high-pitched groan that Max had never heard before. As he dug his fingernails into the armrest, his phone slid out of his lap and onto the floor.

Alex was turning around now. Her eyes were wet and bloodshot, and she mouthed the words "I love you, Max."

Max nodded. "I was thinking the same thing," he said.

"What?" Brandon shouted into his mic. *"We can't!"*

"Can't?" Alex said.

"They're telling all flights to turn back," Brandon said. *"Hello . . . come in . . . come in, ground control! Request clearance to land, over!* I don't believe this. I'm—I'm losing contact."

"Are they going to let you land?" Alex demanded.

"Request landing, do you read me?" Brandon shouted. Now Alex was clutching his arm. "OK . . . we can do this . . ." he said. "Hang tight . . ."

Through the windshield, a mass of black loomed below. *"What's that?"* Max yelled.

Brandon pulled back, hard. The jet began to level. The black mass seemed to spring toward the jet, smacking the windshield. Max lurched forward, his seat belt nearly crushing his ribs.

"Ash!" Brandon yelled.

The word hadn't left his mouth when the engine let out a sputtering wheeze and died.

"What happened?" Alex demanded.

Brandon opened his mouth. No words came out. But a gauge on his dashboard was flickering with the words ENGINE FAILURE.

Then that gauge flickered and went out. Along with all the lights in the cabin.

In silence, the jet plunged into darkness.

And Max began to scream.

11

THE impact jammed Max's teeth together. Unfortunately his tongue was between them.

He brought his hand to his lips. Blood oozed through his fingers to form a small dark pool on the jet floor. And three things occurred to him:

1. His tongue was still intact.
2. So was the jet.
3. And therefore, he was not dead.

He couldn't see much in the darkness, but the cabin was bobbing gently up and down. Water splashed against the hull of the jet, sending small sprays against the window.

Brandon had done it. He'd made a water landing. He

missed the airport but managed to maneuver the jet over the ocean!

"Woo-hoo—*OWWW*!" Max cried out, as the tongue pain destroyed the joyful cheer. *"Brandon?"* he called out, a little more gently. *"Alekth?"*

Neither responded.

Max unbuckled his belt and squeezed between the two front seats. Brandon and Alex were both slumped forward, hair draped over their foreheads. He put his hand to their noses. They were breathing. In the dim light from outdoors he caught a glimpse of an opened compartment on the copilot dashboard. In it was a box marked by a red-and-white cross, and a white, disk-shaped object that had to be tape. On the floor were random Band-Aids and plastic vials.

One of them was marked SMELLING SALTS.

Max had only seen them used in cartoons, but they always worked. He held one just under Alex's nose and carefully opened the bottle.

"Yeeeaaccchh!" she cried out, her head jamming back against her seat.

The scream stirred Brandon in the pilot seat, who let out a moan.

"We made it," Max said.

Alex looked around, her eyes blank and her jaw slack. "We . . . we did?"

"We're in the water," Max said, his tongue still thick and bloody. "Thomewhere near Itheland, I hope."

Brandon was unbuckling his belt, taking deep breaths. "OK . . . OK. We should be just off the coast. The engines sucked in too much ash. Without power, the only hope was to land in the ocean and pray the wings didn't dip underwater and pull us down." He pressed his face against the window, squinting. "We'll have to open the two side doors and paddle this thing to land."

"Paddle a *jet*?" Alex said.

"A small jet," Brandon said. "But seaworthy. And buoyant. We had to do this in training. The oars are long and powerful. I wasn't able to activate the pontoons, which we could have stood on, but we can lean out the doors. We'll have leverage. You'll be surprised."

Max checked his phone. "I have one bar of thell thervice. That meanth we mutht be pretty near thivilization. We can uthe the GP-Eth to get uth to shore. Thorry, I bit my tongue."

"I understood," Brandon said. "You navigate while Alex and I move this baby."

He scooted around to the door, flipped down a lever, and yanked the entire door out of the wall. Watching him carefully, Alex did the same on the other side.

A cold, wet wind blasted through the cabin, rocking it hard. Immediately Max began to sneeze and his eyes stung. "I—I feel like I thwallowed thandpaper!" he cried out.

"Me too," Alex said.

"This is a Class A jet, and we are prepared!" Brandon pulled down a hinged compartment on the wall, revealing a long wooden paddle and a secured rope. As he tied the other end of the rope around his waist, he called out, "There's a pair on the other side too, Alex!"

"Why the rope?" Alex asked.

"In case we fall in," Brandon said.

"Oh, great."

"Just fasten yourself and let's do this."

In moments, she and Brandon were leaning out the doors, paddling as hard as they could, fighting against the thick gush of sea spray. "This is crazy!" Alex said.

Max kept a careful eye on the GPS. "We're moving," he said. "Veer more to the left!"

The blue dot was making its way slowly to some kind of shore. In about five minutes, Max could see the black silhouette of a coastline, and a pale orange swath of light in the distance to the left. "What's that?" Alex called out.

"The out-thkirtth of Reykjavík, I think," Max said.

They both paddled harder. But despite the steady *ploosh . . . ploosh* of the oars in the water, now the jet seemed to be standing still. Max felt his feet getting cold and realized he was standing in a puddle. *"Is this thupposed to be happening?"* he called out.

"You mean water in the cabin?" Brandon replied. "The answer is no. We're taking on water like crazy. But we can't do this without the doors open. Row harder, me matey. Yo ho ho!"

"This is not a time for dad jokes!" Alex shot back. "This water is freezing!"

Max began to shiver. The shore was still a black line on the horizon that seemed not to be getting closer. "I think we're stuck on something," Brandon said.

"How does a jet get stuck in the water?" Alex cried.

Brandon shrugged. "An old mooring, a buoy, a lobster trap?" He leaned his body out through the opening. "I can find out and loosen us."

"Wait—you think you're going to swim in this?" Alex said. "Human beings only last five and half minutes in water this temperature!"

"Really?" Brandon said.

"OK, I made up the number, but it's something like that," Alex said. "It's cold, Brandon!"

"This won't take long." Brandon put down the oar and grabbed a life vest and a helmet with a flashlight from the chest. *"Geronimo!"*

Before they could protest, he leaped through the hatch and splashed into the ocean.

"That was really, really, really dumb," Alex said.

Max activated his phone's flashlight app and shone it out the hatch. *"Where are you?"* he called out.

"Woooo!" Brandon called from the darkness. *"It's awe—awe—awes-s-some!"*

Max's beam caught Brandon swimming though the rough water, until he swam out of sight, around the nose of the plane. *"Stay where Max can see you, OK?"* Alex cried out.

Brandon's tether went taut, and Max could hear him call out, *"I see the s-s-snag, but I c-c-can't reach it! I'm going to unt-t-tie my kn-kn-knot!"*

"You will not do that," Alex said. "You will not even think of doing that!"

As Brandon's rope went limp, Max turned his phone flashlight toward the shore. There, a pinpoint of light shone in the distance. Had it been there the whole time? Max couldn't tell what it was—car? Lighthouse? Lamppost?

Max began flashing the Morse code for SOS—short,

short, short . . . long, long, long . . . short, short, short . . .

"What are you doing?" Alex asked. "Stop playing with the light and help him!"

Before he could respond, a guttural scream cut through the beating rain.

"Brandon?" Alex cried out. *"What's up? Did you find it?"*

Brandon's response was more a series of yelps than a word. Alex and Max peered through the windshield. Brandon's helmet light was moving swiftly—away from the floating jet. "What's he saying?" Alex asked.

"I don't know," Max replied. "But that lookth like an undertow."

"He-e-e-e-elp!"

That word was unmistakable.

"Stay here, Max," Alex said, strapping on a life vest. "See what you can do. Find some flares. Whatever."

"Alex, wait, you can't jutht—!"

But Alex was out the door before Max could finish. As she hit the water, she cried out a very bad word and then began to swim.

Max stood at the doorway, his knees locked. He looked at the shore for the distant light, but it was gone. Max smelled ham when he was confused, and at that moment it was so strong, it nearly made him sick.

But he'd been in this situation before. On a submarine

in water just as frigid. In Greenland. He and Alex had been afraid to jump in. They may not have, if not for Basile's encouragement. The old man knew he would die, but he also knew Max and Alex were strong enough to withstand the cold.

Max would be strong enough now.

The smell was fading. He placed his phone on the rear seat of the plane and grabbed a life vest. Saying a prayer, he jumped out the door.

MAX'S body seized up. He tried to swim, but his arms were locked.

A wave hit him full in the face. As he coughed out seawater, his arms began to thrash wildly.

Don't fight it. Left to its own devices, a human body floats. Especially a human body with a life vest.

Fact.

Panic is one of the main causes of death in the water.

Fact.

Exposure is the loss of body heat, which can kill a person who stays in cold water too long.

Fact.

Max lifted his head. He took a couple of gasping

breaths. A wave hit him on the exhalation, but he did not panic. He allowed it to wash over him. He blinked the saltwater from his eyes.

He could see Alex bobbing up and down at the front of the plane, one arm wrapped around an old log. As Max swam closer, trying to crest the waves, his cousin began swimming toward him. Her free arm was wrapped around Brandon, who wasn't moving at all. *"He got hit!"* she shouted. *"He didn't see the log!"*

Max kicked hard, reaching Alex in a few strokes. He grabbed onto another section of log with one hand and Brandon's arm with the other. "L-L-Let'th get him b-b-back, bef-f-fore we f-f-f—"

"Freeze to death, I know!" Alex said.

Max turned. Together he and his cousin dug into the water. Max could barely feel the tips of his fingers now. His breaths were shallow. A tree branch swept up beside him, and he pushed it away.

He glanced up. He expected to be closer now, almost to the hatch. But the jet was farther away, and it looked like it was moving. *"It's f-f-floating away from us!"* he yelled. The saltwater seemed to be healing his bitten tongue, but it did nothing to stop his jaw from shivering with the cold.

"We're floating away from it!" Alex called back. *"It's the*

current, Max. The undertow. It's taking us out to sea!"

Max thought hard. "An undertow . . . a n-n-natural current . . . doesn't go ffforever . . . c-c-can't f-f-fight it . . . b-b-best to wait it out . . ."

"We're in Iceland, Max, not Mexico! We can't wait. We'll d-d-die!"

The cold seemed to be closing in like a fist. Max had to tell his lungs to expand and contract. Alex was right. Swimming to the ship would kill them.

But not swimming to the ship would kill them too.

"GEEAAHH!"

Max felt a sharp tug. Brandon was awake now, gasping, thrashing in the water. *"Brandon, it's OK!"* Alex shouted.

"Actually, it isn't!" Max shouted back.

Brandon's face was bone white. "The—the j-j-jet," he stammered. "Who's inssside it?"

"No one!" Max said.

"Th-Th-Then why is it moving t-t-toward us?" Brandon asked.

Alex groaned. "Brandon, we can't even see it anymore."

Max looked at the pilot's face. His eyes were not fixed in the direction of the jet, but off to the shore. Max followed his glance. A wave smacked them hard, and Max went under.

When he came up, he heard a low, deep moan. Not from Brandon or Alex, but off in the direction of the shore. He shook off the water from his eyelids and blinked. The sea surface was a constellation of spindrift and whitecaps, like an explosion of stars.

So it took a moment for Max to see that one of those stars was growing larger. He wanted to draw attention to it but the cold was freezing his jaw. "I—I shizz . . . somsh . . ."

As he tried to focus on it, Brandon grabbed him from behind. It was all Max could do to focus on the light. For a moment, it blinded him.

They say when you die, sometimes you see a white light . . .

Max looked away and shoved the thought out of his head. That was not a fact. At least he didn't think it was. The deep moan sounded again, much louder.

It wasn't a human sound; it was mechanical.

As he struggled to stay alert, Max squinted and made out a shape, an outline of something floating on the surface. "What . . . is . . . ?"

"That thing I thought was the jet—it's a boat, dude. Someone saw us!" Brandon said. *"Yo! Yo—over here!"*

Now Brandon was lifting Alex so she could grab onto the log. As she wrapped one arm around it, she waved with the other. She tried to shout too, but her voice was not much more than a whisper.

The horn sounded again, and a small fishing boat cut through the darkness. Max had to turn away from its harsh searchlight. Although his body was nearly numb, he felt a sharp rap to his head. Something bounced off it and dropped into the water a few inches away.

A life preserver, attached to a rope.

And another. A third.

Max, Alex, and Brandon each grabbed one, and Max felt himself moving. Toward the boat.

The hot chocolate made his tongue sting, and it felt like a dagger traveling through his frozen body, but Max eagerly took a second sip. "D-D-Delish—" he said, still shivering uncontrollably.

"Rogers family recipe!" said one of their rescuers, a broad, red-bearded man. "We've also got popcorn, crackers, cereal. A gourmet restaurant, eh?"

Max, Alex, and Brandon were wrapped in blankets, sitting in a cramped cabin with a buzzing light that made everything look slightly green. Another rescuer, a white-haired woman, was swabbing Brandon's head with some red solution. "You took quite a bump there. Are you feeling faint, woozy?"

"Nah," Brandon said with a grin. "Never felt better."

"How many fingers?" she went on, holding up three.

"Six," Brandon said. "Divided by two."

Alex, who was holding his hand, elbowed him gently in the side.

Their third rescuer was a slight young woman with black bangs and black owlish glasses. She was gently wrapping a second wool blanket around Max's shoulders. "Is that better?"

Max nodded. "Th-th-thank you for f-f-finding us," he said.

"Don't thank us," she replied. "Thank whichever one of you sent the Morse code message."

Alex's mouth dropped open into a perfect zero shape. "*That's* what did it?"

"The phone has a surprisingly high lumen count," Max said.

"Max, you are my hero," Alex declared.

The young woman's eyebrows arched over her glasses. "I thought you might be Max," she said, holding out her hand. "I'm Kristin. You texted me."

"From the dating site?" Brandon piped up.

"Don't mind him, he's brain damaged," Alex said.

"I'm the assistant director of the Icelandic Museum of Unusual Phenomena," Kristin said, then gestured to the others. "Sven Rogers . . . Åsa Talo. Sven and I studied together, and now he and Ms. Talo run a rescue boat for Keflavik Airport. Your last name, Max?"

"Tilt," Max said.

"I'm his cousin, Alex, and this is Brandon Barker, our pilot," Alex said.

Max nearly spat out his hot chocolate. "Brandon *Barker*? That's his name?"

"We were afraid for your plane," said Sven Rogers, whose voice was too loud for the small room. "Your timing couldn't have been worse, eh? We managed to get a few small craft in just minutes before you. No one expected that Eyjafjallajökull would blow again like that."

"Don't ever expect me to repeat that name," Max said.

"Wait—those other small craft—you mean other private jets?" Alex said.

Sven stroked his beard. "One, I believe. The others were commercial."

Max caught a quick glance from Alex. She said nothing, but her eyes flashed *Niemand.*

"What about our jet?" Brandon asked.

"We have alerted the authorities about it," Ms. Talo said. "They'll tow it in tomorrow after the weather clears."

"We will pay for repairs," Max said, "as long as it's ready for us when we're back from our tour."

The cabin fell silent, rocking back and forth. Max could hear a whistling gust of wind from outside, and rain hit the porthole like a slap. "Um, this would not be possible for quite some time," Kristin said. "If ever."

Alex and Max sat straight up. "Why not?" Max asked. "The volcano that erupted wasn't Snuffle, right?"

"Snaefell," Alex corrected him.

"That is correct, it was not Snaefellsjökull," Kristin replied, "but you see, Iceland lies on the fault line between two tectonic plates, the Eurasian and the North American. People think of our little country as the land of geysers. And those are pretty spectacular. But a geyser is water released by pressure through cracks in the Earth. And those cracks are created by volcanoes. This little island has produced a third of the world's lava output over the last five hundred years. There are thirty active volcano systems, and many are connected along the fault line. If one goes, another often follows. So we must take precautions."

"What kind of precautions?" Max asked.

Kristin sighed. "The authorities have ordered all tours of caves and volcanoes shut down until further notice."

IN all his thirteen years, Max had never expected to hear the sentence that was uttered by Brandon Barker in the Apotek Restaurant:

"Whale meat is awesome!" he said with a barely covered burp.

"Ha!" shouted Sven. "This is a typical tourist reaction."

Kristin smiled patiently. "We Icelanders—well, most of us—do not tend to order whale meat."

"Well, you're really missing something!" Brandon said, shoveling in another mouthful.

Max swallowed hard against a churning in his stomach. The restaurant was big and cheerful, with twinkling Christmas-style lights and tables full of laughing people.

All of Reykjavík was a kind of picture-book city, full of low-rise buildings along narrow streets, with a view of the ocean on one side and giant mountains on the other. Kristin had shown them to the Viking Manor Hotel, which had soft, comfy beds and humongous TV screens. The walk to the restaurant through the local streets, even over ash-covered sidewalks in the rain, had lifted Max's spirits.

Until he saw the whale meat on Brandon's plate, which was a deep red and looked barely cooked.

"I love whales," Max said. "I love them almost as much as yaks. I think I'm going to get sick."

Brandon forked the entire rest of the whale steak into his mouth. "There," he said, chewing. "It's gone."

"Isn't it illegal to eat whale?" Alex asked.

"Most species, yes," Kristin replied.

"Only the minke whale is served," Ms. Talo added. "It's plentiful here and has the added quality of being legal to eat."

"I want to try auk!" Brandon bellowed.

"Auk?" Alex said. "As in the cute bird that looks like a little penguin?"

Max stood. "I smell wet dog."

The three adults stared at him, baffled.

"He smells wet dog when he feels disgust," Alex said. "It's synesthesia. Associative smells. It's all the talk of whales and auk. I think it's time for a little walk. I didn't mean for all that to rhyme."

As Max bolted up from the table, Alex took his arm. They headed toward the back of the restaurant, winding their way among the tables. "It's been a bad day," Alex said. "How are you feeling?"

Max took a deep breath. He stopped before reaching the restrooms. "Better. I liked the rhyme. It took my mind off those cute animals."

"Max?" Alex said. "Remember when we were in the Yak Restaurant in Kathmandu? And you thought they served yak, but they didn't? And when you went into the restroom, you saw a clue that led us to one of the ingredients?"

"Armando of Kathmandu, yeah," Max said.

"*You* found that," Alex said. "No one else knew about it. But remember what happened when we got to Armando?"

"Nigel. He appeared out of nowhere." Max cocked his head curiously. "Wait. What's the connection? Why are you bringing this up? Are you worried that Niemand might be here?"

"The volcano is shut down," Alex said. "If Niemand and Bitsy didn't make it there in time, they're stuck too. So yeah, Reykjavík's a pretty small city, and they have to eat. All I'm saying is, keep your eyes open. If you see them, try not to let them see you. We can make a plan—"

"To ambush them!" Max said with excitement.

Alex smiled. "I'll meet you back at the table."

As she went into one restroom, Max walked to the other, farther down the hall. Inside, it was dark and moody, with blue lighting and black tiles, and he was the only one in there. The sink was a polished steel bowl, with a spout at the bottom. He put his hand in front of the sensor and it shot up like a geyser into his face.

Stepping back, he shook the water from his face and caught a glimpse of himself in the mirror. In the blue light emanating from below, he looked like a zombie. "Arrrr . . . naaaarrchhh . . ." he growled.

The sound echoed in the room, which made him giggle.

Behind him, the stall door swung open slowly. Which meant someone had heard him. He caught a whiff of gasoline, which to him was embarrassment. So he looked down at the soap dispenser and concentrated very hard on washing his hands.

He wasn't expecting anyone to grab his arm.

With a gasp, he found himself being pulled backward into the toilet stall. He stumbled into the darkness. As the door shut automatically, a voice shushed him.

Max spun around. He was face-to-face with Kristin. "If I go any farther," she said, "I'll fall into the toilet."

"Wh-Wh-What are you doing?" Max stammered.

"Sssh," she said. "In front of Sven and Åsa I cannot speak of certain things. You and your cousin are the ones who found the great hidden treasure of Jules Verne, yes?"

Max swallowed hard. "I smell sweaty feet."

"I beg your pardon?"

"I'm feeling claustrophobic. Can we go somewhere else?"

Kristin reached past him and pushed open the stall door. Taking Max's arm, she exited the restroom and led him back out through the restaurant. She stopped at a corner near the bar, where a row of winter coats hung on hooks. "Sorry, this must seem very odd, but I couldn't think of a way to talk alone. And I didn't want to put this into a text. Security, you know." She lowered her voice to a whisper. "I need to trust you. This conversation must remain confidential. Will you agree to that?"

"I guess," Max said, then lowered his voice too. "But this is weird."

Kristin sighed. "I know who you are. I followed your story in the news with great interest. As you can imagine by my museum's emphasis on Jules Verne, I am a bit of a fangirl. I couldn't help but notice that your adventure seemed to follow closely the plot of *Twenty Thousand Leagues Under the Sea*."

Max nodded.

"In your text, you asked if I'd seen a girl and a man with hair like a skunk and an English accent, and I wrote back, 'No,'" she continued. "Well, it was a strange question, so I asked around. Åsa remembered assisting a pair at the airport, a young woman and older man, who arrived here a day before you on a private jet. She assumed they were father-daughter. She did not catch a glimpse of the man's hair, as he wore a hat. But their rudeness made quite an impression on her, and she believes she caught an English accent. They raced off to a private car, which whisked them away."

"Any other clues? Like, where they went and what they said?" Max asked.

Kristin shook her head sadly. "No, but does this information help?"

Max's brain was kicking. He took Kristin's arm and pulled her out of the coat corner and back into the restaurant. "It sure does. We have to talk to—"

He nearly collided with Alex in the corridor.

"Whoa, slow down, Speedy," she said.

"We were just going to get you," Max said.

"Can you wait till I go to the bathroom?" Alex asked, moving past them.

"I believe I saw your fugitive duo," Kristin said.

Alex stopped. "I can wait."

Kristin quickly explained what she'd said, and Max filled in some details. He watched Alex's brow settle back into place as she listened with close attention.

"It's them," Alex finally said. "Got to be. No question."

"I know everything about Iceland and Snaefellsjökull," Kristin said. "I can help you, if you tell me what you need."

"We're good," Alex said, her expression closing off into a wary coolness.

"We're not good," Max replied. "All we have is a faded old message with half the text missing. They may have a clear copy. If they're headed into a volcano, how will we follow them without a guide?"

Alex gave Max a confused glance. "I—I'm sorry. But

this is hard. We've been double- and triple-crossed so many times."

"I understand," Kristin said. "At least tell me why you've come. You can proceed without me if you like, but I confess I'm dying of curiosity."

Max took a deep breath. If she didn't even know their mission, it didn't seem she was working with Niemand. Carefully he outlined what had happened—the clues, *The Lost Treasures*, the search for the ingredients, the transformation of real-life adventure into novels, the hidden note behind the Verne portrait.

Kristin listened with awed attention. "That is extraordinary," she said. "May I see the note you found?"

Max cast a quick glance to Alex, who nodded tentatively.

Max took out his phone, navigated to an image of the note, and began scrolling down the length of it. "It's in Braille. Alex translated it into French, then English. For some reason Verne and his nephew wanted to take that serum into the Earth. Anyway, the message got decayed over time, especially when you go down past the middle. And the bottom is random squiggles and lines, just total kaka, but—"

"It's not kaka . . ." Kristin said, taking the phone from Max. "At least some of it isn't."

"Well, Braille is an arrangement of dots, and these aren't dots—"

"Exactly." She zoomed in for the lower part of the note. "I see some Icelandic runes. Hieroglyphics."

Max looked closely. "Like the ones at the beginning of *Journey to the Center of the Earth*! Where Axel decodes them because Liedenbrock is clueless."

"That didn't even occur to me," Alex said.

"Max is correct," Kristin replied. "We must show this to Uncle Gunther."

"Gunther?" Max said.

"My boss, the founder of the museum. Dr. Gunther Zax-Ericksson, world-renowned expert on antiquities. Who also happens to be my great-uncle." Kristin's eyes were filling with tears. "You have no idea what this will mean to him. He is quite old and not entirely himself. But he has been waiting a lifetime for this. For a chance to prove the Hobnagian invasion. Which I assume you're familiar with?"

Max shook his head no.

"Can you forward a copy of this to me?" Kristin asked. "I will print it out for Uncle Gunther to see. We will all visit him after dinner. And then we will proceed to Snaefellsjökull in the morning."

"As in tomorrow morning?"

"Of course."

Max looked out the window into the rainy darkness. "But we can't. It's closed."

"To tour groups, yes." Kristin broke into a lopsided smile. "Which will make things much easier for us."

14

"SAY 'cheese.'"

Kristin pointed a tiny camera toward Max. The camera sat on a small reception desk at the Icelandic Museum of Unusual Phenomena, which was a grand name for a modest, slightly sagging two-story house on a residential block.

"American or Swiss?" Max said.

Kristin took the photo, which instantly generated a security sticker for Max. "Now you, Alex."

"Are you serious—do you really need this level of security?" Alex asked.

Kristin sighed. "We had a spate of fossil thefts in 1997, and ever since then my uncle has required photo ID of every visitor. He'll become cross if he doesn't see you wearing it on a lanyard. Come on—'cheese!'"

With a sigh, Alex posed. "Cheese," she said. "Should we call Brandon before we go in?"

Max looked out the window into the dark street. "I think he's down for the night at the hotel. He didn't seem interested."

"He's stuck in Iceland just like us," Alex said. "We need to involve him. Four brains are better than three."

"Unless eating whale meat decays your brain function," Max said.

With their IDs hanging from their necks, he and Alex followed Kristin through the doors of a dark, stuffy library lined with wooden shelves that were crammed full of dust-covered books. It had a sweet-sour smell of old paper, pipe tobacco, and deep thoughts. Sitting by the window on a worn leather armchair was an old man who seemed to be part of the furniture himself. His head sagged alarmingly low, as if it had detached from his neck and planted itself on the slope of his ample belly. Slowly turning his head, he stared at Max and Alex with blue eyes so faint they had barely any color at all.

"Max, Alex, this is my great-uncle, Dr. Gunther Zax-Ericksson," Kristin said.

He extended a shaky hand to Max. "You are the

Australians?" the old man asked.

"No, Uncle!" Kristin said in a loud voice, leaning close to him. "These are Max Tilt and his cousin Alex Verne. You have never met them. They have just arrived in Reykjavík from the United States. They are trying to reach—"

"No need to yell, Katrin," he said.

"Kristin," Kristin said, pulling two copies of Jules Verne's message from a wireless printer. "Katrin was your poodle."

"And where has that infernal pet gone off to?" the old man demanded.

"She passed away, Uncle," Kristin replied.

"What?" he thundered. "No one told me!"

"It was six years ago," Kristin said. "She was very old. We buried her together."

The conversation was not giving Max confidence. He glanced toward Alex, who looked away, trying not to laugh.

Kristin took a leather-bound book from Zax-Ericksson's shelf, then pulled up a seat next to him. Setting the book and the note in his lap, she said, "Max and Alex are ancestors of Jules Verne, you know. They have found a note that he left. They believe it tells something about his motivations for the journey to Snaefellsjökull. I made two copies, one for us and one for you."

"Ah, Verne! I've been talking about him lately. Such vision. Genius! Saw the future like no one besides—"

"Besides DaVinci, yes, we know," Kristin said, gently placing glasses on his face. Then she held his copy of the note close to him, pointing to places on it as she spoke. "The top of this note here is in Braille, which they have transcribed. Would you mind reading from down here, at this spot where the Braille seems to end?"

The old man fell absolutely silent. His shaking subsided. The sad, blank look vanished from his face, and even his eyes seemed to grow darker with the concentration.

"Are they Icelandic runes?" Max asked.

"In a manner of speaking, yes . . ." he replied absentmindedly. "Would you bring me my lap desk, Kristin? And while she is doing that, come closer and tell me how you found this, children who are not from Australia?"

Alex and Max knelt beside him. Carefully, slowly, Alex explained everything—the hidden notes, the voyages, the connections to *Twenty Thousand Leagues Under the Sea* and *Around the World in 80 Days*, the suspicions about Snaefellsjökull and *Journey to the Center of the Earth.* And finally, the emergency that someone else was after the same secret.

Although the old man couldn't lift his head quite vertically, he stared at her above the top of his glasses. When Alex was finished, she took a deep breath. "That's why we're here, sir. We'd like to trace his steps, to find out why he took his healing serum into the volcano."

"Yes . . ." Zax-Ericksson's eyes darted from Max to Alex with great alertness, as if seeing them for the first time. "You are the children who found the treasure in Greenland! I saw you on the news."

"Bingo," Alex replied.

"Yeah, we're famous," Max said.

"You've had great success with these missives from Verne all on your own, haven't you?" the old man remarked.

"Sometimes Verne tells you everything you need to know in the first message," Max added. "But sometimes he lets it out a little at a time. He guides you, step by step."

Now Kristin placed a portable padded desk on the old man's lap. "Thank you, my kind niece," Zax-Ericksson said. "I must say, I am relieved. For a moment I thought these two might be just a couple of the typical crazies who come here. You know, Hollow Earthers, Hobnagian theorists . . ."

"Who?" Max said.

But Zax-Ericksson was pulling a pad of paper and a

pen from a compartment in the desk. "Excuse me for a few moments, I must analyze this."

Kristin led Max and Alex out of the library and into a thickly carpeted side room of the museum, just off the library. The walls were lined with old glass specimen cases and small dioramas. Each was labeled with cards that looked as if they'd been printed in the nineteenth century. In the center was a display of bone fragments, each labeled from A to T.

"These fossils were brought back by Jules and Gaston Verne," Kristin said. "Most seem to be skull bones, some perhaps from Ice Age mastodons, others are thought to be human."

Max leaned over them, looking closely. "Some of these are missing."

"Six, to be exact, all stolen," Kristin said. "The bones corresponded to six of those letters—*H*, *O*, *B*, *N*, *A*, and *G*. Apparently, if you arrange them, you form what appears to be an extremely odd head. It has the thick, armored skull of a pachycephalosaurus, an oval-shaped face, and humanlike features."

"So . . . those six bones are definitely from the same species?" Max asked.

Kristin laughed. "Well, there is no way to know that, of course. But the letters took on a mystical property in the minds of some, and the planet Hobnag was born. People who are determined to believe nonsense are not stopped by little impediments like facts!"

"Yup," Max said. "I'm a fact fanatic."

Kristin smiled at him, adjusting her glasses. "I gathered. I am too."

From the library, Zax-Ericksson's crackly voice sang out, *"Aha! I knew it!"*

Kristin turned. "What is it, Uncle?"

She, Max, and Alex scurried back into the library. The old man was hunched over the lap desk. He was shaking again, but this time it looked like excitement. "Give me your copy of the Verne note, Kristin! Put it on top of my own."

As she did, he circled a portion of it. The three gathered around and stared over his shoulder. "This, children, *this*! Do you see what I circled here?"

"Cave drawings?" Alex said.

"I see the word *ice* on the right," Max added. "And maybe a lobster."

"Is it futhark, Uncle?" Kristin said.

"Not exactly, my dear," Zax-Ericksson said. "Although there appears to be plenty of that underneath, which we shall get to also."

"What's a futhark?" Max asked.

"It's the name we give the Scandinavian system of runic writing," Zax-Ericksson replied. "You see, runes were our form of written communication from about AD 150 until the Latin alphabet was adopted almost a thousand years later. The name comes from the first six letters, which make roughly the sound of *F*, *U*, *TH*, *A*, *R*, and *K*."

Kristin pulled a book from a shelf, opened it, and placed it on the desk, covering Zax-Ericksson's notes. "It looks something like this."

a b c d e f/v g h/x i/j k

l m n o p q/kw r s t u

v w x y z þ æ/ä ø/ö

"You'll notice there are no horizontal markings," the old man said. "This is because they were usually carved into wood. The letters are mainly formed from vertical, diagonal, curved lines. Vertical markings went directly across the grain of the wood. So if you carved horizontally, you would be carving *along* the grain—"

"And it wouldn't show as well!" Max blurted out.

"Bravo, my boy—also, you ran the risk of splitting the wood." The old man reached under the book. Pulling out Kristin's printout, he set it down on the cover and gestured to the section he had circled. "But what you have here—this is something different. It is a more ancient form of runic writing. You see, it took many years for this system of individual letters to evolve. Most alphabets began as series of drawings, and Scandinavian runes were no exception. What did these drawings mean? Well, many scholars believe they were meant to have magical powers—warding off evil, controlling weather, protecting humans against misfortune. They were talismans."

"This section you circled," Max said. "Is it a talisman or a futhark?"

"Kristin, would you remove this book?" Zax-Ericksson asked, craning his neck toward his niece.

She took the book away, revealing the old man's copy

of the note. He had altered it, in his shaky handwriting. "You see," he said, "I filled in the gaps."

"Sweet," Max said. "What does it mean?"

"That does not look like futhark," Kristin said.

"Is it some kind of map?" Alex asked.

Zax-Ericksson began to whimper softly, and it took Max a moment to realize he was laughing. "Young man, your great-great-grandfather thought of everything!"

"Actually, it's three greats," Max said.

"It's Vegvísir," the old man said. "Just as I suspected. One of the most powerful talismans of the ancients."

Max and Alex both looked at Kristin for an explanation, but she shrugged. "What did it do?" Alex asked.

"*Veg* became the word we know in English as 'way.' *Vísir* will be familiar as—"

"'Vizier'!" Max blurted. "Like the evil Jafar in *Aladdin*!"

"Different root," Zax-Ericksson said. "*Vísir* became 'visor.' It means 'face.' While wearing this talisman, you will always face the true path."

The old man leaned over toward his desk and pulled open a flat drawer near the desktop. Rummaging around in some pens and pencils, he pulled out a chain that held a white charm. "Ah, here it is, a scrimshaw Vegvísir, made for me by a student many years ago. Carved from a shark tooth, most likely illegal now."

As he held it up, the shape of the talisman twirled in the light of the office. "Can I hold it?" Max asked.

"You may take it with you, children. If it has the power it's rumored to have, you will never be lost." The old man let out a small giggle, looking up at Alex and then Max over the top of his glasses. "Or so they say."

15

IN a four-door jeep bouncing over lava fields dotted with rain puddles, Max did not feel magically protected. Even with his talisman. He sat sunken into the backseat with his arms draped over the top of his head, next to Brandon the Pilot, who looked out of place without a cockpit. Max's head had already hit the roof twenty-three times, and his seat belt was carving a diagonal stripe down his chest.

"So let me get this right . . . you're going into the volcano because you think Stinky and his daughter are there," said Brandon the Pilot. "And you think they're following Jules Verne's secret message, which has something to do with the miracle cure you guys found and they stole."

"Yes," Alex said, her hands clutching both armrests.

"And if you're wrong?" Brandon said. "If the people they saw at the airport were just some rando rich guy and his daughter, and you're going into a volcano for no reason?"

"Then we'll come back up," Kristin snapped. "But I believe we must commit ourselves to a decision. And that involves a certain amount of optimism and inner strength."

"What she said," Max echoed.

The wipers pounded against the rain but only managed to create greasy arcs across the windshield. Kristin was jerking the steering wheel to the right and left, squinting through the gaps. "Sorry. Visibility is very bad."

Max sat back, fiddling with the Vegvísir medallion that hung around his neck. He fought off the smell of ammonia, which occurred when he thought someone was trying to trick him. Sometimes it happened when people said things he didn't understand. Like Dr. Zax-Ericksson's *Or so they say*. Was that a joke? Did he think the talisman was a dumb old story? Or did he hold out hope that it might be true?

And then there was Jules Verne. The previous night, he, Alex, and Kristin had stayed up way too late decoding one last section of Verne's note. On the positive side, it turned out to be in the runic futhark alphabet.

On the negative side, it didn't sound like it was written by Jules Verne.

He drummed his fingers on the armrest. They had bought good weatherproof winter gear in the morning, but Max hated long pants and these were lined. And itchy. To take his mind off it, Max pulled his copy of the note from his pocket and looked at it for what must have been the tenth time.

Pour entrer dans le noyau:
L'arc de mains en prière dans la plaine centrale
lèvera les yeux vers
Le chameau à trois bosses et aux oreilles tombantes

To enter the core:
the arc of praying hands at the central plain
will lift your eyes
to the lop-eared three-humped camel

"Are you sure you translated this thing right?" Max asked.

"I checked, double-checked, and whatever a-hundred-times-checked is called," Alex replied.

"Sounds like a joke to me," Brandon said.

Max nodded. "Maybe Gaston wrote it. We know he

went bonkers late in life. And this is bonkers."

"Bonkers?" Kristin said. "This is a place near New York City, no?"

"That's the Bronx," Brandon said. "Or Yonkers."

"*Bonkers* is what you are when you decide to drive over lava on a wild-goose chase and your brains are about to fall out," Max added.

Kristin slowed the jeep to a stop and let out a yawn. "I don't know about that. But we are in the center of what I would consider the central plain. Which is good. Because this is where the note told us to go, and if you don't mind, I must rest. I'm having trouble seeing."

Before anyone could respond, the jeep's engine coughed and sputtered. Then, with a wheeze, it went dead. Kristin turned the ignition key, but nothing happened. The only noise was the drumming of rain on the roof and a whistle of wind against the glass. "Guess it wants to rest too," Max said.

"Is there a gas station nearby?" Alex squeaked, gazing out over the wet tundra.

Kristin sighed. "Sometimes it stalls out when you stop in the rain, but most times you can get it going again. Maybe if we wait a few minutes for the weather to clear a bit."

"Sweaty feet . . ." Max pushed open his door and

stepped out. *"Sweaty feet!"*

"Sorry," Brandon said. "I used powder."

"That's claustrophobia," Alex explained. "Max, what are you doing? It's freezing and wet."

Max took a deep breath. Despite the rain and cold, the air felt good. "Figured I'd take a stroll and look for camel noses to pick."

"I don't recommend walking on a'a," Kristin said.

"On *what*?" Max asked.

"A'a," Kristin repeated. "It is a Hawaiian word we borrow, for rough lava."

"Hey, he wants to take a walk, why not?" Brandon said. "As long as he stays in sight. Me, I'm staying here to help get this thing working again."

"My hero," Alex said.

"Ew," Max said, closing the door and pulling his hood over his head. Even with the wind and rain pelting his face, he felt better outside the car than in. The itchiness didn't bother him so much.

Alex cracked open her window. "Just remember Greenland," she said, "where we had to 'look for the bump on the elephant's forehead.' That seemed crazy too."

"Right. We thought we had to look for a real elephant, like maybe there was a circus in town," Max said. "And then we saw that the elephant was an elephant-shaped ice formation."

"Fascinating," came Kristin's voice, muffled through the closed window. "So maybe you'll see something that looks like a three-humped camel."

Max looked around. They were maybe a hundred yards from the base of Snaefellsjökull, which rose into the low, moving clouds. The summit was shrouded, but every few seconds a snow-capped summit peeked through. On it were dark rock crags that jutted upward like thick fingers. *"What are those rocks at the top?"* he yelled toward the car.

"They are lava plugs," Kristin called out her window. *"Left from millennia ago when the volcano was active."*

"They look like a convention of fire hydrants, not a camel," Brandon called out.

Max nodded. "It's all about the angle. I bet from one angle, we'll see the camel. Give me a minute. I won't leave your sight."

He could hear Alex protesting. Kristin too. But they didn't come after him, and neither did Brandon the Pilot. Max began treading carefully over the lava. Even with thick boots, he could feel the jutting rock through his soles.

"Ah!" he cried. *"Ah!"*

Which made him realize exactly why the Hawaiians gave it that name.

As he went on, he tried to focus on the rock formations. But the clouds were thick and mischievous, playing hide-and-seek with the summit. The wind was picking up too, tossing snow and powdery ice into his face. Unlike the anorak he had worn in Antarctica, this one's hood did not have an outer fur lining around it.

He fumbled in his jacket pocket, where he knew he'd kept goggles, but they must have fallen out in the car. By now the jeep wasn't much more than a gray dot. A gray, *unlit* dot, which meant Kristin hadn't gotten it started yet.

So he kept walking, slowly, parallel to the base of the volcano. He could make out a hulking, humanlike shape in the snowy, rainy mix, not too far ahead of him.

He stopped, his heart pumping fast. "Hello?" he called out, but his voice was lost in the wind and precipitation.

Stepping closer, he noticed the shape was not moving. It was much taller than a human, and it did not have limbs. It was a rock. A lava plug, he guessed, from the smooth dark surface.

Curious, he kept going. The wind had blown any snow off the rock. It was slanted slightly away from him, lined vertically with four crevices extending from the middle to the top. Behind it, Max realized, was another formation. It was mirroring the first one, slanted toward it so the two met at the top. Like a tent.

It was a natural shelter. Perfect. If there was room to sneak underneath it, he might be protected from the weather.

"Max!" came Alex's distant voice, carried on the wind.

Picking up his pace toward the two rocks, Max called over his shoulder, *"I'm OK!"*

He slipped underneath. Up close the two rocks were taller than he'd imagined, maybe fifteen feet high. The second rock was exactly like the first, four vertical crevices reaching upward, forming what looked like a thumb and four thick fingers. Like two hands touching.

No, not touching.

Praying.

The arc of praying hands at the central plain will lift your eyes . . .

Max gazed up at Snaefellsjökull. The peak was shrouded in ominous clouds. He kept his eyes glued until the obstruction cleared like a wave bouncing off a jetty.

At the summit, three identical lava plugs stood at equal distances. They were perfectly shaped like thick thumbs. Immediately to the left was a misshapen curved plug. It was angled at the top away from the others by ninety degrees and marked by a moon-shaped mark at its summit. A cave.

Max pulled out his phone and took a photo before the clouds could swallow it again. Staring at the image, he zoomed closer. At the top of the curved rock but below the cave was a curved horizontal crack.

Like an eye. And a smile.

Max dropped his phone into his pocket. With a whoop and a jump, he began running back to the jeep. He didn't care how the a'a' felt under his shoes.

"We have our ca-a-a-amel!" he screamed, his voice cutting through the wind.

PUSHING a jeep over a bed of a'a' was not easy, but it helped to have Brandon the Pilot by your side. "I feel like . . . Ernest Shackleton," Max said, grunting with the effort.

"Who?" Brandon grunted back.

"You know, the guy whose ship got stuck in the ice . . . in Antarctica?" Max said, pausing to take a breath. "And he had his crew drag all their stuff across the ice and snow for miles and miles . . . to a cave near the sea? And then he and five others sailed in a small boat across the Drake Passage with no navigational tools . . . only to land on the wrong end of a snow-covered uncharted island, so he had to walk across it blindly and managed to find a whaling station and then sailed back and rescued everyone? That guy?"

"You know, you are one weird kid," Brandon said with a laugh.

"Thank you," Max said.

The jeep gave an abrupt jolt, and the stalled engine kicked back to life. *"We're good!"* Kristin shouted out her window.

"Woo-hoo!" Brandon smiled at Max. "You're my talisman, little brah! You hired me, but I should hire you to be my history teacher and travel buddy."

"Put it in futhark, and I'll think about it," Max said.

They scrambled back into the jeep, and Kristin drove slowly over the lava. "Will someone guide me?" she asked.

Max glanced back to the twin slanted rocks. "OK, so the praying hands point the direction for us. If you go left . . . *now*, you'll be in line."

"I see them," Kristin said, looking in the rearview mirror. "I'll keep them in my sight."

The rain had subsided a bit, and the clouds were now thinning over the crest of Snaefellsjökull.

"Wowzer," Brandon said, gazing out the window. "I see the camel—up at the top!"

"Good eye." With a smile, Alex reached behind her and patted Brandon's hand.

"He's not a pet," Max grumbled.

The surface seemed to soften as Kristin steered the jeep closer to the volcano. Max kept his eye on the summit until it disappeared from view. "Is there a path up to the camel?"

"I don't think so," Kristin replied. "This is not a commonly traveled area. We may have to wing it. I prepared packs for everyone, with crampons, snowshoes, ice picks, and some food. It's not supersteep, but it will be slippery, so we must stay together. I also packed us some archaeological tools—brushes, compressed air, what have you—just in case."

As Kristin stopped at the base of the volcano, they all scrambled out of the jeep and around to the back. Kristin pulled open the hatch, revealing four sturdy framed backpacks. Each was crammed full of climbing equipment, and next to them was a pile of collapsible climbing poles. "Don't think I'll be needing the poles," Brandon said, strapping on a pack.

"They are crucial," Kristin said. "Do not even think of not taking a pair."

Hooking on his pack, Max peered back at the praying hands. "I can see the lines of the fingers on the right one," he said. "That means we're a little off target. Follow me."

He trudged along the circumference of the volcano, eyeing the hands in the distance. When they were just about lined up, he stopped. "Here," he said.

Alex, Brandon, and Kristin looked up. The slope was rocky but not too steep. "Looks like every other place on the mountain," Brandon remarked. "Except there are some real pathy-looking paths about a mile back. I say we go back. If the point is to reach the camel, what difference does it make where we go up?"

"Good point," Alex said.

"It's not a good point," Max shot back. "It's a bad point. We have to follow directions. And there's no such word as *pathy*."

He began walking up the slope of Snaefellsjökull. The ground was wet and rocky. Max realized Brandon was right about one thing. It didn't look like anyone had walked here in years. He slipped on a rock and caught himself.

"Max?" Alex said. "Don't you think it would be easier if we followed a path someone else has left?"

"I'll race ya?" Brandon said, turning back where he'd indicated.

"It's not a race." Max turned. "We got rich by following Jules Verne. We saved my mom's life and Evelyn's life by following Jules Verne. If Jules Verne says to go up here, we go up here, not any other place. We do switchbacks, we walk carefully, whatever it takes. If you guys want to go all Brandon on me, OK. I will meet you at the top."

Max jammed his pole into the ground for emphasis.

It clanked.

"What was that?" Kristin asked.

Max jammed it again and looked down. "A'a?" he said.

"It sounds like metal," Kristin offered.

"Did we strike gold?" Alex asked.

"An alien ship!" Brandon exclaimed.

"Or a manhole cover," Max said.

"There are no sewers into the volcanoes," Kristin said.

Max dropped to his knees. With the tip of his pole, he began scraping away a thin layer of soil and scrub grass.

Alex joined him, and then Kristin and Brandon. Below the surface was a squarish metal plate. When they scraped out to its edges, Kristin reached into her pack and pulled out a flat box. Laying it on the ground, she opened it to reveal a compact set of tools, including a brush.

As she brushed the soil from the surface of the plate, Max could see raised markings. "Step back!" Brandon said.

He blasted the plate with a tiny compressed air gun, which cleared away a lot of pebbles and soil.

Max sat back, his heart thumping. The square plate was chiseled carefully with tiny characters.

"Futhark," he said, staring in awe.

ᛂᚢᚱᛂ ᛚᛂ ᚽᛂ ᛂᛏ ᛘᛂᛏᛏᛂ-ᚹᛅᚢᛌ ᛅ ᛚ'ᛅᛒᚱᛁ
ᛂᛅᚽᛌ ᛚᛅ ᚹᛅᛚᛚᛂ ᛌᛅᚢᚱᛁᛅᚽᛏᛂ

17

Curez le nez et mettez-vous à l'abri
dans la vallée souriante.

Pick the nose and take shelter
in the smiling valley.

THEY all stared in silence.

"I know what you're thinking," Alex said softly. "But that's what it says."

Max sighed. "Well, Verne never tells us exactly what he means. Sometimes you have to find out for yourselves."

"Personally, I'm not into picking noses in public," Brandon said.

"You can stay here, and we'll save you a booger." Max glanced upward. For most of the volcano's height, the slope was a gradual climb of soil, grass, and exposed rock. The snow cover began about three-quarters of the way up. The smooth white carpet was pimpled and bumped in places, as if a trapped monster had tried punching its way out from inside. At the summit, the camel-rock formations still danced in and out of sight through the clouds. "Think we can make it in a day?"

"If we start now and don't waste time," Kristin said. "But we must also be careful and stay together. There are no paths here, so we will be making our own. It will be slippery. I recommend zigzagging in a switchback pattern. Even if that takes longer than going straight up, it will give us better traction. Also, the angle of climbing will not be so steep."

"That'll take forever." Brandon took a few steps directly up the slope. "Dude, these boots have *awesome* traction. We can get up there in a couple of hours, tops. Last one to the camel is a rotten nostril."

He began striding fast, pumping his arms.

"What are you doing?" Alex cried out.

"Trail running!" Brandon called back. "The best exercise ever!"

Max shook his head. "Did we have to invite him?"

"I'm with Kristin," Alex said, hooking her pack over her shoulder. "We can meet him at the top."

"I promise I won't be slow," Kristin said with a smile. "Now, you may not be used to the altitude, so let me know when you want to stop."

She took the lead, followed by Max, then Alex. Even though she took a good quick pace, zigging right and zagging left, Brandon quickly became a dot in the distance.

Max hurried to keep up. His boots squished into a wet green growth that was something between moss and grass. The rock beneath was uneven and sharp. He tried to tread lightly, but his left ankle jammed into a rocky rut and twisted violently.

It hurt, but he tried not to let it show.

"You're limping," Alex called out from behind him.

"It's only a flesh wound," Max called back through gritted teeth.

As they trudged onward, the rain stopped and the sun began burning away the cloud cover. About halfway up, Kristin pivoted away from a large, flat rock. Max stopped there, catching his breath.

He looked at his watch. They'd started at 7:30 a.m., and it was now 9:08. Glancing down, Max could barely see their car.

"Are we there yet?" Alex called out from behind him.

"No, but look below," Max answered. "We've come a long way."

"Yeah, well, not if you look up," Alex said, pulling up beside him. "Seems like the top half of the mountain stretched, just to annoy us."

Max shifted his glance to the summit. The camel rocks seemed to be about the same size as they had before. "That has to be an optical illusion."

"Can we stop at this rest area?" Alex called out to Kristin. *"I need a gorp break."*

"Five minutes," Kristin replied.

Alex flopped down onto the flat rock and pulled a bag of trail mix from her backpack. She offered some to Max. He had his own mix, but the sight of it made him salivate, so he cupped both his palms. "Nom, nom."

As Alex unzipped the bag, her eyes were trained over Max's head, up the slope. "Do you see Iron Man Brandon?"

"Nom, nom," Max repeated. "Feed me and I will answer."

She poured some mix into Max's hands a little too fast and a few grains tumbled onto the ground. Max dipped his face into his palms and took a big mouthful. "I didn't see him," he said.

Transferring the rest of the mix into his right hand,

he reached down with his left to pick up the stuff that had fallen.

"Ew, don't eat that," Alex said. "Germs."

"I have a trash bag," Kristin said. "We shouldn't leave anything on the mountain."

But Max had stopped in midgrab. The fallen trail mix had gathered into a small pile—inside a large footprint. "Um, guys . . . ?" he said softly. "Maybe Brandon the Pilot *was* here. This is a big foot."

Kristin knelt and picked up a plastic foil wrapper. "He takes Xanax?"

"I doubt it," Alex said. "Xanax is for anxiety. Brandon is Mr. Cool-as-a-Cucumber."

"And half as smart," Max said.

Alex rolled up her bag of trail mix. As she drew back her arm to bop Max over the head with it, he grabbed his pack and began to run.

At the summit, the camel seemed to be smiling down at him. Max didn't like to giggle, but he couldn't help it now. It was a straight path. It looked easy enough. The trail mix had given him energy. Brandon was probably there. Maybe he had figured out the strange message.

And if he didn't, Max would do the job.

Next stop, he thought, *the center of the world.*

NORMALLY Max liked snowstorms. But *normally* meant on a lawn in Ohio on a crisp winter day with the smell of hot chocolate in the kitchen.

Not on a volcano in the middle of Iceland.

For the last hundred yards they'd been tramping through two inches of fresh snow, but that had been easy. The sun was beating down, the air was cold but refreshing.

The storm was an ambush. It rushed over the summit as if answering a 911 complaint about sneaky hikers getting too close to the top. Max drew up his hood as tight as he could. He squinted against the sharp, blowing needles of ice. His body sweat had already chilled, and he shivered hard. Visibility was only a few feet, so all three were sticking very close together now.

"If you get tired of the weather in Iceland, just stick around for a minute!" Kristin cried out from behind him.

"Is that a joke?" Max called out.

"Yes!" Kristin replied.

"Then ha-ha," Max said.

"I think I can see the camel!" Alex shouted. *"We're not too far."*

Max squinted, barely making out the shadowy shapes of the three humps and the head. He was happy, but not too happy. *"A blowing storm is always worse at the top!"* he shouted. *"Once we get there, we better figure out what to do pretty fast!"*

Alex was at his side now, grabbing his sleeve. "Have you seen Brandon's footprints? I'm worried about him."

"I'm worried about us," Max replied.

"He must have gone to another part of the slope," Kristin said.

Max began walking again, but his eyes caught a sudden tiny motion in the snow to the left, and he veered toward it. As the shape jittered in the wind, Max could make out its thin, transparent contour. *"It's a trail mix bag!"*

"Must be Brandon," Kristin said.

"Woo-hoo, he's probably waiting at the top!" Alex said.

"He's a slob!" Max replied. *"Littering is punishable by a fine. I saw that on a sign in Reykjavík."*

But Alex ignored him, cupping her hands to her mouth and calling out Brandon's name louder.

The trail mix bag lifted into the wind and began to swirl. This bothered Max, and he quickened his pace. Snatching the bag in midair, he stuffed it into his jacket pocket. But now he could see a set of footprints leading directly up over the jagged snow-covered rocks from that spot toward the summit. *"There's Brandon's path!"* Max called out. *"I say we follow it. We have to get there before we freeze!"*

Alex took off and Max scrambled behind her, with Kristin bringing up the rear. In the new snow, the rocks were superslippery. Both Max's ankles banged against jagged rock, and he took two falls that bruised his hip and thigh. *"How are you doing?"* Alex shouted over her shoulder.

"I need that healing serum—ASAP!" Max replied.

The wind picked up speed. Closer to the top it sounded like the roar of a locomotive whistle. Snow was blowing into Max's hood. He pulled the strings so tight the hood nearly cut off his vision.

Alex was on all fours practically the whole way, jumping, grabbing, falling, rolling. She scrabbled ahead of Max and Kristin into the whiteness of the blizzard.

"Slow down!" Kristin shouted. *"We can't see you!"*

Alex didn't reply.

Max shouted her name. He picked up speed. He ignored the penetrating pain all over his body. Wetness was seeping through his gloves now, and his fingers were numb. Alex was nowhere to be seen. *"Fish!"* he shouted. *"Fish fish fishy fish!"*

"What?" Kristin shouted.

"I said fish!" Max replied.

It was the last thing he wanted to smell. Fear was the worst smell in the world. As he picked up the pace, he thought he would pass out. His lungs heaved like a cheap accordion. He'd felt like this before, when he'd gone running with his dad at the gym track. All those big people with serious faces looked like they wanted to run into him. Like they wanted to steal him away from Dad. Fear plus running equaled hyperventilation. That was a fact. *Exhale*, his dad had advised him. *Exhale and let the inhalation take care of itself.*

Max blew the air from his lungs and peered upward. A gray form was emerging from the snow—the "head" of the camel. It seemed to be moving toward him as he climbed, but Max knew that was an optical illusion too. *"Alex!"* he called out again.

"Dear Lord, now I've lost two of them," Kristin murmured, racing past Max. Her sure, swift strides climbed the remaining rock embankments that led to the camel head. When she reached the rock, she disappeared around the other side.

Max closed ground as quickly as he could. Up close, the rock really did seem to come to life. It curved forward like a bent neck. At the top was a shape so much like a camel that Max could swear it had been carved—a jutting snout, split by a horizontal crack that looked like an impish smile. Two crags in the rock looked like lopsided eyes, and two other crags resembled nostrils.

Kristin peered out from behind the camel rock, signaling Max to hurry. *"Found her!"* she cried out.

As Max hoisted himself over one last outcropping, a blast of wind knocked him backward. He managed to hold on with one hand until Kristin ran over and grabbed his wrist. Her skin was bright red from the freezing wind. *"We have to stop meeting like this!"* she said.

Max knew that was supposed to be a joke. Joking was good. It chased away the fish. *"Snow problem!"* he said. "Where's Alex?"

Before the words left his mouth, he felt himself being yanked up over the last rock outcropping. Kristin helped him to his feet and linked arms with him, leaning into the wind. Together they headed behind the camel rock.

Alex was there, crouched against the snow, a scarf covering her face. She was staring at the ground, facing away from the "head."

Max followed her glance. They were at the top of a small hill. It dipped downward, then rose again. On top of the next hill was the next lava plug, the first "hump."

The snow was deep up here. So, in spite of the wind, a trail of footsteps was still visible. It led from exactly where they were standing down the side of the small hill.

Halfway there, the steps ended.

"He just . . ." Alex swallowed hard. "Disappeared."

Max stood there, mentally cycling through all the possibilities of what might have happened to Brandon:

He had fallen asleep and died under the snow . . .

He had been taken away by a rescue helicopter . . .

He was playing a prank and was about to jump out of hiding . . .

But there was no sign of a body, no sound of rotors, and no Brandon jumping out of a snow bank yelling "boo!" Alex was next to him, screaming Brandon's name as loud as she could.

He began following the footprints, but Alex grabbed him by the arm. "Something happened to him."

"That's pretty obvious," Max said.

Alex held him tighter. "Whatever it is, I don't want it to happen to you. Think before you do anything. Put yourself in Brandon's shoes. I am trying very hard to imagine what he would have done when he got up here."

Kristin was by their side, shielding her face from the snow with an arm. "He knew what the message said. He wouldn't have stood here waiting. He would have tried to solve the mystery."

"'Pick the nose and take shelter in the smiling valley . . .'" Max recited. "The camel has a nose," he continued. "What's a *smiling valley*?"

"I sang this song in chorus once," Alex said. "It's called 'Shenandoah.' One of the lines is 'I long to see your smiling valley.' Our director told us it was because all valleys looked like smiles."

"So why not just say *valley*?" Max said.

"Because Jules Verne wasn't as logical as you?" Alex shot back. "He liked complicating things? He liked that song? I don't know, Max. Whatever. Look at where Brandon's footsteps ended—that's a valley!"

"And the camel does look like it has a nose," Kristin added.

Max turned. He looked at the rock's odd shape—the thick neck and curved head, the snout, the strange droopy ear, the crags that looked like eyes and nostrils. As he walked closer, he realized the head began at least ten feet above the snowy ground. "Can someone give me a boost?"

Alex lifted his left leg and Kristin his right. As Max rose to within reach of the nose, he could swear the camel was staring at him. "Hey, sorry about this. I'm Max. Mind if I stick a finger up your nostril?"

He wasn't expecting to hear an answer, but asking permission just seemed like the right thing to do. Max pulled the glove off his right hand. The cold numbed his fingertips. In one quick motion he reached upward and jammed his finger into the nostril crag.

He felt something inside give. Just a fraction of an inch, like a loose section of rock. He flinched, expecting something to fall out of the hole, but nothing did. "I think I impacted a booger," Max said.

"Charming," Kristin said.

Silently Kristin and Alex let him down. All three of them looked back over the sloping area between the head and the hump. "Well, we picked the nose, so now I guess we take shelter in the smiling valley. Who goes first?"

"We go together," Alex said, linking arms with them both.

As her scarf fell away from her face, her lips were blue and trembling. Max held tight. The snow had turned Brandon's footsteps into subtle indentations, barely visible. They followed them carefully until they reached the bottom of the slope.

There they came to a stop.

"Now what?" Kristin said.

"Now n-n-nothing," Alex said, her body shaking violently. "This is creeping me out. This is an epic fail, Max. I don't know what went wrong, but Jules Verne did not want us standing at the top of a volcano. The only thing that can happen is a thousand-mile-an-hour wind that can blow you clear to Norway. Which is probably what happened to Brandon."

She let go of Max's arm and wriggled away, turning to face down the big slope to the bottom. "Where are you going?" Kristin called out.

"To look for Brandon," she replied.

"Alex, we can't just give up!" Max shouted.

"Come with me!" she pleaded. "Both of you. Because

we need to rethink this whole thi— ”

Before she could finish the word, Alex vanished from sight.

And Max could feel the earth rumbling beneath his feet.

MAX was falling.

He could hear Kristin screaming in his ears. Her arm smashed against his head, and his body went horizontal in midair. He was tumbling now, until his shoulder made contact with something hard. As Kristin landed on top of him, he let out a scream.

"Sorry!" Kristin shouted. *"Are you OK?"*

For a moment Max couldn't move. He breathed hard and looked around. In the dull light that filtered from above, he could make out a hard rock floor and a wall that curved into blackness.

He felt an arm behind his head and turned to see his cousin staring down at him. She had a gash above her left eye. "You got hurt," he said.

"It's only a flesh wound," she said.

Max smiled. "That's my line."

A deep mechanical throb echoed through the chamber, and Max sat up sharply. Above them, an enormous rock slab hung downward from the ceiling on a hinge. "By Leif Eriksson's ghost," Kristin said. "That thing is a trapdoor."

Slowly it was moving. Two thick metal rods were bolted to its underside, each one attached on the other end to a kind of pump. The pump wheezed and roared, with a painful metallic scraping sound that echoed in the chamber.

Max was OK with most sounds, but not scraping rock. *"That's too loud!"* he screamed.

As he put his fingers to his ears, Alex and Kristin reached into their packs, took out flashlights, and shone them upward as the rods pushed the rock upward. With a deep scraping noise that jarred Max's teeth, the rock settled back into place. A small storm of dirt and pebbles rained downward, and they all dropped to their stomachs.

Kristin was the first to stand. "What . . . in Odin's name . . . just happened?"

"The nostril . . ." Max grunted, pain jolting through his shoulder as he stood. "It was some kind of button. It triggered the door . . ."

"Door to what?" Alex said. "Where are we? *Brandon? Are you down here?*"

Now Kristin was shining her flashlight around, slowly. The walls were rough, casting shadows that seemed to move. These walls surrounded the platform where they all stood, which was roughly round and maybe twenty feet in diameter.

Her beam stopped at the far side of the platform's circle, where the wall bowed outward and the floor angled down into darkness. "It's a ramp to the underworld . . ." Max murmured.

Alex smacked him in the elbow. "Don't say *underworld*. That means death."

"Ow," Max said. "You didn't complain in Greece when they said the Cave of Vlihada was the entrance to the underworld."

"Ohhhhhh . . ."

The deep, distant moan stopped the conversation cold. It was coming from the direction of the downward-sloping ramp.

Max jumped. "It's Bigfoot," he said.

"There's no Bigfoot here," Kristin said, stepping closer. "We call it the yeti."

"It's not Bigfoot or the yeti—it's Brandon!" Alex shouted. *"Bra-a-ndon!"*

Kristin led the way across the flat circle. The top of the ramp was marked by three sturdy rock formations that thrust upward from the rock like stalagmites. Her flashlight followed the ramp down into darkness. The stone floor was marked with rough horizontal stripes. "That's not natural," she said. "Someone carved that."

Max nodded. He had seen photos of just this kind of thing. "They did this in ancient Greece," he said, "to prevent slipping on stone ramps, where they led animals to ritual slaughter."

"Stop that!" Alex shouted, peering out over the ramp. *"Hey! Hello?"*

Her call echoed, unanswered.

"There's only one way to find out what's down there." Kristin tested the surface of the ramp with her boots. "Carved lines or not, it's pretty slipperyyyyyyyy—"

The ramp echoed with her shout as her arms flailed and she slid out of sight into the blackness.

Max's breath caught in his throat. He felt Alex gripping his hand. "I d-d-don't like this," she murmured.

Max quickly unhooked his pack and pulled out his own flashlight, shining it downward. *"Kristin?"*

A moment later her voice piped up: *"I'm OK! But I don't recommend doing what I just did."*

Alex was rummaging around in her backpack. She

pulled out the end of a thick coil of rope. *"We're coming right down!"* she called.

"We are?" Max said.

"Dude. You're not the only smart one. I think you have some rope too. Can you give it to me?" Alex asked. As Max reached into his pack, Alex tied the end of her rope around one of the stalagmites and pulled it tight. Then she took Max's rope and knotted it to the other end of hers. Leaning over the ramp, she tossed the long part of the rope downward. *"Geronimo!"*

A moment later Kristin's voice echoed upward: *"Yeow! That hit me in the face!"*

"Guess it's long enough," Alex said.

She turned her back to the bottom. Facing Max and clutching tight to the rope, she took a couple of steps backward onto the slope and began to lean back until she was perpendicular to the slanted stone floor. Then she began walking upright and backward down the ramp. "You could slide if you want," she said. "But rappelling is more elegant."

As she descended, step by step, the rope held tight to the rock. Max took a deep gulp and grabbed on to it. His arms shook as he turned his back to the ramp. He took a couple of tentative steps backward, but his foot slipped. He leaned forward and gripped the rope tight, but that just made him slip more.

"Lean backward!" Alex cried upward. *"You need to be perpendicular. It's counterintuitive, I know. It doesn't feel safe. But it's much more stable. You get used to it immediately!"*

Perpendicular. The stone floor was angled downward, so he would have to angle too. *"I can't!"* he shouted.

"What do you mean, can't?" Alex shouted back.

"I smell fish!"

"Just do it! Plant your feet, let the rope slip from your hand as you lean back."

Max planted his feet. He stood, leaning forward. Leaning forward was natural, backward was not. He let the rope slide in his palm, forcing himself to lean back. But that made him feel completely off-balance. Which gave him a stench of spoiled flounder. So he pulled himself forward again, and his feet gave out from under him.

With a scream, he fell to the rock and slid downward on his stomach. *"What are you doing?"* Alex shouted.

"You said I could slide!" Max replied.

"Not if I'm rappelling behind you!"

Max was picking up speed. He held on to the rope but now it was hurting his hand. As he loosened his grip, his feet made contact with Alex. He knew it was Alex even though she let out a curse he had never heard her say before.

Together they tumbled downward in a tangle of arms, legs, and rope.

They came to a stop in total blackness. Max unwrapped himself and stood. "Sorry!"

"Next time," Alex replied, "you go first."

Now Max could see a flicker of light, but it was coming from a distance of maybe fifteen feet. *"Nice of you to visit,"* Kristin's voice called out. *"Wish we could celebrate, but we have an emergency."*

Max scrambled toward her, with Alex close behind. As they neared, Kristin shone her flashlight toward the ground near her feet.

Lying flat on his back, eyes closed and mouth hanging open, was Brandon.

20

MAX wasn't about to provide mouth-to-mouth resuscitation.

It wasn't that he didn't know how. He'd done it with Alex in Greenland, but that was because he'd *had* to. Her heart had definitely stopped beating. Brandon's chest, at the moment, was moving up and down. So the fact was, he didn't need it.

Still, that didn't stop Alex.

As she leaned over the pilot and lowered her lips, Max turned away. "I can't watch this."

Ignoring him, Kristin ran to Alex's side.

This seemed like a good opportunity to explore, so Max trained his flashlight on the surrounding walls. They were just as smooth and dark as the walls above.

He slowly rotated. When he reached 180 degrees, he saw Kristin and Alex both leaning over Brandon. He was moving, which was a good sign, so Max kept spinning, slowly, the rest of the way around. This chamber wasn't round like the one above. To the right, at about three-quarters of the way around, the wall extended out into a tunnel that was wide but not very deep.

Max fixed the beam and walked closer. At the end of the corridor, the wall was decorated with carvings.

A sudden moan made him spin around. Brandon was sitting up, coughing. "Whoa . . . they booby-trapped this place!" he sputtered.

"Max, come back!" Alex shouted. *"He's alive!"*

"I know, his chest was moving," Max said.

"Just come help out, Max!" Alex shot back. "Brandon took a bad fall!"

Max approached, training his flashlight on the pilot. Brandon's reddish-blond hair looked dark and matted like a wet dog. Kristin was swabbing his head with a white cloth that stank of medicine. "It's a pretty nice scrape," she said. "Best keep it covered."

Max remembered seeing a bandanna in his pack, so he pulled it out and handed it to Kristin. "I won't be needing this. You can wrap his head with it."

"There we go," Alex said. "Max, that's so sweet."

"It won't be after he wears it," Max replied.

"Thanks, little buddy," Brandon said. "I don't know how I got here. I went to the camel head and did what the message said. Nothing happened, so I figured I'd walk to the next lava plug—"

"And you walked into the smiling valley," Alex said. "Which is exactly where Jules Verne wanted us to go."

"That's how we got here too," Kristin said.

Alex smiled. "And now we're together and alive for the start of the adventure!"

"Wait," Brandon said. "We nearly died. You're thinking of going on?"

"We have to!" Max said. "Guys, there's a message on the wall, down that corridor behind us. In futhark, I think."

Kristin stood. "Show me."

"Wait—" Brandon protested. "Futhark?"

"I'll explain the way this works, Brandon," Alex said, as Kristin scooted away. "Verne leaves these clues. Remember, he explored this volcano and came back alive. So he's instructing us how to do the same thing."

"And a gazillion years have passed between then and now," Brandon pointed out. "Rocks shift, paths change. What if there are crevasses and molten lava and poisonous snakes . . ."

"Are you chickening out?" Max asked.

"No! I mean yes! I mean . . ." Brandon took a deep breath. "I fly. I skydive, I do scuba rescues and I have EMT training. But look at what's happened since we got here. Already you guys have had to rescue me twice. I don't have what you have—Jules Verne DNA. And I don't spelunk. All I want to do is fly planes and travel the world."

Max looked up. "Your only other choice right now is sitting on your butt because the trapdoor is shut."

"Max, Alex!" Kristin cried out from behind them. *"It is futhark. Come. I'm transcribing for you!"*

"Woo-hoo!" Max cried.

Alex put her hand around Brandon's head and examined his wound. "It's already stopped bleeding. Come on, pick up your stuff and come with us."

Brandon stood shakily, looking down at a couple of slips of paper and a dollar bill. "That's not my stuff."

"Whose is it?" Alex asked.

"Doesn't matter," Max said, leaning in to pick it up. "We're responsible for taking out what we bring—"

His voice caught in his throat. In his hand was a Snickers wrapper, a receipt from Beantown Nuts from Logan Airport, and a crumpled dollar bill.

But the only thing Max was really seeing was a scrawled message on the back of the bill.

MT Savile, OH www.TraceMyMoney.com.

"What's wrong, Max?" Alex said.

He looked up, and the chamber felt like the bottom of the ocean.

"Bitsy. Niemand," Max said. "They're already here. In case you had any doubts."

21

ALEX took the dollar bill from his hand. "How can you tell?"

"Now that we have so much money, I've been marking the bills," Max said. "To see where they travel. I use this app called TraceMyMoney. You copy the bill's serial number, your location, and the date into the app's database. Then you write 'TraceMyMoney' on the bill, so other app users will know. When another user finds it, they record when and where. I have a twenty-dollar bill that I marked on a Wednesday, and by Saturday someone changed it for foreign currency in the Dubai Airport. A five-dollar bill was used in Bangs, Texas—"

"I don't understand," Brandon said. "It sounds like *you* dropped this here."

"It's my money, yeah," Max said. "I always write my initials and location on the bill. But my pocket was picked by a woman outside Bilgewater State Prison. It was Spencer Niemand in disguise. They'd locked down the prison, but there he was, walking away with all my money. And this is some of it. Which means he dropped it. Which means he must have fallen through the way we did. Which means he knew about the camel nose and the smiling valley."

Alex nodded. "The only question is, how far ahead of us are they?"

"And what do they intend to do with the serum?" Kristin asked.

"In Verne's note, he said he wanted to propagate it," Max said. "Make it grow."

Alex nodded. "Something involving a large body of saltwater."

"Which Verne's character, Professor Liedenbrock, finds at the center of the Earth," Kristin added.

"So that must be it, just like we thought," Alex said. "Niemand plans to mass produce the serum."

"Or maybe already did it," Brandon suggested.

Max held his nose against a sudden foul stench. "Fish."

"Max?" Alex reached to him, but he recoiled.

"Fish fish fish fish . . ." he said through his pinched nostrils.

Alex was trying to grab his shoulders, but he didn't want to feel her hands. Or smell her breath. Brandon was saying something, but he had a smirk on his face.

He backed away from the smell. He felt like it was melting the skin on his face. His eyes darted left and right. He could see Kristin reaching toward him and Alex holding her back.

His legs were moving now, as if they had a will of their own. They were taking him down the corridor, to the wall. The runes seemed to be dancing before his eyes. There was a Vegvísir symbol above them, carved deeply into the rock, and it looked like it was throbbing. He wanted the motion to stop. All of it. He reached out and rubbed his hands on the wall, trying to erase the runes. *"Go away!"* he screamed.

Alex was telling him to stop, but he couldn't.

Brandon grabbed him by the shoulders, but Max turned and kicked him.

He could hear Kristin's voice, but it sounded like she was in an echo chamber, calling *"Fire!"*

Fire?

As Max spun around, he felt as if he would explode. He wasn't thinking straight about much, but he knew fire consumed oxygen.

Deep breaths. When you're spinning out of control, recognize it is happening. And take deep breaths. Because you need to think even more clearly than usual. His therapist, Ilyssa, said this to him a lot. And now he was spinning. He could recognize it.

He inhaled slowly. Alex was staring at him, waiting, holding Brandon back. And Kristin was not saying "Fire!" In his panic, he hadn't heard her right.

"Higher!" she shouted, pointing at the wall.

Max turned. He exhaled hard, trying to blow away the acrid, fishy smell. And he forced his eyes to travel upward, to the top of the carving.

To the Vegvísir.

It was not carved *into* the wall, really. More like *out* of it. Someone had gouged a big round circle into the rock, leaving the shape of the talisman jutting out.

"Max, we can do this," Alex said. "I really believe we can. Are you with us?"

Max nodded. "I'm breathing deeply."

"That's the same shape as the talisman, right?" Alex said. "The one Kristin's uncle gave you?"

"Vegvísir," Kristin said. "Yes."

"OK, cool, because there's a connection to the futhark message. I'm going to read you the translation, OK?" Alex began reciting: "'To use the talisman to your advantage, one must advance from three to six.' Does that make any sense to you?"

"Three to six . . ." Max said.

"It makes sense to me!" Brandon blurted. "Look at the ends of those lines on the right side. They look like three-pronged rakes. They're shaped like threes!"

"They're pointing the wrong direction," Max murmured. "They're more like uppercase *E*s. It's got to be something else."

"Three to six could be a time," Kristin said. "Like three minutes to six."

Max thought about that for a moment. But it didn't make sense. The hint was to advance *from* three *to* six.

Which could mean three o'clock to six o'clock.

Those were times, but they were also positions. That was a fact. On circular sundials and old analog clockfaces, three was on the right. Twelve was on top, six on bottom, nine on the left. All the other numbers filled in between.

Max had no clue what the shapes meant, but he knew exactly what to do. In his mind, he imagined the Vegvísir as a kind of old-timey clock, as if it had numbers printed on it:

One part of the Vegvísir was in the three position. To move it to six, you had to imagine it as a turning wheel. You could push the three part down to the six position.

He dug his fingers in and tried to yank it down, but it wouldn't move. "Help . . . me . . ." he said through gritted teeth. "All we need to do it push it ninety degrees downward . . ."

Now Brandon's arm was reaching over Max's shoulder. His beefy fingers interlaced with Max's. Together they pressed. The shape turned about a quarter inch, exactly like a wheel. Debris crumbled from the wall.

"It's like a latch!" Brandon said. "A big disk in the wall. Come on. Harder!"

Now Kristin and Alex dug their fingers in too. *"Heave . . . ho!"* Alex yelled.

With a deep rumbling sound, the disk turned again, slowly. It took four more tries before the entire shape had been turned one quarter of the way around. Ninety degrees.

The "three" had clicked firmly into the "six" slot.

Max, Alex, Kristin, and Brandon stood back. "Now what?" Brandon said.

The chamber was quiet again. Max was beginning to sweat. It seemed like an hour had gone by before Kristin finally broke the silence with a sigh. "It is a nothing hot dog," she said.

"Burger," Alex corrected her. "A nothing burger."

With a growl, Max smacked the wall. Then kicked it. "That feels better," he said.

Brandon laughed. "I like your thinking, little dude." He leaped in the air and gave the wall a big, thudding martial arts kick.

"Yeoow . . ." he yelled, hopping on his good foot.

"Um, it's made of rock," Alex said. "Like your head."

But before anyone could speak again, the room began to shake. Everyone looked at Kristin. "Is that an earthquake?" Max asked.

"My bad," Brandon said.

As if in answer, the wall began to move inward.

22

THE sound of hardened lava scraping against hardened lava was like a fleet of cars being put through a meat grinder.

The wall was swinging inward like a massive stone door, inch by inch. Max covered his ears and staggered backward. Alex was shouting something to him, but he couldn't hear her.

When it finally stopped, the wall was tucked into an inner wall, revealing a square of total blackness. In the sudden silence, Max could hear everyone's panicked breaths.

"If Niemand really is here," Alex finally said, "after that racket he knows we are too."

Max stood, training his flashlight into the darkness.

Beyond the entrance was a narrow tunnel into the rock that went straight for a few yards and then curved away out of sight. As Max stepped closer, he heard a scraping sound. It was coming from above, from Vegvísir. The dial circle was moving counterclockwise, back from the six position toward the three. "Guys, the dial is going backward," he said. "I think it's a timer."

"Like, a timer to get through the door?" Brandon said. "Like, it's going to move back?"

The wall answered by moving slowly toward them.

"That's a yes!" Alex said. "Let's go!"

"What?" Kristin shot back. "No! We can't! We don't know anything about that tunnel—like where it goes, or if it goes nowhere. And we have no way to get back. It's insane!"

"These two, Max and Alex—they do *insane*," Brandon said.

"Our great-great-great-grandfather hasn't let us down yet, with any of his clues," Max said. "Spencer Niemand and his daughter are down there, and if we leave now, we will all regret it."

Alex was the first through, and Max followed. Behind them, he could hear the wall scraping shut another few inches. He did not look back. *"Are Kristin and Brandon with us?"* Alex shouted over her shoulder.

"I don't know," Max replied, training his flashlight on the ground. "Just keep going. And watch your step."

The tunnel was slanted downward, uneven and low. Max placed each step carefully to avoid slipping. Soon Alex was bent into a crouch. *"I am so happy to have this hair!"* she shouted over her shoulder. "I can feel where the ceiling is."

"*I* can't!" Max banged his head against a low-jutting rock. His boots hit a slippery patch and went out from under him. With a cry, he fell on his back. His flashlight clattered to the stone floor. As he slid, his feet tangled with Alex's. Together, screaming, they tumbled in the darkness.

Max felt his back smack against another wall. Then it smacked again when Alex banged into him. "Get . . . off me," Max grunted.

"Sorry, cuz!" Alex sprang away. "Did I hurt you?"

"It's not you," Max said, lifting up his rear end to extract his flashlight. "I landed on this."

He flicked it on. They were sitting on a level stone landing, a break in the slanting tunnel. They'd been stopped by a wall, about ten feet across. On either side of the wall were separate, smaller tunnels that also angled downward.

"We're in a fork," Alex said, brushing herself off. "A

few feet to the right or left, and we'd have kept going."

Max nodded. He swung the flashlight from one path to the other, but the beam wasn't strong enough to penetrate to the end of either tunnel. "How do we know which one to take?"

"Eeny meeny miny mo?" Alex said.

"Can you give me a signal when you're telling a joke, like shutting your mouth halfway through?" Max was shining his beam on the wall now, which was overgrown with a kind of brownish-green moss. As he swept some of it aside, the wall seemed to shake. "Wait, *another* moving wall?"

At the sound of a distant squeal, Max spun around, back toward the tunnel he and Alex had just come through. A voice sang out: "Just hear those sleigh bells jingle-ing, ring-ting-tingle-ing too . . ."

He shone his flashlight upward, back to where they'd come from. Brandon and Kristin emerged sled-style, both sitting, with Kristin in front and Brandon hugging her from behind.

"Keep them away from the tunnels!" Max shouted. He and Alex jumped away, each standing at the mouth of one of the tunnels. With a loud *swooosh*, Brandon and Kristin swept across the small platform and tumbled into the mossy wall. Brandon was laughing hysterically.

Kristin sprang to her feet. "You find this funny? We could have died!"

"Sorry, just trying to be cheerful," Brandon said.

"Glad you're here," Alex said. "I thought you weren't coming with us."

"We thought so too," Brandon said. "For about a nanosecond. Until we realized we didn't want to leave you guys alone."

"Thanks," Alex said.

Brandon shrugged modestly. "That's just the kind of people we are."

"OK, we need to figure out what to do next," Max said, turning his flashlight back toward the wall. "We're at a fork with no instructions. I'm hoping there's something behind this moss. Help me out."

"All for one and one for all," Brandon said. As Max began brushing away the moss, the others joined in. The moss came loose easily, but so did a lot of stone. It flaked off in four narrow crevices that formed the outline of a square about three feet long on each side.

But Max was noticing that the wall itself was completely free of any markings, inside or outside the three-foot square.

"Weird," Alex said. "Why would someone carve a square into a wall and put nothing in it?"

"A painting with invisible ink?" Brandon suggested.

Kristin was feeling around the edge of the square. "Nothing hidden in these crevices . . ."

Max stood close to the wall. "OK, we already found one really old-time mechanical contraption. We had to dig our fingers into the Vegvísir and turn it. Maybe we have to do the same with this."

"You can't turn a square embedded in a wall!" Brandon said with a snicker. "There's no place for it to go." To demonstrate, he dug his fingers into the top crevice and pulled down. "See?"

Pebbles dribbled out from the other crevices, showering the stone floor with a small cloud of dust.

"*I* see that there's something behind this." Alex hip-checked Brandon to the side and dug her fingers into the left crevice. "OK, when you feel deep inside the crack, you can work your fingers under the square. It's loose. I think it's some kind of plate, with something behind it. I want you all to pull outward. Max, you help me pull on this side. Brandon and Kristin, you pull on the right side. And do not position yourself directly in front of it, because this thing is heavy and it will fall."

Brandon's brow furrowed. "If we step aside we won't get the right torque—"

"No mansplaining—just do it!" Alex said. "On three!"

They scrambled into place. Max felt inside the crevice. He felt under the edge of the square, jamming the pads of his fingers so that they pulled outward, into the chamber. It felt awkward.

"One . . . two . . . three!" Alex cried out.

As they pulled, more rock dribbled out from the edges of the square.

"One more time!" Max said. "One . . . two . . . three!"

Max gritted his teeth. His fingertips felt wet. He realized they were bleeding. But the square was moving again.

And then it completely dislodged.

All four of them jumped away from the wall as the square crashed to the cave floor. Max rolled away in a shower of rock.

He sprang to his feet. The square was in pieces about three or four inches thick. It looked like someone had carefully carved the whole thing out of the wall and then plugged it back in.

"Max . . . ?" Alex was saying. "Look."

He trained his flashlight on the wall behind the fallen square insert. A message stared back at them, carved across the top:

"Carte," Kristin said. "That's what it says."

Alex nodded. "It means 'map.'"

"It's like our Holy Grail," Kristin said. "It's our route to the center of the Earth. So to speak."

But Max was not cheering. He stepped closer to look at an intricate carved series of lines at the top.

About halfway down, the wall was a beat-up mess of destroyed rock. It wasn't a map. It was about one-third a map. The rest was rubble.

"I think," Max squeaked, "we pulled too hard."

"Brandon's influence," Alex said with a sigh. She looked toward Brandon, but all she saw was Kristin. "Um . . . Brandon?"

Kristin spun around. There was nothing behind her on the platform except the right-hand part of the fork. *"Is this a joke?"* she called out. *"Because if it is, it's not funny!"*

Max spun his flashlight around. There was no place to hide on the round landing, and Brandon was nowhere to be seen.

He moved toward the right-hand part of the fork and shone his flashlight into the dark tunnel. *"Are you here?"*

he shouted. *"You need to come back. On the wall we exposed? There's part of a map. It says we're supposed to go left!"*

After a few moments of silence, Alex came up behind Max and shouted Brandon's name again. It echoed distantly with no answer.

"I don't think he's pranking," Alex said. "When he fell back from the wall, he must have slid in here."

As Max stepped into the tunnel, he felt a cool, wet breeze. "That's weird."

"What's weird?" Kristin asked.

"I feel wind," Max replied. "And moisture. Maybe there's some underground river."

The tunnel was six or seven feet wide. Max could see how Brandon could have slid in. But it was no more than three feet high and sloped sharply downward. "If he went in, there's nothing stopping him," Max said softly.

"I think it would be wisest if we tied the rope to your foot," Kristin suggested.

She had the knot tight before Max could reply. He was glad. It made him feel more secure as he crawled inside, examining the walls with his flashlight.

He pressed against the walls with his free hand and both feet, for traction. About ten feet in, there was a sharp left turn. Max took it and then stopped short. The stone floor ended abruptly, falling away into . . . nothing.

As he let out a gasp, Alex shouted, *"What happened?"*

"Hold the rope tight!" Max called back. He flattened himself onto his belly and inched forward, peering over the edge of the abyss. His flashlight searched around in a wide circle, but the beam dissipated into nothingness. From below came the distant rush of water.

No one could have survived a fall of that distance.

"Is Brandon OK?" Kristin called out.

Max swallowed deeply and replied, *"I don't think so."*

23

HUGGING was Max's least favorite human activity, just below crying. But right now Alex was doing activity number two because she was sad. And he was doing activity number one because he knew it would make her feel better.

Sometimes you had to.

Max was sad too. He could not shake the smell of skunk. And Kristin was sitting against the wall with her knees pulled up around her face. "It's my fault," she said. "I should have forced him to stay behind. We could have waited behind the rock door and opened it for you when you got back."

"Maybe he's OK . . ." Alex said. "You heard water, right, Max?"

Max nodded. “Really far down, though. So if it was deep, he might have done a big belly flop and survived. But if was shallow, he probably cracked his skull open and died instantly.”

Kristin grimaced. “I . . . I will choose optimism.”

“It’s about all we can do,” Alex replied, wiping her eyes with her sleeve. “Brandon can be crude, but he’s a wonderful pilot and a sweet man. And we owe him. He saved our lives by landing on the water. And he was the one who led us here.”

“Let’s see if we can find him,” Max said, standing up. “Or his corpse, before it rots.”

“Max!” Alex snapped.

“Sorry.” Max stood. He flicked on his light and walked toward the carving on the wall.

"The top part of this map is pretty clear," Max said. "It's the bottom that's messed up. Worn away over the years. So . . . we definitely take the left part of the fork. Looks like it leads to another room. From there it gets . . . um, a little complicated."

"*Obliterated* is the word," Kristin said. "This isn't going to do us much good."

Max stood back, aiming his phone camera and snapping an image.

"I think we need a rubbing too, in case the phone runs out of juice," Kristin said, fishing around in her backpack.

As she pulled out a big white sheet of paper and a thick charcoal pencil from her pack, Max looked over toward Alex. She was still staring wordlessly down the right-hand tunnel. "Hey," Max said softly, "can you help us?"

Alex turned to Max with a blank, red-eyed stare. He wanted to cheer her up, but he wasn't sure how. It looked like something inside her had died.

As Max pressed the top left corner of the paper tight against the wall, Alex held the upper right. With great care, Kristin traced the map's upper section until she had a decent image. She rolled up the paper and stuffed it into her pack. Her eyes moistened as she looked at Alex. "We'll find him," she said.

Alex nodded.

"Go slow," Max said. "Every path we've been on is slippery."

Taking the lead, Max shone his flashlight into the left-hand tunnel. It angled downward too, but it wasn't round or square. It was shaped more like two parentheses joined at the top—maybe eight feet tall but no floor, really. Max had to plant each step on the V shape formed at the bottom. His ankles bowed outward with the effort. It helped to steady himself against the wall with his free hand.

The path meandered downward in an irregular zigzag pattern. At times it inclined upward for long, long stretches, and Max feared they would never go any deeper, just cross from one end of Iceland to the other. Other times it switched back so it seemed they were returning to where they'd started. Max lost track of time, listening for the sound of water, hoping they would get to the place where Brandon had landed.

Sweat was soon dripping from his brow and stinging his eyes. They were on a level section now. The seam in the rock had widened so they actually had some solid, flat stone to stand on. Just ahead of them, the tunnel branched off into a kind of oval-shaped chamber. "Can we take a break in there?" Kristin asked.

"Twist my arm," Max said.

But as he entered the room and dropped his pack, he smelled mercaptan again. Anxiety. Big time. "Guys," he said, "I'm nervous. What if we're wrong about this whole route?"

Kristin's and Alex's faces were beaded with sweat, and they were breathing hard. "We . . . have no choice . . ." Alex said. "It was . . . this path or . . . Brandon's."

"Still . . ." Max said. "Something's telling me this is a mistake. I smell gas. I think we're going around in circles."

Kristin locked eyes with Max. "Anxiety and claustrophobia are normal for underground explorers," she said, holding up a squarish metallic device. "I've been consulting a compass and depth measurements. We have descended about a thousand meters. That is nearly a half mile, a substantial depth. We are not spinning our wheels." She smiled. "Besides, my uncle gave you the Vegvísir, and that means we can never be lost."

Max fingered the talisman around his neck. Holding it out, he examined the shapes. The nasty smell was dissipating, and he felt calmer. Not that he believed in magical properties. He didn't. It was not scientific. But the design itself was comforting, like the blueprint of a cool maze you could run through and solve. He loved the beauty and complexity. The most truly magical thing about it was how Uncle Gunther had put the shape together from the vague lines they'd seen at the bottom of the Braille note.

Lines.

Not runes. Not talismans. *Lines.*

There were other lines under the text of Jules Verne's message. They were under the Vegvísir. Max tried to picture them in his mind.

And as he did, they seemed weirdly familiar. He needed to see them again.

As he reached into his pocket for his phone, Alex touched his arm. "Max . . ." she said. "Your talisman? I'm seeing it."

"Where?" Max said, scrolling to find the Braille message.

"Around your neck," Alex said. "I'm *seeing* it—and you. But I shouldn't be. No one is shining a flashlight. Why is this?"

Max looked up. Kristin held out her flashlight to show him it was turned off.

His flashlight was off too, and so was Alex's. Yet both of his friends were faintly visible, as if they had wandered into a room on a cloudy afternoon with the shades down.

"What the—?" His eyes passed over Kristin's and

Alex's shoulders to the walls beyond. They were glowing a faint brownish green. But it wasn't a steady light. It moved and winked and pulsed softly, traveling from crag to crag like a mist, as if a billion tiny fireflies were flitting just over the surface.

"Where is it coming from?" Alex said, glancing up to the ceiling. "Do you see some kind of fissure?"

Above them, the roof's ceiling seemed to be hung with a netting of moss and thick cobwebs. No skylight there.

"Whoa, that's weird," Kristin said. "It's like a sagging tent top, only made of cobwebs."

"I think the light is coming from the stone," Max said. "It's making its own."

Kristin rubbed her hand along the wall. When she turned her palm inward, her fingers glowed too. "Ha!" she exclaimed. "This is awesome! Nitrogen-based bioluminescence . . . Jules Verne wrote about this. Since his time, it's been detected—but not like this!"

Tracing his finger along the wall, Max wiped off moss and made a smiley face. It wasn't until he turned full circle that the breath caught in his throat.

Alex and Kristin were staring at the other end of the chamber. There, where he would have expected the path to continue, was a small opening not any bigger than a basketball. "This is crazy," Alex murmured. "Verne couldn't have made it through that."

Max pulled moved closer, pulling out his flashlight. Before he could flick it on, he felt something catch on his foot.

He looked down just as a taut filament snapped in two.

"Max!" Alex shouted.

A clattering echoed from above. Kristin and Alex were gaping at the ceiling. As Max craned his neck upward, the thick, tentlike netting of cobwebs split wide open.

First a white object dropped to the ground. A bone.

Then a grinning white face burst through.

As Alex let out a piercing shriek, Max dove to the ground. He covered his head as a cascade of bones and skulls rained on top of him.

24

HE expected the pain. But not the squeaking and chittering.

Max rolled away onto a pile of bones. Above him, black shadows skittered across the chamber in the faint light. Tiny pairs of eyes winked into sight and disappeared, and little teeth flashed dully.

"I hate bats!" Alex screamed. *"I hate hate hate them!"*

Max cowered, feeling the rush of wings just touching the top of his hair. Above him the cloud thinned out and disappeared up into darkness, like smoke into a chimney.

As he listened to their tiny screeches grow fainter, he glanced up at Alex.

She looked like she was about to get sick. "That is the

most disgusting thing I've ever seen," she said, staggering over to Max's side.

"Are you going to throw up on me?" Max said.

"If I did, it couldn't be worse than being beaned with a million bones," Alex said. "Are you OK?"

"I smell ammonia. That usually happens when someone is trying to trick me. Which actually just happened." Max gestured toward the tiny opening. "The trap was set off by a trip wire. I didn't see it."

"OK, but I smell ammonia too," Alex said. "That's bat poop. It really stinks."

The bones, scattered on the ground, were dim shapes in the phosphorescent light. But even in the dimness he could tell they were stained with black guano.

His eyes watering with the acrid smell, he leaped up to move away. Kristin and Alex were both wrapping their bandannas around their faces. "This is awful," Kristin said through a coughing jag. "Why did they do this?"

"Well, bats eat just like we do," Max explained. "But mostly mice, I think. So as the meat passes through the digestive system—"

"Not why did the bats poop!" Kristin retorted. "Why did Jules Verne set this trap?"

"There's got to be a reason, or we are stuck here with nothing to do but go back." Alex paced the floor, as far from the guano-stained bones as she could get. "Let's think about this. I'm Jules Verne. I'm heading down to what I think is the center of the Earth. I probably have a team. I get there and head back—and along the way I leave clues. For some reason I didn't succeed in my mission and someday I want a descendant to finish the job . . ."

Max's brain was churning. "Right! But maybe I would be scared that the wrong person would stumble into my mission. Some random person from Iceland would wander down here and go, 'Oh, look, clues!' And maybe that person would be a good clue solver. Because Icelandic people are smart. So Verne figures he'll make it harder than just secret messages and square plugs and futhark. He'll use a booby trap!"

"Makes sense to me," Alex said.

"You two are the weirdest people I have ever met." Kristin sighed, looking up into the void. "But it does make some kind of twisted sense."

"Of course it does." Max shone his flashlight upward—to the space that was opened by the collapsed ceiling. "Because *that* is our only pathway out of here."

Even in the faint light, Max could see Alex's eyes grow as wide as baseballs. "You expect us to climb up into a . . . a *bat cave*?"

"Bruce Wayne did it all the time," Max said.

"That's not funny," Alex shot back. "That is so not funny!"

"I don't hear the bats, do you?" Kristin said, her ear cocked toward the ceiling.

In the silence, tiny hisses and whistling noises swirled in the darkness over their heads. "Yes, as a matter of fact, I do!" Alex said.

Kristin shook her head. "That's pressurized air, squeezing through cracks in the rock. Bats don't like company, especially human, and they can fit into small spaces. I'm betting they've made it through all kinds of crevices, and we won't see them again."

"What happened to my brave, daring cousin?" Max asked.

"Fine," Alex said, looking upward. "OK. But how are we going to get up there?"

Kristin switched on her flashlight and shone it straight up. The hole was easily wide enough to fit a person, but it was tough to see what was beyond it.

Alex reached into her pack and took out a length of climbing rope. She tied the end into a noose and tossed it upward into the hole. "Let's see if it catches on anything."

The rope fell back to the ground once . . . twice . . . three times. Max moved backward, shining his flashlight upward to get a different angle. His foot clattered against the edge of the bone pile, kicking the bones aside.

Recoiling, he glanced down at his shoes. And he caught a glimpse of something he hadn't noticed before.

A section of slightly frayed rope stuck out from the pile. "Kristin, did you drop this in here?" he called out.

"No." Kristin stepped over to him, training her flashlight beam on the bones. She reached down and pulled at the rope. It was filthy and slimy, but as she lifted it off the ground, several bones came with it. "I didn't see this before."

"We weren't looking," Max reminded her. "We were running away."

Alex quickly rummaged in her pack and pulled out her winter gloves. She, Max, and Kristin yanked the rope free.

Or *ropes.* Plural.

Two of them, to be exact. Each was tied at intervals to the end knobs of the bones. The trio pulled as much of the arrangement free as they could. The ropes were parallel, tied to the ends of the bones every few inches, like a ladder.

They laid them carefully on the ground.

Max looked up toward the ceiling. There, along the rim of the opening, he saw a long lip of rock that looked as if it had been carved to dip upward, like the blade of a bottle opener.

It was about the width of the bones that were attached to the rope.

"That's a hook, and this is a ladder," Max said. "And bats or no bats, we have a way out."

25

ALEX watched in horror as Max lifted the top "rung" of the bone-and-rope ladder. "Stand clear!" he announced.

As he reared back to throw it upward, Alex grabbed his arm. "No way, cowboy!"

"We need to get it over that lip," Max protested. "That's what Jules expects us to do."

"That contraption is heavy," Alex countered. "You won't make it. What if the bones crash and separate from the rope?"

"Do you have a better suggestion?" Max asked.

"Let's use our heads," Alex said. "Jules would expect that too. He wouldn't give us something impossible to do. Maybe there's some other clue. Something we can use to guide the ladder up there."

"But—" Max protested.

"Alex is right," Kristin said. "If we fail, we're stuck. So we have to take all precautions."

Disappointed, Max dropped the ladder. Kristin and Alex were sifting through the bones with their feet. Most of them were the length of a human forearm or smaller.

But Max's eye was on a really big one that had rolled to the wall. "Guys, look at this baby," he said.

He lifted one end of it and propped it against the wall. It was nearly his height, but not as heavy as he expected.

"Extraordinary," Kristin said, snapping a photo of it with her camera. "I've never seen anything like it. It must be from some prehistoric mammal. A mastodon, maybe."

"Or a dinosaur," Max said. "It's not superheavy. Which means it may be hollow inside. Some of the dinos were probably cold-blooded. They developed into birds, so the bone structure had to be light."

"I studied paleontology in college," Kristin said, pulling the bone from the wall until it was upright. "This has the stresses and thickness of a mammalian bone. But that doesn't explain the lightness. How strange. You're right, it should weigh a lot more."

Max knelt by the bottom of the bone, where Kristin

was pivoting it away from the wall. "Can I turn it upside down?"

As he stood, Kristin backed away and let Max hold the bone upright again. He rubbed his palm on the top of it. "This end looks pretty normal, right? It's a joint. It's where the bone will connect to the next bone. But the other end doesn't look like this."

He spun the bone around so that the bottom was at the top. It was flat. "Looks like the bone was broken off at the joint," Alex remarked.

"Or maybe sawed off," Max said. "It's really clean. I'm not sure bones break that cleanly."

"They don't," Kristin said.

Slanting the bone toward him, Max was able to look inside. "It's hollow too. I mean, *really* hollow."

Now Kristin and Alex were crowding him from both sides. The bone's walls were as thin as a sheet of plastic. "This isn't normal," Kristin said.

"I think someone hollowed it out artificially at one end," Max said.

"Why?" Alex asked.

Max set the bone back against the wall. Holding his breath, trying to ignore the stench, he rooted around in the smaller bones and skulls. At the bottom was another long one, which he grabbed and pulled out. It was exactly like the first—one end jointed, the other cut off and hollowed out. "OK, I'm thinking one of these fits into the other," Max said. "But check out the joint end of the bone, the one that's not hollowed out."

He turned the bone so they all saw the jointed end. It had been carved into a perfect, concave U shape. "A smiling valley," Alex said.

Max smiled. "More like a hook. I'm thinking you're supposed to rest something inside it."

He lay both bones on the ground, cut end to cut end. With one hand on each bone, he jammed them together.

With a dull snap, one slid perfectly into the other. "Bingo. Now we have a superlong pusher. We hook the ladder in and lift it up into the hole."

Alex's jaw dropped. "Cousin, that is the awesomest thing you have ever done!"

Max thought about it. "I'll go with flying a balloon."

Kristin brought over the end of the bone-and-rope ladder. She inserted the topmost rung into the U-shaped joint at the top of the long pole.

"Fits like a glove," Max said.

Lifting the top of the long pole off the ground, he thrust it slowly upward, watching the ladder rise. The two long bones together, plus the two ropes and the rungs made of bones, were too heavy for one person, so

Alex joined him. "We're . . . not going to . . . reach it," Alex said.

Kristin knelt, cupping her hands together near Alex's boot. "Step into this."

Grunting with the effort, Kristin lifted Alex off the ground. Max let go of the pole to help.

"Little more . . ." Alex said, reaching as high as she could. Now the top of the ladder was rising into the hole, and Alex slowly set it down until it fit onto the stone lip. "Got it!"

Max pulled down. It held fast. He placed his foot on the bottom rung, which now hung about two feet off the ground. "Jules thought of everything," he said with a confident smile, then backed away. "Who wants to go first?"

"Heck yeah, I will," Alex said. "But if I see bats, be ready to catch me."

As she grabbed the ladder and began to climb, the ropes swayed back and forth. Max and Kristin grabbed on to steady it. Alex rose steadily until her head was over the rim. *"Not much phosphorescence up here,"* she called down. *"And it could use a little air freshener."*

"Can you see anything?" Max called up.

"Not much—no, wait, hang on." Alex stepped

farther up, until her torso was completely in darkness. "Whoa. What on earth is—"

With a scream, Alex was sucked into the void. The toe of her boot caught in the ladder, and it jerked upward and out of Max's hand.

26

MAX never could have predicted he would be smacked in the face by a guano-covered bone, let alone choose to grab onto it.

But it all happened so fast. Alex's screams from above were growing muffled. Above him the ladder was disappearing into the ceiling rung by rung. Once the ladder was gone, Max would never see his cousin again.

Under the circumstances, there was only one choice. As he clamped his fingers around the rung and held tight, his feet left the ground.

He was rising too.

"Max, wait!" Kristin shouted.

The bottom rung whooshed up beyond her head.

She bent her knees and sprang upward, her hand barely closing on Max's ankle.

The ladder jolted with the added weight. *"Sorry!"* Kristin yelled.

"Just hang on!" Max called out. As he rose into the hole, his fingers scraped the rim. The ladder pulled him over and onto a narrow chute. For a moment he was horizontal and then sliding downward.

He tightened his grip and felt the rope and the bones beneath him, clattering loudly over the hard lava. The ladder gave him some protection from the rock floor, but it sounded like some insane underground roller coaster. Max tried to see Alex ahead of him, but the tunnel was pitch-black. *"Alex, are you there?"* he called out.

"Yes!" her voice answered. *"Look up, Max!"*

Max tried to raise his head, but he banged it against something metallic. Before he could try again, the ladder yanked him with sudden speed. The rung ripped out of his grip. He was sliding on his own now, grabbing for the rungs that slid faster beneath him.

"Watch it, Max!" came Kristin's voice.

She smacked into him from behind. Now they were both careening downward. Max tried to press his hands against the walls of the chute to slow himself down, but in a moment the walls and floor vanished.

He shot out into a vast underground cave. Its floor was pebbly and flat, and as he landed, he executed a perfect somersault. Kristin thudded to the ground beside him.

"Are you guys OK?"

Alex's voice.

Max sat up. His eyes adjusted to an even brighter greenish light than the one they'd seen above. Alex was leaning over him. Her right cheek was scraped and bloody, pebbles had lodged in her hair, her winter coat was gashed down the left side, and every inch of her was stained with black. "I—I've never done that before," Max said.

"Slid down a chute?" Alex asked.

"No," Max said. "A somersault. I try to do them in gym class. Everybody laughs at me."

"I . . . should have done one too," Kristin said through a grimace. "I landed on my coccyx."

"Your what?" Alex asked.

"The bone at the bottom of your spine and just above your butt," Max answered. "Lots of nerve endings there."

"You're both covered in black," Alex said.

"Coal," Kristin said. "Which indicates organic matter, compressed carcasses of dead prehistoric animals. It also indicates that we are pretty far down into the Earth."

"We got here alive because of *that*." Alex pointed back to the chute.

A metal handle in the shape of an upside-down T was dangling from the top. Like a miniature ski lift.

Max moved closer. "It's on a track that runs down the ceiling of the chute! *That's* why you asked me to look up."

"The handle was way up at the top of the chute when I climbed through the ceiling," Alex said. "But I didn't see the track *or* the chute. I could barely see anything. The dumb thing I did was grab that handle without knowing what it was. The smart thing was that I didn't let go. It controlled the speed of my descent. Otherwise we'd all have been sliding down at a zillion miles an hour."

"So the whole point of it was to guide you down here safely!" Kristin said.

Max moved closer to examine the mechanism. "This has Jules Verne written all over it."

"I think so," Alex said. "He knew we'd be climbing through that hole into darkness. He also knew the chute was narrow and steep. A recipe for disaster. So he installed a track."

Kristin walked to the chute opening. Just below the

bottom ledge, a horizontal groove had been carved into the rock, running about six feet wide. She crouched, shining her flashlight into it. "Come look at this."

Max ran to peer inside. Kristin's beam shone on the handle of a hidden wooden lever that extended directly into the dark. Max grabbed it and pulled it to the right. "Nothing," he said.

But when he yanked it to the left, he heard a metallic clanking noise. The T-handle shook and began moving back up the track. Max kept pumping the lever all the way to the left, pulling it back, and then pumping it again.

"Amazing," Kristin said. "It's a ratcheted mechanism against a flywheel buried into the rock!"

"A what?" Alex said.

"Inside the rock is a set of pulleys," Kristin explained. "They must be connected to a cable that conveys the T-handle up and down the track. Constructing this in Jules Verne's time would have been a scientific marvel."

Max smiled. "He hung with people who made submarines. What do you expect?"

Alex was looking around the room nervously. There were several holes in the wall and three possible tunnels. "This place is giving me the creeps. Do you smell anything funky?"

Max let go of the mechanism. The T-bar dangled overhead, a few feet along the track, but a barely audible thumping of the inner gears continued. "I smell pee," he said, "and I'm not angry."

"I smell it too," Kristin said.

Alex cupped her hand to her mouth. *"Brandon?"*

"Wait, you think Brandon *peed* here?" Max said.

"I don't know!" Alex said. "But he's down here somewhere, Max, and our number one mission is to find him."

"Ssshhh, guys, come here!" Kristin whispered. She was standing against the wall, her flashlight trained on the ground. "Look at this. The ground is covered with coal dust, so it shows us who's been here. Or *what*."

Max and Alex ran to her side. Her flashlight beam was illuminating a dirt floor carpeted with black dust. A few inches inside the wall was a set of three-toed footprints.

Max leaned down, holding his outstretched fingers just inches above the print. "That's like one and a half times as big as my hand."

"You didn't tell us animals lived down here!" Alex asked.

"They don't," Kristin said. "Especially animals this size."

"Do you know what kind?" Max asked.

Kristin shook her head. "A kind that does not exist in any reference book that I know. Let us pray that it's friendly."

Kristin's flashlight followed the prints along the wall, past the first tunnel and into the second.

"I say we make our first left!" Alex said.

Kristin looked at Max. "I say we ask Vegvísir."

Max smiled. "It's an inanimate thing," he explained. "It can't help us."

"Then why are you fingering it so nervously?" Kristin asked.

Max hadn't noticed he'd been holding his talisman. He was about to unclutch it, but he didn't.

He couldn't help noticing that Vegvísir was heating up in his hand.

It sort of made sense. Body heat did that sort of thing. But it sort of didn't. Because it was pulsing, ever so slightly. And a pulse was coming from the other side of the room too.

From something on the opposite wall.

Max moved closer. It was a blemish in the stone, a roundish shape just to the right of the entrance to the second tunnel, into which the animal's footsteps had disappeared. “Bandanna, please?” he said.

As Kirsten handed Max her bandanna, he walked toward the shape. It was grimed over with coal, and he began wiping it until a clear pattern emerged—a totally symmetrical shape made of some kind of steel that had been embedded in the stone.

Kristin gasped. She reached out to touch the shape.

“What is it?” Alex asked.

“It is a different talisman,” Kristin said.

“Maybe we need to turn this one like a clock also,” Max said.

“It does not appear to be embedded in a disk, so I

don't think it's a dial," Kristin said, running her fingers along the raised iron lines. "May I examine? I do not have your solving skills, but I think I can be useful."

Max and Alex nodded as Kristin felt along the lines of the talisman, pinching, grabbing, shaking. Finally she grabbed the circle in the center and pulled. The design moved a fraction of an inch, releasing a small cloud of coal dust.

"Hmmm . . ." With a loud grunt, she yanked harder. Outward.

This time the entire shape came loose in a small dust explosion. As she held it up, she smiled. "Ægishjálmr," she said softly.

"Gesundheit," Max replied.

Kristin smiled and shook her head. "Ægishjálmr is known as the helm of awe. One of the most powerful protectors against harm. It looks like it was housed very loosely in the rock, so it could be easily released."

"Cool," Max said. "I didn't see that."

"What does it do?" Alex asked.

"If you carry it with you," Kristin said, "it will instill fear into any enemy."

Max took it from her. "Does it also have powers of communication?"

Kristin and Alex stared at him curiously.

"Because I know this sounds weird, but I think the two talismans called to each other," Max said.

"Say what?" Alex said.

He stared at the two shapes. The Vegvísir shape around his neck was crazy and creative and asymmetrical. In a way, the design was everything Max was not. Maybe that was its real power. It was helping him get through the maze by giving him what he didn't have. By completing him.

Ægishjálmr was a different kind of shape. Each spoke was exactly identical. Steady and predictable, the same no matter how you looked at it. "This one," Max said, holding it out to Alex, "has your name written all over it."

"What do you mean?" Alex asked.

"I can't really explain it," Max said. "But may it help you the way Vegvísir helps me."

"Ohhhh-kay," Alex said. She tucked the talisman into her jacket pocket. Then, with a deep breath, she turned toward the entrance. "Whoa."

"Whoa what?" Kristin asked.

Alex turned toward Max. "I don't believe in magic. But this is so strange. I feel like I can do this. I feel like the Cowardly Lion after he gets his heart."

"The talismans," Kristin said softly, "are very powerful."

"Lead the way, Lion," Max said.

"Rrrrrufff," Alex growled, as she stepped in first.

27

"**JOHN** *Jacob Jingleheimer Schmidt . . .*" sang Alex in a loud, way-out-of-tune voice.

They'd been walking a long time. Silence had become too boring. Everyone was sweating and stir-crazy. So Alex had begun to sing. She'd said it was a song she learned in camp. It was about the twelfth tune she'd sung.

It made Max very glad he had never gone to camp.

But he wasn't really listening to her. His ears were picking up something else.

The pulsing had not stopped.

It had begun, very faintly, in the last chamber. At first he thought it was the talismans. Then, when it didn't stop, he'd figured it was the sound of creaky old gears from the sliding track. He'd first heard the pulsing when

Kristin used the hidden lever to move the T-handle. *Maybe,* he thought, *the mechanism lost its stopping ability and it needed oiling.*

But that was then. They had been traveling in this passageway for a long time. Max had no clue *how* long—maybe three hours, maybe thirty minutes. It was so hard to tell. The temperature had climbed steadily, and everyone was exhausted and achy from the steady descent. Max's eyes stung from the coal dust running down from his forehead in rivers of sweat. And through all of that, the sound had just gotten louder.

The trouble was, it was too hard to notice over Alex's performance. *"Guys?"* Max called out. *"Do you hear that noise?"*

"His name is myyyy name toooo—" Alex cut herself off in midverse. "Excuse me, it's called singing," she snapped. "And I won Best Vocalist of the Summer in Gosling Cabin—"

"I'm not talking about your singing," Max said. "I mean the thumping noise. Listen. It's not normal."

Alex fell silent for the first time in way too long. Her heavy footsteps grew light. Kristin leaned forward, her eyes narrowed, as if that would help her hearing. "I hear it too," she said. "Sounds like a dance club."

Stopping in her tracks, Alex let out a cackle. "Maybe

that's where the creature with the huge footprints was going. The Dinosaur Disco."

"With its famous Mastodon Mosh Pit," Kristin added.

"And a paw-cranked Jurassic Jukebox."

As the two broke into laughter, Max shook his head. "Are you doing that because you're scared?" Max said.

Both Kristin and Alex looked at him blankly.

"Laughing at jokes that aren't funny is a sign that you're really scared. That is a fact I learned from my mom. I used to do it a lot. And now when it happens I just *shh-hhh*." Max put his finger to his mouth.

In the quiet, the thumping echoed again.

Alex and Max crept forward in the tunnel. The sound was getting louder. As they followed a sharp bend to the left, Max could see a rectangle of greenish light at the end of the corridor.

And a shadow passing across it.

He stiffened. "Did you see that?"

"Y— " Kristin said, choking on the word.

Alex fingered her talisman. "This thing isn't making me feel brave anymore."

"What should we do?" Kristin asked.

Thump thump thump thump . . .

The sound was distracting Max. It was different now. A little slower. And he could hear other sounds too, high-pitched, like distant instruments and voices. The fear of the animal was short-circuiting with the absolute weirdness of the pulse. The two things canceled each other out, and all Max wanted to do was rush into the light.

"That's music," he said, rushing forward.

Kristin held him back. "That's impossible."

"Don't . . . make . . . any . . . sound," Alex whispered. Creeping forward, she held tight to her talisman with one hand and trained the flashlight straight ahead with the other.

As the green rectangle grew larger, Max could hear the distinct plinking of a piano. The wail of a saxophone. He stopped short. "'Born to Run,'" he said.

"We've come too far for that," Kristin whispered.

"No, that's the name of the song," Max said. "Bruce Springsteen. He's my dad's favorite. Listens to him all the time. He says this was the only music that calmed me down when I was a colicky baby. But I don't feel calm now."

They quickened their pace. The rectangle of light was coming from a big hole in the tunnel wall to the right.

Ahead of them the tunnel kept descending, but they weren't interested in that right now. Max, Alex, and Kristin flattened their backs to the wall as they neared the sound. The chords of the song were clear now. As they edged toward the green-lit opening, Alex peered inside. Max wanted to see too, so he dropped to his knees and crawled around her.

"Aaaaaah!" Alex screamed.

"What?" Max said.

"Sssshhhh!" Kristin shushed.

"Why did you do that? I thought you were that animal!" Alex whispered.

But Max didn't reply. He was staring into a room about ten feet high and ten feet across. The walls glowed with green moss, and against one of them was a lopsided table made of stones. On top of the table was a small metallic object barely visible in the dim light.

"Is that . . . a cell phone?" Kristin asked.

Max stood. As he walked into the room, he looked right and left. It was empty. It was also too small for anyone to hide in, human or animal.

The song ended, and another one began. It was some Europop dance tune Max had never heard before. He was close enough to see the phone now. Its screen was off, so he lifted it up and pressed the On button. The light was so bright, he had to turn away for a moment.

When he turned back, the screen showed a keypad, with an image underneath. It was a selfie of a smiling blonde girl about Alex's age with duck lips and dark sunglasses in front of a pool.

Max's hand was shaking so hard he nearly dropped the phone, but Alex cupped her hands under his.

"Is that—?" Kristin asked.

Alex nodded. "Bitsy."

28

"SHE'S here . . ." Alex's face was growing redder.

"I'm not so sure," Max said softly.

"I hate her, Max. I hate her with all my soul." Alex held up the phone and screamed into the screen, *"I hate you, Bitsy Bentham!"*

"Alex," Max said, "maybe she's not here—"

"This is her phone, Max, of course she is!"

As she reared back to throw Bitsy's phone against the wall, Max snatched it out of her hand. "Just listen to me—"

Alex ran for the entrance and called out into the long passageway. *"Where are you? Come back here and give us back what you stole!"*

Max raced out and blocked Alex's way. "You are five

years older than me, and you are acting like a baby. If Bitsy is here, we should be quiet and sneaky. We don't want her to know."

"Too late now," Kristin said. "You just woke up the reindeer in Siberia."

"Take a deep breath and think," Max said. "We just found a phone on a table, with the music playing. Don't you think that fact is weird? I mean, who would ever do that? It's bonkers, right? Like something in a movie."

Alex and Kristin exchanged a silent, baffled glance.

"OK, so I'm thinking if this were a movie, what happens in the next scene?" Max went on. "Boom. Booby trap! Or evil scar-face person jumps out of hiding! Or a note on the phone says, 'Darling, will you call for takeout, I'm going to sleep,' even though—*dun, dun, dun*—there's no Wi-Fi. Depending on the kind of movie. But none of that happened. Which makes me think, maybe she didn't mean for the phone to be here. Maybe someone else brought it. Or some*thing* else. Do you catch my drift?"

He looked hopefully from Kristin to Alex.

"No," they said together.

Max gestured toward the ground, shining his flashlight around. "All these footsteps in the coal dust? They're ours. But when we got in here, there were no human footprints. Just the creature's."

Alex looked up, her eyes growing wider. "And in the chamber we slid into, prints were under the T-bar."

"And in the tunnel on the way down here," Kristin added.

Max nodded. "Those footsteps were in all those places. All belonging to that . . . thing."

Even in the darkness, Max could tell Kristin had grown pale. "Oh dear. Do you think . . . ?"

"That the creature ate Bitsy while she was trying to get help on her phone, hoping there might be cell connection, out of total irrational desperation, only to accidentally activate her playlist and drop it to this table?" Max said. "Yes."

"Max, that is horrible," Alex grumbled.

Kristin gulped. "But plausible. We don't know what this creature is, or how it looks, but it does appear to be four-legged, so in a worst-case scenario I suppose it could happen."

"What if there are more of them?" Alex said. "What if Brandon . . . ?"

As her voice trailed off, Kristin took a deep breath and looked out into the long tunnel. "What do you think we should do? I forgot to pack artillery."

"I noticed something else," Max said. "The bioluminescence is getting brighter. The temperature is rising and the air is wet. We're getting closer to a water source. If Bitsy and Niemand are still alive, maybe they'll be there."

Alex smiled wearily and pulled her talisman out of her pocket. "I have the . . . chrysanthemum . . ."

"Ægishjálmr," Kristin corrected her. "Supposed to ward off all harm. According to legend. I repeat—*legend*."

"Right." Max set down his pack, yanked it open, and pulled out the two bones he had taken. Setting them down on the ground, he rooted around for a hunting knife.

With the knife, he scored a diagonal line near the ends of each bone. Then, one by one, he smacked both of them into the rock wall. They shattered cleanly on the diagonal lines.

Now each of the bones had an end as sharply pointed as a shark's tooth. He held them out to Alex and Kristin with a smile. "I'll take the knife, and you take these."

The two tentatively grabbed their weapons. Max pocketed the knife and slung his pack over his shoulders. "In this movie," he said, "we win."

They left the room carefully, moving slowly, stopping at any strange sound. They'd only gone a few hundred feet when Alex stopped. She shone her light on the wall of the cave, on an inscription Max had missed.

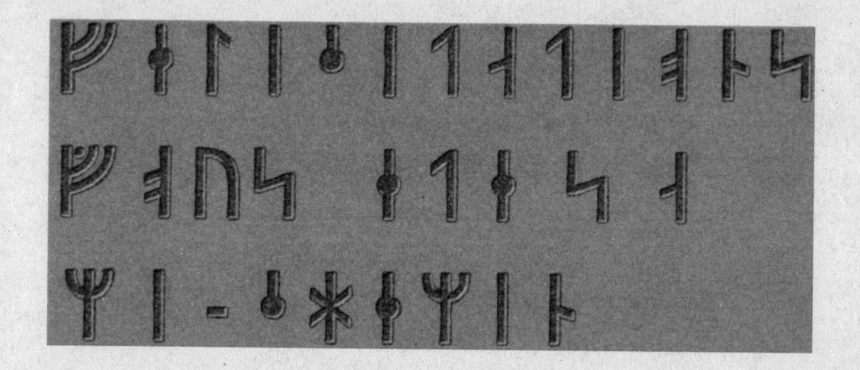

Kristin pulled out a pad of paper and pencil and translated the tunes into letters.

Felicitations, vous etes a mi-chemin

"No . . ." Alex said, her chest heaving in and out. "Just . . . no."

Kristin and Max were staring at the carving in the wall with curiosity. "That's what it means—'just no'?" Kristin asked.

"'*Félicitations, vous êtes à mi-chemin* . . . '" Alex let out a deep breath and leaned against the wall. Her eyes were red and her skin had become blotchy. "It means 'Congratulations, you have come halfway.'"

Kristin moaned. "Oh, dear."

Alex sank to her knees. "I—I need to rest . . ."

Max knelt next to her. "Halfway is awesome, Alex. The second half always goes quicker."

"You're so eager. I like that." Alex gave him a wan smile.

"What does the second line say?" Max asked.

"Follow the North Star," Alex replied.

"That's helpful," Kristin said.

"That's sarcastic," Max said.

Alex reached into her pocket and handed Max her talisman. "Take this. You and Kristin do a little reconnaissance if you want. Tell me what you see. Keep an eye out for Brandon. By the time you get back, I'll be ready to do wind sprints."

Kristin sat down next to her. "We will not leave without you."

Max looked down the tunnel. It had all looked exactly the same for such a long time, but now he was hearing a soft whooshing sound, like a waterfall. "I think we're close to something," he said. "But sound is so weird here."

"Tell me we're near a waterfall," Alex said, "and I'll be the happiest person on earth."

"I don't like the idea of splitting up," Kristin said.

Alex put a hand on her arm. "It's OK, Max, if you

stay within our eyesight. If you don't, I will personally kill you. That was sarcasm, but you get the message."

Max nodded. The moss down here was almost enough to light the way. With his flashlight in one hand and his knife in the other, he began walking. The slight rest had only made the pain in his legs worse. He grimaced as his muscles seized up. The tunnel walls had gradually changed from hard, undulating, moss-covered lava to a rockier surface, like stacks of small boulders.

Granite, Max figured. They were down into the bedrock of the Earth. As he paused to wipe sweat from his brow, he felt a rumbling from below him.

He stopped. His legs stiffened, as if tiny creatures were pulling on each of his leg muscles like cello strings. "Ow ow ow . . ." he moaned. "Charley horse!"

"It's all the downhill walking!" Kristin called out. *"Your legs aren't used to it. Stretch them in the opposite direction! Work against the pain."*

Gritting his teeth, Max turned to the wall. He let his body drop forward, arms extended. His palms hit a flat slab of rock not much larger than his hands. He planted his feet behind him, lowered his heels to the ground, and pushed.

The rock shuddered. Then with a grinding *ssshhhhuck*, it slid into the wall.

Max gasped. He had no reason to expect the wall to be hollow. But the rock dropped out of sight, leaving a big hole.

Max grabbed onto the hole's ledge for balance.

From inside, a pair of eyes stared back.

29

MAX sprinted back up the tunnel, too shocked to scream.

Kristin and Alex were frozen, staring at him. "What happened?" Kristin asked.

"Eyes . . ." Max glanced back over his shoulder. A small pile of rubble marked where he'd pushed the rock into a wall. He exhaled hard, trying to the release the fishy stink from his nostrils. "The rock . . . I pushed it all the way through . . . there was a room . . . two eyes . . ."

Alex was sitting forward, her face beaded with sweat, her eyes bloodshot. "Max, are you saying you saw some-one in a room in the wall?"

"Yes!" Max blurted.

As Kristin sprinted down the tunnel to see, Max

helped Alex onto her feet. They both followed after Kristin, gathering around the hole formed by the missing stone. Kristin was beaming her flashlight inside the room.

It wasn't very large, maybe eight feet across. On the opposite wall was a painting of three men. One was wearing a stuffy-looking suit and carrying a cane. He was stroking his gray beard and looking down skeptically at a chest-high world globe on a stand. Next to him was a younger, hatless man with dark hair and angry eyes. He was staring at the third guy. With long, stringy hair, dressed in a long robe, the third one seemed like a lost wizard from a Harry Potter movie. His robe was decorated with runic symbols, but his strongest feature was his eyes. They were large, wild, and sad. And they looked straight out from the painting toward the hole.

"Wait," Alex murmured, "*that's* who you saw? A painting?"

"My bad," Max said. "Those eyes looked so real."

Kristin was backing away from the wall. "Saknussemm . . ." she whispered. "Max, stand back a minute and look at the hole you made. There's a reason the rock pushed inward so easily. It fell from above and was never secured. There used to be a doorway here. Look at the whole wall, and then look at the pattern right in front of us."

Max and Alex stepped back. Looking left and right, up and down the tunnel, Max could see that the wall was smooth and unbroken. But the section right in front of them was different. There, rocks had piled up from floor to ceiling, about five feet wide, sealing up what must have been an entranceway. Above them the ceiling looked like it had partially collapsed. A boulder plugged up most of the space up there, and Max figured it had probably fallen into place from above and got stuck.

"The caves can be unstable," Kristin said. "With each shift of the earth, each quake or eruption, things like this happen. Nature wants to fill space, and these tunnels are spaces. They collapse. New seams form in the rock. Then everything's stable again until the next event. Obviously there was a collapse here many years ago."

"But why is that room here?" Alex asked. "Who are those people in the painting? And who painted them?"

"There's a series of paintings all around the room," Kristin said. "You can't really see all of them from the outside. They're covered with moss and cobwebs."

"I think the bearded guy is Verne," Alex said. "Let's

get in there and see the other paintings. These could be his next set of clues."

"How? We can't take apart the wall if it's not stable," Max pointed out.

"I think we're OK," Alex said, examining the stones. "Look at the rocks above the hole—they're huge. And they're really jammed in there, holding all the weight. The ones below are sitting there like loose change. We just need to knock a few over and climb inside. Come on, it won't take long."

Alex picked up a rock that was directly under the one Max had dislodged. With a grunt, she pulled it out into the tunnel. Max and Kristin joined her, and before long they had made a hole big enough to fit through. Kristin was the first to step in. Max helped Alex, who was still sweating like crazy and breathing hard.

Kristin got to work wiping away coal dust and moss from the walls. One by one, all four paintings were revealed. Each had the same three guys. In the first, the shabby, bearded man was at a desk, bent over a scroll filled with futhark letters. The other two guys floated in the air, facing each other angrily, like figures in a dream. The older one was leaning on his cane and the hatless guy looked young, handsome, and angry. "Jules and Gaston

Verne!" Alex said. "It's got to be them! But who's the dude in the center?"

"That would be Arne Saknussemm," Kristin said.

"You said that name before," Max said.

"He was in *Journey to the Center of the Earth*," Alex said. "The fictional scholar who left all the Icelandic runes for Liedenbrock."

"He was not fictional," Kristin said softly. "He was a brilliant man, a sage like Nostradamus or Rasputin—and like them, he had some unorthodox ideas. He was the one who believed the continents floated above one connected sea. Gaston revered Saknussemm. He convinced Jules to meet him in Reykjavík. This second painting represents this meeting, where they are agreeing to penetrate the Earth! They believed they would release the healing serum into the water supply and let it spread like an elixir of life throughout the world!"

Alex was wiping clear the third painting, in which the three men, with a team of workers, were hiking down a tunnel. Everyone was covered with grime but Gaston Verne, who glowed with health. "What's with the halo around Gaston's head?" Alex asked.

Kristin moved close to the image, shining her flashlight on the initials GV painted at the lower right. "Looks like the artist was Gaston. Guess he had a high opinion of himself."

But Max was staring at the final image, on the wall through which they had entered. It was a sea of grotesque faces, some wild-haired and completely bald, some with missing eyes and teeth. They were grasping at each other, screaming, clawing each other to pieces. One of the figures in the painting was a man whose face was covered with scars. Some of the scars were oozing fat worms. His hair was on fire, and he was screaming. In the back of his wide-open mouth was a T-bar, exactly like the one Alex had slid down the chute with.

"This is crazy," Max said. "It doesn't have anything to do with the others. But it's signed GV. And the guy in the center with the worms in his face? It's Gaston."

"Weird," Alex said. "Is he trying to tell us *that's* what happened down here?"

"We know he survived," Max said. "And so did Jules Verne. This does not look like a survival scenario."

Alex nodded. "We also know Gaston was committed to an institution late in life. Maybe something happened down here. Maybe this is when he began to snap."

Max couldn't take his eyes from the worm man's—Gaston's—face. The man seemed to be speaking to him, begging for help. "This is giving me the creeps," he said. "Can we go now—?"

Gaston's left eye exploded, spewing rocks outward.

"Aaaahhh!" Max fell backward, losing his balance, falling on his rear end.

Alex picked him up and wrapped her arms around him, shieldeing him with her body. Stones were dropping from the ceiling now. A jagged crack came down from the ceiling through the painting of Saknussemm in his study, cracking the globe in two. The ground shook as if a train were passing inches underneath.

"Move! Move!" Kristin said, shoving them both toward the opening. They made it through before it collapsed, and the entire outer wall imploded into the room.

All three of them dived farther down the tunnel and scrambled to their feet. *"That could have been us!"* Max shouted.

"What is going on here?" Alex screamed.

"I told you the area was unstable!" Kristin replied.

"Where do we go now?" Max demanded.

Kristin's mouth had dropped open. Her eyes were staring at something over Alex's shoulder.

Max and Alex spun around. Farther up the tunnel, something was moving toward them. "Is that an animal?" Max asked.

"I don't think so," Alex said.

It took the concentrated beam of three flashlights to reveal a round surface, round and pocked with holes, moving toward them.

It was an enormous lava rock, filling the entire circumference of the tunnel.

And it was rolling downhill toward them, like a killer bowling ball about to make a strike.

"RUN!" Kristin shouted.

"*No kidding*!" Alex replied.

They were practically flying down the tunnel.

Running wasn't the hard part. It was staying upright. The boulder was picking up speed, pushing air through the tunnel as it rolled. Max felt a gale wind at his back. He didn't dare look over his shoulder. As he forced his legs forward, each step turned into a jump. Kristin was taking advantage of this, leaping with long strides. *"Hurry!"* she shouted.

Alex lost her balance, tumbling forward as if she were falling down stairs. Max grabbed her hand and pulled her to her feet. *"Step with me!"* he cried out. *"Right . . . left . . . right . . ."*

They leaped like dancers, side by side, down the

steep path. From behind them came the boulder's steam-engine rumble. The thing was picking up speed. Spitting pebbles forward, directly into Max's back.

He tried to go faster, but his legs were killing him. To make matters worse, with each jump Alex's head seemed to just barely graze the ceiling. *"Keep your body lower!"* Max said.

"What?" Alex replied over the noise.

"I said, keep your body—"

With a dull *crrrack*, Alex's head made contact with the stone above him. As she fell to the ground, her hand unclasped from Max's. He stumbled and hit the ground himself, tumbling once and catching sight of Kristin's panic-stricken face.

"No-o-o-o-o!" came her voice from below them.

Max had always heard that when you were about to die, your life flashed before you. But that was not a fact. All he could think about was that in about two seconds he was about to be Flat Stanley.

He felt Alex's hand reach for his as they slid out of control. Even though he didn't like hand-holding, he felt lucky he was able to grab it.

GRRRRRROCK!

The sound was like a punch to the ears. Max felt his body lurch violently.

And then, silence.

Max curled himself into a ball. He could hear his own heart beating. That was a good sign.

"Max?"

It was Alex's voice, soft and plaintive.

Max swallowed. "Can you swallow when you're dead?"

"I don't know," Alex replied.

Max looked up, directly into the face of the boulder. *"Gyyyeeeeeh!"* he screamed.

It wasn't moving. For a moment, Max thought he was caught in some bizarre slo-mo state, where everything seems frozen just before you die. He could see a tiny gnarled twig embedded in the boulder's side, a pattern of dirt and rocks shaped a little like the continent of Antarctica. A couple of confused and very ugly beetles were crawling out a hole in the rock's side.

"Move!" came Kristin's voice from down below. *"Before that thing gets loose!"*

Gets loose. That meant it wasn't loose. Meaning it was *stuck*. Physically. The tunnel was too narrow. The rock had jammed.

Max didn't have time for relief. Tunnels, he knew, could be altered. He lifted Alex to her feet. Linking arms, they stumbled after Kristin. All three of them crouched low, until the tunnel was little more than a crouch space.

One by one they crawled through, curving left and then right, until the space widened again.

Gasping for breath, Kristin dropped to her knees and then sat against the wall. "I . . . can't . . ." she moaned.

Max and Alex joined her, and for a long moment no one said a word, until Alex finally asked, "Are we safe?"

"Maybe," Kristin replied. "The boulder is not likely to fit through the tunnel we just crawled through. It's stuck for now. But the stability of this whole volcano is compromised, so anything can happen."

"Plus," Max said, "safe or not, we're the ones who are stuck. We can't go back."

"Oh, that little thing," Alex said.

Kristin began shivering, despite the heat. "I—I never said good-bye to Uncle Gunther. I didn't leave a lunch for him. I was supposed to shop yesterday. How will he get by—"

"Stop that!" Alex said. "You'll see him again. We're going to get out of here."

"You don't understand," Kristin went on. "He had such hopes for this mission. To him, you were like gods dropping from heaven. A chance to redeem the name Saknussemm."

Max and Alex stared at her. "Was he a big fan?" Alex asked.

"Wait . . ." Max said. "*Your* name, Zax-Ericksson . . ."

"Is made up," Kristin said. "It sounds similar. I'm sorry I haven't been completely honest with you. Arne Saknussemm was my great-great-great-grandfather, as Verne was yours. His career and worldwide reputation were flourishing, until the journey with the Vernes. That changed him. His theories became outlandish and embarrassing, his public demeanor eccentric. The Hobnagians—the ones who believed in the alien invasion—they took him as their patron saint. Many named themselves after him. Some died trying to replicate the journey to the center of the Earth. Saknussemm died a laughingstock and a desperate man. Over time, people began to assume he never existed. Such was the power of *Journey to the Center of the Earth*'s imaginative story that people assumed Saknussemm was part of that fiction. That he was a figment of Verne's imagination."

Alex struggled to stand. "Why didn't you tell us?"

"I didn't think you'd believe me," Kristin said. "Or respect me."

"What? I would believe and respect anything you said," Max said with a shrug. "Because you're you."

Kristin smiled wanly. "Thanks. That's nice to hear. No one ever says that to me. I guess it's a good thing to know. Before we all . . . you-know-what."

"Dude, we'll do this," Alex said, taking her hand. "We are a special breed, the doofus descendants of geniuses. We complement each other. You're the competent one with the water glass half empty. I'm the maniac with the glass half full."

"I don't care how much is in the glass, as long as it's water and not hydrochloric acid," Max remarked.

"Remember what Mark Twain said," Alex said. "'Never, never, never give in!' Or something like that."

"That was Winston Churchill," Max corrected her, starting off down the tunnel. "And I agree. We may or may not get out of here, but I want the satisfaction of finding Niemand and Bitsy."

Kristin and Alex joined hands and began following. "I guess," Kristin said, "that makes about as much sense as anything else."

The air became so thick and warm, it felt like they were swimming instead of walking. Max's breaths rasped like a buzz saw. He was beginning to smell his own body odor. On the positive side, he'd put his flashlight away. The bioluminescence was washing the entire tunnel in a greenish light, brighter than ever. The walls seemed to be alive, undulating like giant serpents, but in the humidity Max found himself only able to walk a few steps before pausing to catch his breath.

"Max! Maaaaaax!"

Behind him, Alex was calling out his name, so he waited. Max had to blink away the sweat from his eyes to see her. It looked like Kristin was completely supporting Alex's weight.

"What?" Max said.

Alex looked up wearily. "What what?"

"You were calling," Max said. *"Max! Max!"*

"I thought that was you," Kristin said.

"Me calling myself?" Max replied.

"Maaaaaax!"

The hair on Max's head stood on end. If his veins had hair, they would be standing too. Neither Kristin's nor Alex's lips were moving. The sound echoed upward from behind them. From farther down the tunnel.

"B-B-Bitsy . . . ?" Alex whispered.

Max shook his head. "The accent isn't right."

"It's one syllable, Max," Alex said. "How can you tell— "

"Maaaaax! Mack-mack-mack-maaaaaaa . . ."

"See, that's not British," Max said.

"It's not humanish either," Alex replied.

"And it's not really saying 'Max,'" Kristin said. "I think it's a caw. From a bird."

For the first time in hours, Alex's face brightened. "Which means there must be an exit!" she said.

Max spun around. There was light ahead. Birds. A way out of the volcano.

"Wooooooo-HOOO!" He jumped, spinning in the air, then began running down the sharp slope of the tunnel. "Maaaax! That's me! Max Max Max Max!"

His feet slipped on the moss-covered rock. He slid, bracing his body like a skier. The tunnel angled right again, and he leaned into it.

As he took the turn, the path dropped sharply. Max's feet went out from under him. He windmilled his arms, trying to keep his balance. Panicked thoughts flashed through his brain. But below him was a wide circle of light. Light was better than dark. It meant something was there. Another chamber, with a floor.

He grasped at the walls, but they were wet. There was no hope of any traction. As he tumbled, the opening drew closer, and now he could see that something was in it.

It was a shape as round and dark as the boulder they had escaped.

Great. Their hope for salvation had finally arrived, and he was about to become a human pancake. Max's body caromed from wall to floor. He screamed, curling himself into a ball as he hurtled toward the big black lump.

He hit hard. The air rushed from his lungs like a burst balloon. For a long moment he saw a field of black and red through his closed lids.

Before he opened his eyes, he moved his fingers, toes, arms, legs. They were all there, all intact, nothing broken. He had no idea how he had managed to survive, but sometimes it was best not to question.

As his unclosed his eyes and tried to focus, he heard a deep growl.

He blinked. The boulder was covered with hair.

And it was moving.

MAX tried to spring away. But whatever this thing was had a different idea. It held Max tight—with arms, legs, or tendrils, he couldn't tell. But it was smothering him, smushing his face into its fur, lifting his feet off the ground.

As he rose upward, Max kicked as hard as he could. His boots sank into the creature's flesh but didn't seem to have much effect. His face was jammed into a mass of mossy, dust-choked fur. He also caught a blast of something so rotten and foul that he almost passed out.

Coughing, he jammed his flashlight upward. He was hitting something soft, so he repeated it again and again, as hard as he could. The creature's grip loosened. It snorted and seemed to stagger. As Max tried to wriggle free, he heard a scream. Something sharp struck his left ankle.

"Let go of him!" bellowed Kristin's voice.

The beast let out a guttural moan. It let go of Max and he fell to the ground. As he rolled away, Kristin flew over him, attacking the beast with her backpack. Behind her, Alex was just emerging from the tunnel, sliding headfirst. She scrabbled to her feet, took a moment to look, and raced toward Max.

She pulled him away. They retreated far behind Kristin, who was now chasing after the beast with her backpack raised high.

Max's eyes were adjusting to the location. It was another "bubble" in the long tunnel, a widening, with a ceiling at least five stories high over a flat stone floor. By now they'd been in several of these underground openings, each deeper than the last. Each was hotter, more humid, and greener with the glow of the strange light-giving moss. Now the air was so thick, the fleeing beast seemed to be moving through tiny green clouds. Its outline was soft in the haze, almost liquid. It seemed to float along the wall, first upright and then on all fours—or maybe sixes or eights. It was impossible to tell much about the beast under its long, matted hair, which covered every inch of its body and dragged on the ground like a street sweeper.

"What is that thing?" Alex whispered.

"I don't know," Max said. "But compared to Kristin it's a chicken."

They watched as their screaming Icelandic guide chased the creature, until it slinked into a cave in the wall and disappeared from sight.

Kristin paused by the opening, panting. "What . . . did I . . . just do?"

"That was awesome!" Alex said.

When she looked up at them, her face was pale. "I . . . I was thinking about Uncle Gunther. About how he would protect me when we hiked volcanoes."

"He chased monsters?" Max asked.

"No, muskrats," Kristin said. "But still. I didn't know I had that in me. I guess you guys are family now. This is what families do."

"Awww," Alex said, putting her arm around Kristin.

"It was hideous," Kristin murmured. "All that hair. Maybe some kind of subterranean bear?"

Max crept closer to the cave. "It's a carnivore, that much I know. It was very happy to see me. And its breath smelled like half-digested dead human."

"Did it smell like Chanel perfume?" Alex asked tentatively. "That's what Bitsy wears."

Kristin put her hand over her mouth. "I don't know whether to laugh or puke. That is disgusting."

"Snaefy?" Max called out, leaning into the cave opening. *"Here, Snaefykins, nice Snaefy!"*

"Max, stop that!" Alex said. "That thing nearly killed you, and you're giving it cute names and trying to lure it out?"

"It's scared." Max paused by the cave entrance. "I surprised it. I don't think it knew what to do with me. Maybe it never saw a human before."

"I will forbid us to go in there," Kristin said.

His eyes drifted to the top of the cave, where a crude star had been carved into the stone. "Do you see what I see?"

"Cave carvings from primitive beasts?" Alex said,

Let the North Star guide you. That had been Verne's message. "Remember Verne's message, about letting the star guide us?" Max asked. "A star is carved over this opening. Maybe we're supposed to go inside."

A deep belch echoed from inside the cave opening, followed by a blast of putrid air. Max jumped back with a startled yell.

Alex groaned and sank to the floor. Whatever energy she had summoned was draining again. "Let's see . . .

chase a monster and get eaten . . . stay in a cave and suffocate to death . . . eeny meeny miney mo . . ."

"OK . . . OK, Verne said the *North* Star," Kristin said. Her hands shaking, she was pointing a compass at the opening in the wall. "That opening is facing east."

"Right," Max said. "I'll keep looking."

Max gazed around the wide cavern. From what he could see, the walls were unbroken, solid except for the small cave. But in the eerie phosphorescent light, the stone seemed fluid and strange, weirdly alive. Despite the light, he cast no shadow of his own—yet other shadows appeared and disappeared. For a moment he saw Kristin fanning Alex with a paper folder, and the next moment they blended into the stone and disappeared. "The light plays tricks," Max said.

"Is it tricky enough to hide an escape route?" Alex called out.

Max kept walking slowly along the wall. Shady forms seemed to pass before him like ghosts. Black holes bubbled and closed like fish mouths. So when he spotted a grayish circle in the floor, he slowed down and approached warily.

He fell to his knees, crawled forward, and looked over. There wasn't much to see—inside was the same wash of greenish light, the same shapes and shadows, only deeper. But the dull whooshing sound was unmistakably louder. So was the burst of salty, wet air.

This close, he could make out a strange symbol beneath the bottom rim of the hole, which looked like some kind of new runic talisman. But his eyes were drawn to a star at the top.

"Kristin!" he blurted. "Am I north?"

"Yes!" was Kristin's instant answer. She and Alex emerged from the eerie thick light and stopped by his side, looking downward.

With a shrill caw, something enormous passed from right to left. Max recoiled and sprang to his feet. "Gahhh!" he gasped.

"It's a *hole*," Alex said with a look of horror, "deep enough for a *bird* to be flying below us."

"What's a bird doing down here?" Max squeaked.

"Good question," Kristin said. "But we must be getting close. This was the more northern star of the two. Verne may have left the other star as a decoy. I'm guessing he was nervous that the wrong person might stumble onto this secret."

"It's different too," Max murmured. "It's not like the other star. One ray is way longer than the other."

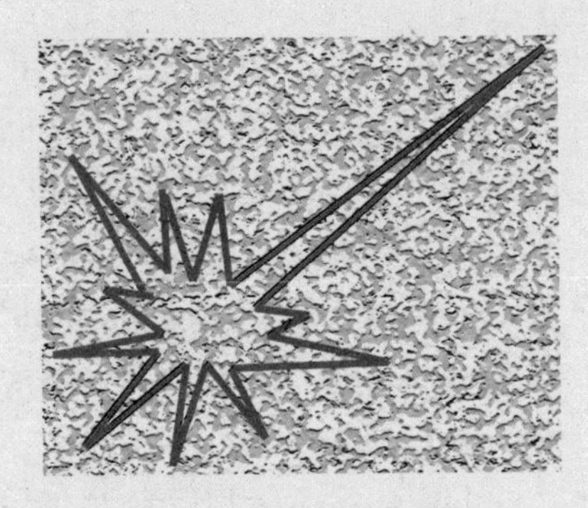

"Maybe it's pointing to something," Alex suggested.

Max's eyes snapped to the right, following the path of the long pointer. The wall was thick with moss, but he could see the faint outline of a carving. In a moment Kristin was wiping the area clear with a cloth.

As the carving underneath became clear, she smiled. "Max and Alex, say hello to Lásabrjótur."

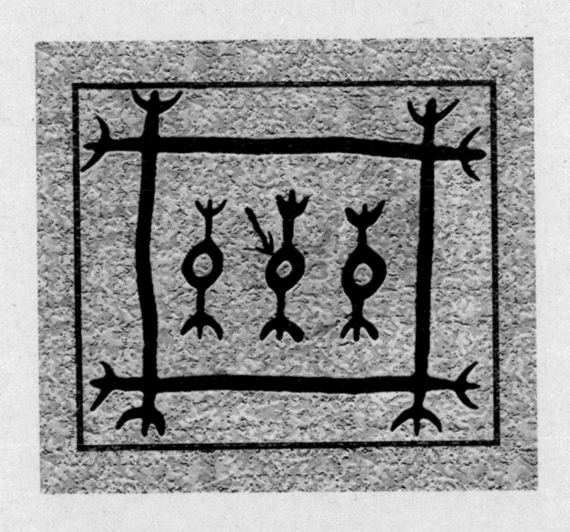

"Hello, Las . . . L . . ." Max tried. "I don't think I can."

"What does it mean?" Alex asked.

"Lásabrjótur is the lock breaker," Kristin said. "It allows the bearer to open any lock without needing a key."

"I don't see a lock," Max pointed out. "Also, even if we did find a lock, how are we supposed to use this thing? It's not removable like the last one."

"Excellent questions." Kristin drew closer to it. "I also don't understand the little arrow. That's not supposed to be there."

"Monster graffiti?" Alex suggested.

Max shrugged. "Well, OK, it's pointing to the middle, right? So maybe he's giving us an instruction. Like, 'Press here.'"

He held up his right index finger. Carefully he touched the carving at the place the arrow pointed to, the circle at dead center.

Nothing happened.

"I felt a little give," Max said. "I think."

"It's old," Alex countered. "Press harder."

Max reached into his backpack for one of his retractable poles and unsnapped it to its full height. "Hey, dude," he said, "I didn't use you in the climb down here, so maybe you can help me now."

Rearing back, he shoved the end of the pole into the

little circle. It sank into the rock with a dull click.

As the button slowly popped back out, the square around the carving moved outward. *"Stand back!"* Kristin shouted. *"Keep your feet clear!"*

But the whole thing did not fall out. It was trying to open like a lid, hinged at the bottom. Max leaned forward, grabbing firmly along the top side of the square. Alex and Kristin joined him.

"Heave . . ." Alex said, "ho!"

They pulled as hard as they could. The square fell open along the bottom edge, breaking its old, rusted hinge and crashing to the ground. Max, Alex, and Kristin jumped aside as a crowd of small creatures scurried out of the hole—lizards, salamanders, ants, spiders, and a small furry mole with one eye.

"Ew," Max groaned.

"Party time," Alex said.

Waiting for the animals to clear, Max stepped onto the rubble and peered inside. Just behind the broken door was a kind of metal plate, a square carved with yet another Lásabrjótur symbol. "Whoa, there's your talisman," Alex said.

"You have one and I have one," Max said. "Maybe Kristin can wear this one around her neck."

He dug his fingers around the edges of the metal

square and pulled it outward. It came loose easily, and Max handed it to Kristin. "Now we're even. If only we can figure out how to get down there."

"Um, Max?" Alex said.

She was looking at the square. Her flashlight was trained on a thick chain that lay inside, coiled like a giant sleeping snake.

Max reached in and began pulling. It was rusted, and it shed cobwebs and insects as it emerged into the light. Kristin and Alex joined him, yanking out the heavy chain onto the ground, where the end of it spilled out over the debris.

They pulled and pulled. Yards of chain slid out, enough to completely cover the debris with coiled links. But the other end of the chain remained inside the square hole. It seemed to be jammed. "Pull harder!" Kristin urged.

"No . . ." Max was shining his flashlight into the depths. "I think that's all there is. Looks like it's attached at the other end. Bolted right into the rock at the back wall."

Alex stared over the expanse of metal, shaking her head in bafflement. "Why on earth—?"

"I think we're supposed to take it from *on* Earth," Max said, looking down the hole, "to *in* Earth."

32

AS Max slid down the chain, he thought about evolution.

It made absolutely no sense to him that human beings could not fly. If evolution was survival of the fittest, and dinosaurs evolved into birds, then why didn't mammals?

"How are you doing, Max?" called Kristin's voice from the top of the hole. *"We can't see you!"*

He swung gently on the chain, which was wrapped around him in a complicated arrangement that Kristin assured him would prevent falling. *"I am very uncomfortable!"* Max called back.

"Keep doing what I told you!" Kristin shouted back. "If the chain is too short, or you lose your nerve, we'll pull you back up. Remember, loosen, slide, loosen, slide—and whatever you do, don't look down!"

Holding tight to the chain with his feet, Max slid his upper body down into a kind of squat. Then he slid his feet lower, clamped them, and started the process again. He tried looking down once, but all he saw was a thick green soup of moving shadows. That was scary. In his life he had hang glided into a river valley in Russia, flown a hot-air balloon in Mexico, and swum through an underground cavern in Greece. But at least in those places you could see where you were going. Not seeing was worse.

Loosen. Slide. Don't look down.

It all seemed so awkward and unnecessary. He had thought about human flight a lot, in his bedroom, while making models of prehistoric creatures. Rhamphorhynchuses and pteranodons always looked angry, predatory, and not so bright. But their descendants sixty-five million years later, hawks and sparrows, did fine. People with wings would be awesome. And they would never have to drop into a green underground cavern hanging from a hundred-fifty-year-old chain.

Loosen. Slide. Don't look down.

"Still there?" Alex called down.

"And what about gills?" Max called back. *"We should have them too!"*

"*What are you talking about*?" Alex said.

"It's so unfair!" Max replied.

The air had definitely thickened. It was salty and wet. You could bite into it. It smelled weird too. It was how the shower water smelled in a campsite in Canada when he was little. Sulfur, his dad had explained.

So maybe Iceland was connected under the earth—to the RV camp in Canada!

"Ha!" Laughing at that thought was not a good idea. It made Max slip down the chain. The metal links hurt if you weren't controlling the speed. He couldn't help crying out in pain.

"Do you need us to pull you back?" Alex shouted. *"What's up?"*

He was swinging now. The chain had slipped, and his right leg dangled. He tried to pull the leg back, but that made him rotate. And rotating made him sick.

"My leg let go!" he called upward.

"Was that a no?"

"No!" Max said. *"It was a yes!"*

"Yes?"

Max's swinging had become spinning. The distant shadows bubbled in and out of sight, like he was trapped in a gigantic green lava lamp. The distant whooshing sound had grown to a roar. He wanted to puke.

"Yes yes yes yes yes yes!"

"OK!" came Alex's answer.

The sudden upward jerk made him loosen his grip. The chain was coated with wet, slimy moisture, and he slipped downward. *"Not so fast!"*

The next pull was even more sudden. As he gripped tight, one of the shadows began darkening, growing before his eyes. It angled toward him from above, its sides churning up and down until they became unmistakably the shape of wings. A shrill squawk penetrated the green, goopy air. Two bright yellow eyes emerged, the eyeballs vertical black slits that were focused on Max.

"Faster!" he shouted, trying to pull himself upward, hand over hand.

He could see it clearly now, its blood-red skin a stark contrast against the green air. Its body was scaly and thin, and it seemed too small for its own long, torpedo-shaped head. Three crooked fingers poked out from the top of its leathery wings, which were hinged like those of a giant bat.

With a final thrust, it tucked its wings into its torso and dived. Max spun one last time and found himself staring at an orange-red tongue and four rows of gleaming, pointed teeth.

33

MAX did the only thing he could do, which was let go of the chain.

The creature did the only thing it could do, which was to grab whatever it could with its talons.

Which, unfortunately, happened to be Max's hair.

Max felt himself rise, in ridiculous pain. He let out a scream that seemed to come up from below his toenails. He couldn't imagine anything worse than this.

Until the flying beast let go. Or maybe it was the hair that let go from his head. At any rate, the pain had ended, but he was plummeting. His mouth dropped open to scream again. His arms and legs pumped, as if that would do anything. For a moment he thought about his mom.

His legs hit the surface below. But instead of being

squashed, he broke through. He felt his body jerk backward as he kept plunging. Air rushed from his lungs as if they'd been squeezed by a fist. He couldn't inhale, and he couldn't see. He was tumbling slowly, gritting his teeth against the pain.

It felt like he'd landed in water. Or maybe some kind of warm underground pudding.

Instincts kicked in, and he thrust his arms downward into the liquid. He opened his eyes into a thick green murk. He could see light coming from above but couldn't gauge if it was inches or miles away.

Thrust . . . thrust . . .

His lungs began aching and he felt light-headed. He wished he had paid more attention in swim class, instead of running around the pool stepping on only blue tiles.

"Gyyyaaahh!"

His head broke through the surface. Air slammed into his mouth. As his chest heaved, his gulps sounded like the barking of a sea lion. He flailed his arms to stay afloat. This stuff didn't taste much like water, but more like a cocktail of obnoxious flavors—rusted metal, rotten eggs, dead fish, salt. He spat out as much as he could, but the taste lingered. His eyes scanned the thick atmosphere, but the flying creature was gone. All he could hear now were distant screams.

"Maaaaax!"

That one, he knew, was Alex.

"I'm OK!" he yelled back. Now he could see the chain swinging above him. The last link was about ten feet above the surface. *"Come down, the water's warm! But bring a weapon! There's a pterodactyl!"*

Not too far away, Max spotted what looked like a coast, so he swam toward it. It took about five strokes before it dawned on him that he shouldn't be able to do this, because he wasn't a good swimmer.

He panicked for a moment. But even that panic did not sink him. He was floating without having to do much. That meant the water was buoyant. Like the Great Salt Lake. People could float easily in the Great Salt Lake because of the salt. They could float in oceans easier than lakes. These were facts. So he stopped being afraid and made his way toward the coast. After a few minutes he felt his boots touch the bottom and began to walk. He was nearly out of the water when he heard a loud splash behind him.

Alex's head was emerging from below. And Kristin was jumping in after her. *"Over here!"* Max shouted, waving.

The two swam toward him. Or rather, Kristin swam with her arm around Alex, who was trying as hard as she could. *"Are you hurt?"* Kristin called out.

"No," Max replied, "I let go of the chain before the pterodactyl's beak cut me in half."

Now the two were on their feet, slogging toward him slowly. "That's weird," Alex said. "Everything sounds muffled down here. I thought you said pterodactyl."

"It might have been a rhamphorhynchus," Max said. "I didn't get a chance to examine it that closely. Although it did pull a clump of my hair out."

Alex headed toward him with a weak smile and open arms. "Your hair looks bad, but I'm just glad you're alive, cousin!"

"No hugging." Max ran away, his boots crunching on a surface that looked like sand but felt like a sea of broken glass. He stopped, scooping a handful of bright-green flakes. "Whoa, what is this stuff?"

Kristin was craning her neck, gazing around as if trying to memorize every detail. "Shushed crells, I believe. Erm, crushed shells. Perhaps stained by a high concentration of algae . . ." She let out a deep exhalation. "I'm sorry. Everything is distracting me. This is the strangest ecosystem I've ever seen."

The massive soupy fog was rising up from the water now, billowing on a breeze and separating into clouds like green balloons. In an instant, a luminous neon-green lake began bursting into sight as if a curtain was rising over it from front to back. The water stretched to a horizon Max couldn't see, its surface smooth and unbroken.

"This thing is as big as Lake Michigan," Alex said under her breath. "And . . . that light! It's like someone snuck a green moon down here and hid it behind the clouds."

"We are a kilometer under the Earth," Kristin said. "It should be pitch-black. The bioluminescence should be a smattering of pinpricks from plankton and moss. This volume and brightness—it's the stuff of fiction! It's *not* like a moon. It's like someone collected the material of all the world's fireflies, magnified the light to a power of a thousand, and exploded it across this sky. No wonder Verne never tried to convince anyone this was nonfiction. Who would believe him?"

"Somehow that makes me want to cry," Max said.

Kristin nodded. "What do you think is the likelihood that Niemand and his daughter made it this far alive?"

"Not very," Alex said. "After that phone, we haven't seen any sign. I'm not even thinking about them at this point, guys. I'm thinking about us. And getting home. We are in survival mode." She began walking along the shore, squinting into the distance. "We have to be careful. We know there's wildlife down here. I thought I saw something in the water just as we dropped from that chain, Kristin. I think that's it—that *thing* down the shore."

Max glanced in that direction. The lifted fog had revealed a big dark lump swimming toward the shore.

No. Not swimming. Floating. Bobbling like some lifeless piece of driftwood. "Looks dead to me," Max said.

But Alex was headed toward it. She was trying to run, but her ankles were buckling beneath her. *"Wait up!"* Max shouted.

He and Kristin ran after her and caught up quickly. "That's not your normal way of running," Max said.

"No kidding," Alex growled. "I think I have Snuffle sickness."

"Is that a real thing?" Max asked.

"No, but *that* is."

The floating carcass had washed up onto the shore. It did not have a torpedo-shaped head or red skin or a body covered with matted hair.

It was wearing clothes, and it looked human.

Max and Kristin picked up the pace and reached the body first. It was facedown in the green flaky sand, half immersed in the lake. Up close, Max could see it was a man, and he wore a soggy shirt and khaki pants.

As Max knelt before him, Kristin ran around the other side.

Alex staggered up to them at the moment they carefully turned over the body of Brandon Barker.

34

ALEX was kneeling by Brandon as Kristin applied chest compressions. This time, the resuscitation was not working. Brandon's skin was pale, and his chest wasn't moving. His head, which still had the gash from his first fall, now had a new one, twice as long and much bloodier.

"Sorry . . ." Kristin said softly, pulling away for the last time.

Alex nodded, holding back sobs. "Yeah. I was kind of expecting this." She let her head sink into Brandon's chest, wrapping her hand gently around his head. "He wasn't as lucky as we were."

Max felt numb.

Death was numbness. Brandon would never not be numb.

It didn't feel right. Brandon had slid the wrong way. He'd done exactly what Max had done, but he'd leaned too far to the right. And that was it. His airplanes would never feel Brandon's hands on their controls. People would not hear his stories as he flew them to new places. Alex really, really liked him. And now he had been taken from her forever.

Max liked Brandon too. He'd never really thought about that. Brandon could be annoying, but that was only because he took Alex away from Max. You never really knew how you felt about someone until you thought about your life without them. And when Max did, it was as if he were surrounded by skunk. Sadness all over. Brandon was a part of everything he and Alex had done.

He began rocking on his knees. Alex came close to him. She was crying about Brandon, but despite that she put a hand on Max's shoulder. To make him feel better. She was connected to Brandon and also to Max. Which meant Max was connected to Brandon. That's how things worked. "I feel bad," Max said. "For him. And for you."

"Yeah," Alex said softly.

"What do we do?" Kristin asked. "Do we just leave him? It doesn't seem right. What about his friends and family?"

Max thought for a long moment. He knew two people who had died. One was Basile, the captain of the *Nautilus*, who had saved their lives. "We left Basile," he said. "At the bottom of the sea. Where the fish ate him."

"We had no choice," Alex said.

Max nodded. "When my grandfather died, our family had a burial. I didn't like it. There was a lot of crying and fuss about the coffin and the service. It seemed weird to bury people in the ground. But I don't like thinking about Basile on the seafloor. And I don't like thinking about leaving Brandon out in the open like this."

"Yeah, me too," Alex said.

"We should bury him," Kristin suggested softly.

Alex nodded. "If we survive, we'll tell people what happened. We'll get professionals to come back for Brandon's body."

Alex stood. She looked out toward the vast underground sea, empty but for a tiny island at the horizon. Her eyes took in the high, green clouds gathered at the cave's dome, the lava walls that stretched into the fog.

"*All for one and one for all* . . . that what was one of the last things he told us," Kristin said. "He would want us to continue. To get back what was stolen and find out Jules Verne's secret."

Max held out a fist. "Family, remember? Till the end."

Alex smiled weakly. With one arm, she wrapped Kristin in a hug. With the other, she extended a fist bump to Max.

A distant call that sounded something like *breeeeee-aaaahhh* made them all sit up straight.

"Maybe we should do this really quickly," Alex said.

"I put trowels in our backpacks," Kristin quickly added. "We'll start digging here."

"Is this body of water tidal?" Max asked.

"What?" Alex said.

"Because if it is," Max replied, "and if it happens to be low tide right now, the water may rise over the grave and eventually undo the burial. Which is why, in the old Inuit culture, bodies were buried far up from the water's edge. That's a fact."

Kristin gave Max a pained smile. "I am impressed you know that. And it's a good point. Let's move him up the shore."

Alex groaned, staggering to her feet. She and Max took one shoulder and Kristin took the other, and together they began pulling Brandon up the sand. His dragging heels made a soft *sssshhh* sound as they moved across the surface, in a sad rhythm with Alex's muffled sobs.

Breeeeeeaaaahhh . . .

The sound seemed closer now. But with the echo, it

was impossible to tell where it was coming from.

They set Brandon down on the green sand, about fifteen feet beyond where the hill leveled off. One by one they opened their packs, took out their trowels, and began to dig. The sand was light, almost sugary. With each shovel full of sand they removed, more slid in from all sides.

Now Max could see something distant in the water, floating toward them. It was hard to make out exactly what it was. Despite the lifting of the clouds, the light was still dim and shifting. But from what Max could see, it seemed to have a wide, low body and a thin head like some crazy form of squid.

"What the heck is that?" Alex whispered.

"I don't know, but it sounds hungry to me," Max said.

Even in his peripheral vision, Max could tell the creature was moving toward them very quickly. They plunged the trowels in harder and faster. The sound hissed against the walls, along with the chuffing of their labored breaths. But the fine, shifting sand was making it hard to get any depth.

Max glanced up. Now the thing was close enough to see. What he thought was a wide body was actually a stout raft. What he saw as a thin head was the creature itself. It was a tall, thin animal that looked like a broom with no handle, a mass of long hair from head to toe—although below the hair, it was impossible to tell if it had any toes. Two arms, also long masses of hair, were maneuvering a pole, pushing the raft forward. Behind the creature, a long tail dragged in the water like a rudder.

"What the heck is that?" Kristin asked.

"I was hoping you'd know," Alex said. "We've never been to Iceland before."

As the hairy creature poled closer, Max stared at the area where he imagined its face would be. He spotted three speckles of brightness shining from within the cascade of hair, in the place where he expected two eyes. And just beneath the three, where its mouth should be, a red-rimmed black hole opened wide.

BREEEEEEAAAAHHH . . .

Max winced, doubling his grave-digging efforts with the trowel.

"Max . . ." Kristin said. "Stop that. Get back!"

She was pulling him away from Brandon, up the shore. Which was not right. It was against their agreement. They were supposed to take care of Brandon's body.

Max lost his balance and tried to fight against her, but she was stronger than he expected. "But . . . family . . ." he protested.

The beast was stepping off the raft now. It resembled a walking haystack, and it was impossible to see its legs. Pulling the raft to shore, it lay the two poles on top and turned toward the group.

With a grunt like an agitated elephant, it was gesturing toward Brandon. Alex rose to her feet. But instead of running, she stood between the beast and the body. "You have to get past me, Cousin Itt," she said.

"I don't think insulting it is the best idea," Max said.

The hairy creature moved closer to Brandon. Max and Kristin fanned out to both sides. With its three eyes, it glanced up from one to the other. Kristin said something to it in Icelandic.

"What did you say?" Alex asked.

"I told him Brandon was dead, and he should leave us alone," Kristin said.

"Does it even have ears?" Max asked.

"Hard to tell," Alex said. "But if it comes any closer, it's going to be toast."

As it let out another roar, Kristin jumped backward. Then, swallowing hard, she said, "Sorry, but you need to go back."

She stepped in front of the beast as it reached out with its right arm.

Max leaped forward. He grabbed the arm, and the creature let out a squeak of surprise. Kristin quickly grabbed its other arm.

Taking advantage of the distraction, Alex lunged forward with her trowel.

The beast's three eyes swiveled toward her. Its mass of hair quivered. Max and Kristin held tight to the arms, but that wouldn't be enough.

From the front of the creature's torso, hidden under the thick mass of hair, an orange tentacle whipped forward. It wrapped around Alex's arm and tossed her to the side like driftwood. She screamed in surprise, her trowel flying away and into the water.

Max let go of the creature and ran for his cousin. *"Get away from that thing!"* he shouted, grabbing her by the ankles to try to pull her away. "You too, Kristin!"

Kristin was lying half in the water, maybe ten feet by the creature. Snorting through nostrils buried under its hair, the beast stood over Brandon. Its tentacle, which had disappeared back into its hair, now emerged from its torso again. This time it was holding a strange metal object, round and elaborately carved like a ninja nunchuck.

"What the heck is that?" Max murmured

"Leave Brandon alone!" Alex screamed.

BREEEEEEEAAAAHHH . . .

The shriek was like a quick slap in the face. Max, Alex, and Kristin all recoiled. The mass of hair was kneeling beside Brandon Barker, rearing its tentacle back with the silver weapon.

"Get that thing!" Max shouted. He was the first to race back toward the beast. But as he approached, one of its arms rose out toward him. It was rubbery like a Gumby, and the tips of its four hairy fingers glowed and blinked.

Like eyes.

The sight made Max stop short, his body paralyzed. The beast's tentacle was holding the silver object high, tilting it toward Brandon's body. From one of its metallic points, a clear liquid dripped on Brandon's forehead. Moving quickly, the creature ripped open the pilot's shirt, letting the liquid course down his chest. Brandon's skin let out a hiss, sending up wisps of green smoke.

"It's burning him with acid!" Alex screamed. Despite her weakened state, she dived toward Brandon.

As she landed on him, the liquid splashed onto the back of her neck. Kristin blindsided the creature from the other side. With a roar like a creaky door, the hairy thing fell back. Kristin was yelling in Icelandic, pounding the beast wherever she could with her trowel. It let out a scream like a creaky door. Alex fell on it from her side, pulling it away from Brandon. *"Hit it, Max!"* Kristin shouted.

Max stood over the struggling creature. He held his trowel high. The thing was squeaking and snorting now, its three glowing eyes whirling and its red-rimmed mouth opening and closing. Its hair swirled as it struggled, revealing not one but four tentacles hidden under it, along with its arms. Two of the tentacles were waving wildly in front. The other two were digging into the sand along with its arms, trying to push away from Alex and Kristin.

"What are you waiting for?" Alex demanded.

But Max couldn't bring himself to stab it. "It's not attacking anymore," he said. "It—it's trying to get away from you."

"What?" Kristin said.

Alex glanced up at him in shock.

With a sudden lurch, the beast leaped away, out of Kristin's and Alex's grip. Now its arms and tentacles were carrying it along the sand, scuttling like a crab overgrown with seaweed.

Kristin sprang to her feet and began to run after it, screaming angrily. Alex overtook her, running faster than Max had seen her move in a long time. *"And never come back!"* she shouted.

"Alex?" Max said. "You just ran like a world-record sprint."

She stood there, staring down at her own body. "I know. Wow. I guess I wasn't as sick as I thought."

But Max's eyes were fixed on Brandon. Where the hissing liquid had touched his body, his pale greenish skin was darkening. From a series of thin lines along his forehead and torso, it spread like the branching of nerves, setting off blotches of deeper color that grew and joined until he no longer had the same tinge as the lake. The bloody gashes on his head seemed to knit up with fibers of his own skin, the streaks of blood drying and flaking.

Max stepped closer.

Brandon's head lolled toward him. His eyes fell open, and Max jumped back with a scream.

"I feel like I just died," said the corpse. "What's for lunch?"

35

FOR a dead person, Brandon the Pilot sounded pretty cheerful.

"Anybody got popcorn?" he asked, looking around at the gaping faces of Max, Kristin, and Alex. "If you don't move your mouths, I bet I could land three for three—ping, ping, ping!"

As Brandon stood, Alex nearly tackled him to the sand again. Throwing her arms around him, she shouted, "*You—you—*you're alive!"

"Hit me a little harder and I won't be," he said.

Alex's eyes were full of tears, as were Kristin's.

Max didn't know what to do, so he started to spin. That made him feel pretty good, because each time he came around, Brandon's smile got bigger and bigger.

"Max!" Brandon cried out. *"Dude!"*

"Welcome back," Max said. "I promise I will always say nice things about you."

"You were dead, Brandon," Alex explained in a rush of words. "Like, flatlined. No breathing. You slipped through a hole, way up near the top of the volcano. We were devastated. We kept going, hoping we'd find you alive. We traveled for so long, down through tunnels. This is incredibly deep in the Earth. No human being could have survived a fall this distance. So seeing your body was our worst fear confirmed—"

"There are creatures down here," Max added. "Flying reptiles and superhairy beasts. And one that was like a yeti and a spider and a squid all in one, and he poured out this magic fluid from a nunchuck and uncrushed your skull and brought you back to life after you were a carcass."

Brandon looked confused. He flashed a smile and said, "Yetis and spiders and squids, oh my!"

"Actually it might not have been a he," Max said. He was standing still now but rocking from side to side with dizziness. "Or a she. It seemed pretty gender-nonspecific. But the point is, this is real, Brandon. No sarcasm. Something happened down here that does not happen in real life as we know it."

Brandon's jokey expression was tightening as he looked from one face to the other. "I don't really remember any of this. . . ."

"You don't have to." Alex hugged him tight. "Funny, the moment you revived, I felt better too."

"It was the liquid," Max said, pacing the shore. "It doused you too, Alex. *That's* why you felt better. Guys, I think we've found what we want."

"Oh . . . my . . . gosh . . ." Alex's eyes went wide. "Is this what we found, the serum? In the hands of some hairball with tentacles?"

"Exactly!" Kristin said, walking beside Max. "It had an immediate effect. Brandon must not have been dead very long."

"Maybe it wouldn't have had the same effect if Brandon's body had stiffened," Max said, "or if animals had, say, eaten his eyes or any of his vital organs—"

"I was enjoying this," Alex said. "Can we lighten up the conversation?"

"So wait," Brandon said. "It may take me a while to catch up, as I am a pilot of little brain. Jump in if I'm wrong here. So I flew you all over the world to catch these two creeps who stole this tiny batch of some crazy healing formula, and now this monster Muppet brought me back to life by pouring all over me and Alex . . . wait for it . . . some crazy *healing formula*. And now we're all alive, we're all down here together, and we're not doing cartwheels?"

"Why should we?" Kristin said.

"Because if Trickle Me Elmo just happens to have some of this stuff, then you guys don't need to find Skunky McSkunkface and his daughter. We have a source!" Brandon said brightly. "We found what we needed! We'll be rich!"

"We're already rich," Max said.

"We could win the Nobel . . ." Kristin said dreamily.

"Just a few pesky details," Alex said. "First, we have to actually get our hands on the stuff. It's not as if we can text Bad Hair Day Creature and say, hey, float on back to us and lend us some healing formula. And second, we'll all die if we can't get back up. And third, even if we get back up, what do we tell people? Mutant prehistoric creatures . . . daylight from plants . . . an underwater sea . . . a journey deep inside the Earth where no one burns up from heat or gets squished from pressure . . . who's going to believe us?"

"We can deal with three if we nail one and two," Brandon said.

"We'll take photos," Max said. "We've been bad about that so far."

"We'll have the formula, Alex," Kristin said. "That's all that matters."

Alex started to answer, but her voice trailed off, her eyes focused on something over Max's shoulder.

As he turned, so did Brandon and Kristin. For a long moment, no one said a word. Far down the shore three figures were taking form, emerging from the lingering green fog. As they passed a cave opening in the big arching stone wall, Max heard distant whistles and shrieks. Two dark shadows spilled out of that cave and joined the others. From high overhead, a flying creature descended. With a flapping of wings, it perched on the shoulder of one of the walking creatures.

"Holy moly, an underground army," Brandon murmured.

"M-M-Maybe we can . . . talk to them?" Kristin said.

"In what language?" Alex shot back.

Kristin pulled a white handkerchief from her pocket and waved it. *"We come in peace!"* she shouted.

"They can't hear you," Max said. "And put that away! Maybe to them a white handkerchief means 'Go suck on a rock' or something. Crazy cultural differences down here."

He kept his eyes trained on the procession. More

beings were emerging from the caves along the sand. They were hulking beings, about seven feet tall and dressed in tunics. Their faces were humanlike but covered with hair, and their eyes stared out from shadowy ledges under their foreheads. Their shoulders were broad, their legs bowed. In the center of them all was the creature who had saved Brandon, a completely different species than the rest, its tentacles gyrating all around.

Kristin, Max, and Alex started instinctively walking backward.

"Hang on," Brandon said. Fishing a phone from his pocket, he scooted behind the others and held it up, pointed toward the advancing horde. "Smile, guys."

"Are you out of your mind this is no time for selfies and besides you fell from a gazillion feet so your phone is busted!" Alex yelled.

Max grabbed Alex's and Kristin's arms and turned. Together the three ran away, back down the beach. Max glanced over his shoulder to see Brandon scooping a rock out of the sand. "Fastball, ninety-three miles an hour, down the pike!" He went into a pitching stance, kicked, and hurled the rock into the advancing crowd.

"Don't antagonize them!" Alex yelled.

"Steeee-rike!" Brandon yelled.

"KRIIIIIIIIIAAAA!" came a shriek that was way closer than Max wanted.

He and Alex turned. The gang of creatures had doubled. One of them writhed in pain in the sand. The others were picking up speed. Sand spewed in all directions like a greenish-white cloud as they flew toward their attacker.

"You fool!" Alex raced to Brandon and pulled him back. Caught by surprise, he lost his balance. But this time, he wasn't going to disobey.

He, Max, and Alex ran toward Kristin, who was heading toward a cave opening farther up the beach. *"Guys, over here!"* she screamed.

"How do you know it's safe?" Brandon called out, but Kristin was already inside.

A deafening *CAWWWW!* split the air behind them. Leathery flying creatures were swooping down from high above now.

"I think, yeah, the cave," Brandon said.

But now Kristin was screaming. She ran out, followed by a slithery yellow reptile. And at the same time, Max felt a hand on his shoulder.

No. It wasn't a hand.

It was a paw.

"Ahhhh!" Max yelled in shock, twisting his body away, instinctively spinning and kicking. His right foot landed square in the face of a furry, monkey-like beast with wings. It fell to the ground, whimpering, and immediately ran away.

"Whoa," Max murmured, "did I do that?"

"Max, help me!" came Alex's voice.

She was surrounded by three of the odd hairy humanoids. Max reached into his backpack and pulled out a squeeze bottle filled with raspberry Gatorade. "Forgot I had this," he said. "Don't say I never gave you anything!"

As he squirted the liquid as close as he could to their eyes, they screamed in surprise and Alex crawled away.

Out of the corner of his eye, Max saw Brandon fighting off two more of the creatures. They were bigger, but Brandon had better speed. Max and Alex both ran toward him, but they were stopped by a piercing scream from above.

"No! No-o-o-o-o!"

Max and Alex glanced up to see Kristin's legs dangling as a flying reptile lifted her toward the sea.

"That thing almost killed me . . ." Max murmured.

He did the only thing he could think of, which was

throw the Gatorade bottle toward the beast. He knew it was about the weakest thing ever. And it only grazed the reptile's tail. But the impact was enough to throw the thing off-balance. It squawked, loosening its talons. With a scream of terror, Kristin hurtled downward. She landed in the soft green sand with a thud and rolled.

As Alex ran after her, Max stopped short.

To their left, another phalanx of the humanlike beasts was approaching from the opposite direction. Kristin was groaning and struggling to her feet with Alex's help. Brandon was running toward them. *"They're not so tough!"* he shouted.

And just beyond Kristin, still floating in the sea, was the raft that had been left by Trickle Me Elmo. On it was one long pole; the other floated next to it. Beyond it was a wide-open sea with no signs of life. Now, in the clearer sky, Max spotted a dark lump near the horizon.

An island.

"Follow me!" Max shouted over his shoulder toward Brandon, who was already passing him by.

"With you, dude," the pilot said.

Max urged Alex and Kristin toward the water. The sea seemed to have no current, so the raft had floated only about fifteen feet out. Together the four sloshed out in the shallows and climbed aboard.

It was a tight fit, only about six feet square. Brandon lifted the floating pole out of the water. Max took the other pole and stood. Together he and Brandon thrust the planks into the water and pushed the raft farther out. Not daring to look up, Max poled as hard as he could. At any moment he expected a furry paw or slimy claw to grab him off the raft.

But the creatures had gathered on the shore in a clump, staring out to them, grunting and babbling to each other.

"Can you do the 'Hallelujah' chorus?" Brandon shouted.

Kristin narrowed her eyes. "The jaw shape . . . the cranium . . . if I didn't think it was such a crazy concept, I'd say they were Neanderthals."

"With a random pterodactyl, flying monkey, and walking hairball," Max said.

"Well, it's a good thing no one taught them to swim," Brandon said with a sigh.

"It's not much of a comfort," Alex said. "We're heading into the middle of a sea with no way out."

Max's eyes were focused on the creatures. Their chattering didn't seem so random to him. It seemed more like a discussion.

And it looked like they had reached a decision.

A squad of about a dozen was making its way into the water, following in the wake of the raft.

"It looks to me," Max said, "like we have some company."

BRANDON stared down the approaching mob, lifting a pole over his head. *"Yeeaarrgh!"*

"Chill, Brandon the Pirate," Max said. He was watching the creatures closely. They were keeping their distance. "We're not going that fast. If they wanted, they could swarm us. But they're not."

"Why aren't they?" Kristin asked.

"Because I'm scaring them away?" Brandon replied.

"Maybe," Alex said, her eyes on the slow-moving mob. "But I'd try putting the pole down for a minute and helping Max move the boat."

Reluctantly Brandon lowered the pole and dipped it into the water again. The creatures kept their slow, silent pace. Now they were fanning out around the raft on both sides, keeping a safe distance.

"So strange," Kristin said. "It looks like some kind of escort."

"But they were attacking us a couple of minutes ago," Brandon asserted.

Max gave the pole a hard shove. "Maybe," he said, "they weren't."

From above, a crying screech broke the silence. Out of the green clouds, a prehistoric bird dropped like a missile.

And another.

And a third.

Brandon lifted his pole out of the water again. This time so did Max. The animals around the raft were chattering again. The three birds circled above the raft like buzzards, and then one dropped like a dive-bomb. It was heading straight for Max, its saw-toothed beak hinging open.

"Maaaax!" Alex screamed.

Max swallowed hard, praying he could jam the pole into the creature's beak. But now a second lizard-bird was dropping fast.

And a third.

Brandon was bracing himself for attack. But there were two of them and three attackers.

"What are we supposed to—?" Max yelled.

From his left, a black coil shot upward into the green sky. With a whiplike *snnnap*, it knocked the first lizard-bird out of the sky.

Snnnap! The second screeched, its head jolting backward, and it plummeted to the sea.

Snnnap! The third had come close to the tip of Max's pole, but it never reached it, as a pink tentacle flicked it away like a fly.

Three of the hairy creatures—just like the one who had poured the liquid over Brandon—were picking the birds out of the sky with their tentacles. "Dear Lord," Kristin said, "those are like frog tongues! They just expand and expand."

Now a flock of the deadly birds was hovering warily above them. They squawked, crisscrossing each other in the sky. And a moment later, they were gone.

Max smiled. He scanned the faces of all the creatures that surrounded them, although with some of them it was hard to tell where the faces were. "Thanks!" he called out.

They responded with grunts and moans. Two of the hairy creatures clapped hands, crying out, *"Aaaaannsa! Annsa annsa annsa!"*

"Same to you," Brandon replied.

"Sounds like they're saying 'answer,'" Alex remarked.

"I don't think they would actually know English," Max said. "It's probably Hairballer for 'See what I did there?'"

"What just happened?" Kristin said. "They're our friends now? I'm so confused."

"I think they were trying to be friendly, but we didn't understand," Alex said. "The lizard-birds, I guess, are the real predators. This gang may have saved our lives." She looked warily at their new allies. "Let's go back to the shore. We can make nice with them. We know at least one of them has serum. Maybe they'll give us some."

Max gave Brandon a look. He nodded, and together they jammed the poles into the bottom of the shallow sea and reversed course.

BREEEEEEEAAAAHHH!

The hairy things started shrieking, wagging their tentacles threateningly at the raft. They, and the horde of Neanderthal-like creatures, started to crowd the area, blocking the path back.

"I guess we're not doing that," Max said, as he and Brandon stopped the raft.

"What's up?" Brandon said. "They *want* us to float out to sea?"

Max looked back over the water. They were closer to

the island now, and he could see wisps of smoke rising from its midst. "Looks like that place is inhabited."

"Maybe that's where they cook their dinners," Kristin said. "And we're tonight's special guests."

"Or," Alex added, "we're the main course."

They were trapped, but Max tried not to think of it that way. The creatures seemed peace loving. He reminded himself that one of them had healed Brandon. They hadn't attacked, really, when you thought about it. They had just approached. It was Max and his friends who had overreacted.

He said those things to himself over and over.

The island was drawing closer. Its surface was covered with rubbery-looking trees draped with moss. They sagged of their own weight, bent over from the top like elderly gardeners. In the distance, Max once again heard a deep whooshing noise. "What is that?" he asked. "I heard that all the way down here."

"Geysers," Kristin said. "They go off regularly. You can time your clocks to them. Who knows where that one is, maybe many kilometers away."

Where the raft was headed, a green sandy path led up through the trees into the island's interior. Animals were scurrying down that path now, emerging from farther inside the island. They gathered noisily on the shore. Most of them were smaller than the creatures around the raft—furry, rodent-like beings who reared back on two legs, jumping up and down. Out of their tiny mustached mouths came a song like the calls of tiny whales.

Kristin winced. "Out of tune," she said, "but fascinating."

"Annsa!" the winged monkeys shouted. *"Annsa annsa annsa!"*

Kristin stood, staring at the commotion on the shore. "I am not feeling excited about this . . ."

"I hate rats too," Max said.

As Max and Brandon poled the raft closer, the monkeys began impatiently gesturing toward the island. *"Annsa annsa annsa annsaannsaannsaannsaannsa!"*

Max gulped. He gave his cousin a wan smile. "Let's do this."

"Let's do *what*?" Alex said. "Walk up to those little hungry-looking critters? They look way too eager."

The raft was beaching now, its front edge scraping against the soft sand. Max stepped off first, letting his boots sink into the muck. Brandon followed. The rodents were hopping excitedly, twirling around, keening little tuneless songs.

"Hey, buddies! You guys are the cutest!" Brandon said.

"They're *rats*, Brandon!" Alex blasted.

"More like lemmings," Kristin said, her voice hushed and awestruck as she stepped out of the boat. "With a bit of pika mutated in there. And maybe fox. This area is an extraordinary evolutionary laboratory. Don't you see, Alex? It's like the island of Komodo!"

Alex gave her a why-are-we-talking-about-some-place-I-never-heard-of look.

"Explorers found a giant lizard there, which existed nowhere else on Earth," Kristin explained. "It had been allowed to evolve, because in Komodo there were no predators for that sort of creature. And this is what we have here! Up on the Earth, millions of species have gone extinct by natural selection over the millennia. Entire branches of the developmental tree, snapped off because of predators. But here, in this unique biome . . ."

Her voice trailed off as she gazed around.

"Mutant madness," Alex said.

As Brandon pulled the raft up onto the sand, the rodent-like creatures began tugging at their hems and shoelaces, pulling all four of them forward. "Don't bite me, don't bite me, don't bite me," Alex said, shaking her leg.

The animals didn't seem fazed. Letting go, they led the way up the path, nudging ankles, singing, pointing with their tiny paws. The other beasts, dripping green water from their fur, hair, and scales, followed close behind.

Together they all trudged up into the odd jungle. The path was winding and exactly the same width all the way, framed on each side by thick hedges of gray-green moss that were trimmed perfectly flat.

After about five minutes, a house came into view. It was constructed of jagged lava rocks, irregularly shaped and different sizes. A couple of crude, glassless windows peeked out the long side. On the shorter side was an archway with no door, and Max thought he could see movement within.

At the top of the path, they stopped short.

"More Neanderthals," Kristin murmured.

A team of the hulking humanoids turned toward them. At the sight of Max and company, they backed away. Some shuddered, a couple of them screamed, and all began chattering excitedly.

"This is extraordinary," Kristin said. "They aren't exactly what the fossil record shows. I believe they're what the Neanderthals may have looked like if they'd survived extinction."

"I thought they developed into us," Brandon said.

Kristin shook her head. "Different species. They were thought to have died off."

Now the monkeys were shouting *"Annsa!"* again, and the rodents were back to leg-pulling, guiding Max and the others toward the open entrance to the building.

On the slanted rooftop, which looked like it had been made of pasted-together shells, smoke puffed out of a crude rock chimney. The Neanderthals were slouching away, back to their work.

Max stopped for a moment to watch them. A team of four was pushing against the arms of a huge horizontal wheel, turning it slowly. Others were lugging pails, stacking what looked like wood, trimming hedges with knives, talking to one another in what sounded like a real language. *"Kristin,"* Max called out, *"is that Icelandic?"*

"Max, come!" hissed Alex.

He spun around. Standing in the doorway was a grizzled old man, maybe five and half feet tall, dressed in a white robe. Skin hung on his facial bones like worn-out clothes, wrinkled and neglected and nearly transparent. His eyes were pure white, one higher than the other, but both were sunken in deep sockets. The skin around his mouth was so thin, you could practically see his teeth. Max couldn't tell if he was smiling or frowning.

The monkey-like creatures were bowing, throwing their arms to the ground in some strange kind of salute, squeaking *"Annsa! Annsa! Annsa!"* as if afraid the old guy would bonk them over the head.

Outside, the Neanderthals were making noises again, grunting and snorting and squealing *"Annsa!"* in high-pitched voices.

"Are they mocking these guys?" Max asked.

"I guess there's a pecking order everywhere," Kristin said

Now the old man was stepping forward onto the sand. His steps were mincing and light, and his robe made a swishing sound as he walked.

It took Max a moment to realize the sound was not the robe's material but actually the man's speaking voice. It was a papery whisper, mostly clicks, whistles, and hisses.

"Can anyone understand him?" Brandon asked.

"Yes, it's Icelandic," Kristin said. "He's welcoming us."

The old man stopped speaking. As his head cocked to the side, Max panicked for a moment that it might fall off.

"Would you prefer English?" the old guy whispered.

"I understood that," Alex said.

Max walked closer to hear more clearly. "Th-Thank you. I'm Max, and these are Alex, Kristin, and—"

"Brandon Barker, pleased to meet you," Brandon blurted, stepping forward with his hand outstretched. "And you are . . . ?"

The old man's mouth twitched. Ignoring the hand, he turned his eyes to Brandon. Where his pupils should have been was a grid of thin, lightning-like blood vessels. "They call me Annsa," the old man said. His laugh was like the creak of an opening door, and it lasted a few nanoseconds too long. "So I suppose that is my name. Come."

Turning slowly into the house, he called out in his raspy whisper: "We have guests!"

"There are more of him?" Alex asked, as she took Max's hand.

Shuddering, Max followed Kristin and Annsa into the house. It was dark and smelled a bit like seaweed, divided into two rooms by a wall in the middle. A stone fireplace was burning some dried green substance. Above the fire hung a stone pot of some not-bad-smelling stew.

Annsa stopped at the opening into the next room. His mouth twitched again as he stepped back.

Inside was another roaring fireplace, and a modest table made of carved stone. Sitting at the table were two figures in hooded sweatshirts, hunched over a table that contained two cups of a steaming green liquid and a plate of dry-looking seaweed snacks.

"Humans, thank goodness," Kristin sighed. She walked in first, extending her hand. "Hello, Kristin Zax-Ericksson."

As the smaller of the two looked up, her hood fell back to reveal her face. "Bitsy Bentham," she said. "And this is my pa—"

She never finished the word. As Max and Alex walked in, her jaw dropped open.

"Surprise," Max said.

He could feel the heat of Spencer Niemand's glance even before seeing his slate-gray eyes.

"I hope," Niemand said, "that one of you brought a Snickers bar."

"GIVE me one good reason," Alex hissed, staring at Niemand, "why I should not wring your neck."

Niemand smiled brightly. "My boyish good looks?"

"Oh, Papa, please!" With a fluttery laugh, Bitsy gently elbowed her father and stood. "You know his unique sense of humor. It really is so lovely to see you all alive and well. Er . . . how did you get here?"

She extended her hand, but Max and Alex stared at it like it was a dead fish. "Are you serious?" Max said. "I'm not shaking your hand, and it's none of your business how we got here."

"A bit harsh, don't you think?" Niemand said.

"Kristin," spat Alex. *"Get. Away. From. Those. Villains."*

As Kristin jumped away, Spencer Niemand barked a

laugh. "Aren't we being a bit dramatic, dear girl? Consider our last meeting. As I recall, you had cruelly trapped me in a dangerous, unhygienic relic on a remote Arctic island. With a slavering German engineer who had communication issues. Textbook villainy if you ask me."

"Our last meeting," Max said, "was outside a prison in Massachusetts. Where you had escaped after being jailed for multiple crimes. I think they were kidnapping, attempted murder, and grand larceny."

"Ah, glad you reminded me!" Niemand pulled a wallet from his pocket and slid it across the table to Max. "I believe this is yours. Sorry, old bean. I needed the cash, and you were such an easy target."

Alex lunged across the table, reaching for Niemand's throat. With a yawn, he calmly veered aside. She went sprawling over the table, landing on the stone floor with a sickening thud and crashing into the wall.

"Oopsy," Niemand said.

Max, Brandon, and Kristin raced toward her. Behind them, flying monkeys were rushing into the hut, cackling and hooting.

"Sssssssss!"

The sudden sound was barely louder than an insect's buzz, but it stopped the monkeys' voices cold. They stood at the entrance to the inner room and stared, slack-jawed.

Annsa was just inside the door, facing them, his skeletal hand raised high over his head.

As Max helped Alex sit up, Annsa rasped a few unintelligible words to his minions. Immediately they backed into the other room.

"Are you OK?" Max asked his cousin.

"Remind me never to do that again," Alex said, holding her head.

"I merely stepped away from an attack." Spencer Niemand stood, offering his seat to Alex. "My apologies. You caught me by surprise."

"Stuff it," Brandon said, clenching and unclenching his fists.

"Where on earth did you find Dudley Do-Right?" Niemand said

"Papa, that is not called for," Bitsy said, turning to Max and Alex. "Please don't be angry. We can explain—"

"Give us back the serum!" Max blurted.

"Don't ask us," Niemand said, gesturing back to Annsa. "Ask the Zombie from the Green Lagoon."

"Sssssssstop! Sssssit!"

The tiny sound of Annsa's command managed to cut through the noise like a siren. In the sudden quiet, the crackling of the fire sounded like breaking bones. Obediently Niemand, Bitsy, Max, Alex, Brandon, took seats or perched at the edge of the table.

Annsa walked slowly to a small green cabinet made of tight rubbery cords. He pulled out an enormous conch shell and held it to his mouth. When he spoke through it, his voice was still raspy but extremely loud.

"I have the serum," he said. *"And it will stay here."*

"You see?" Niemand said. "This . . . erm, fine elderly gentleman set his hench-creatures after us. We were simply attempting to do the right thing, to carry out the noble mission of Jules Verne. For the benefit of the world. So Annsa is the thief here. Not I, not dear Bitsy. We were in the midst of delicate negotiations when you so rudely interrupted us."

"Papa, they did not interrupt," Bitsy scolded. She looked pleadingly at Max. "I know you and Alex are angry at me, and I don't blame you. But please know that my concern was for the good of humankind. I could have explained my plans, but you would not have supported them, so I had to act alone. I could have taken the serum earlier, but I waited for your mother to recover. I do have a heart. You were so emotionally involved. You also desired the serum for yourselves, and I understand that. But my father possessed the secret to replicating it, and it was important to—"

"Steal it from Martin Hetzel?" Alex said.

Niemand held up a bony finger. "Free it from obscurity," he said. "Into which it was about to fall, had we not rescued it. In this age of interwebbery, you know, it's just so easy to find people."

"You snuck into his files while he had a heart attack," Max said.

"The word," Niemand said, "is *sneaked.* At any rate, how were we to know the old fellow would fall ill?"

"How was he to know he'd be fleeced by an escaped convict?" Alex snapped. "Who'd been freed by a thief?"

"Imprisoning a man like Papa—that was an injustice," Bitsy said. "His life's goal is the safety of the world in the aftermath of climate change! We all want that. So now that you're here, now that we are trapped together, what is there to lose? We can choose to be partners. I plead with you to trust us." She turned to Annsa. "And I plead with you, sir, to give us back the serum. Let us all heal the world together."

"Not so fast," Alex said. "*Trust you?* We heard that in the *Nautilus.* We heard that from Nigel, from your mother, from you. And each time we were betrayed."

"Mr. Annsa," Max said, "I know you're superold and, like, really set in your ways. But this serum is a big, big deal. One of your buddies, the hairy, tentacle-y one, brought Brandon back to life with it, after he was toast.

The person who brought it down here in the first place, long before you were born? He was the one and only Jules Verne, who was my great-great-great-grandfather—"

"By the light of Loki," Annsa said, "I can see the resemblance."

Max stopped in midsentence. "Wait, what? You *do*?"

"And also a resemblance to you . . ." he said to Alex.

She raised her eyebrows. "Well, no one's ever told me that. I mean, the skin and the hair and the gender and all, plus no beard, but I can write like a fiend."

"No . . . no, it's in the eyes, the confidence, the quick intelligence," Annsa said. "It is him all over again."

"So . . . you're a fan," Max said. "That's cool. You've seen pictures, huh? We have a portrait in our living room."

"Ck . . . ck . . . ck . . ." Annsa said.

"That's his laugh," Bitsy explained.

"I do not need portraits," the old man said. "Not for a man to whom I became closer than anyone in the world. *Annsa*, you see, may be what these loyal creatures call me . . ."

"Annsa! Annsa!" agreed the winged monkey guards.

". . . But my real name," he continued, "is Arne Saknussemm."

Max exhaled. Claiming to be someone who died in

the 1800s was definitely a sharp turn into cuckoo-land.

Alex laughed. "That's a good one, sir. I'm Joan of Arc."

"No, Alex, I believe him. There are many with this name." Kristin gave the old man a weary smile. "This is another Hobnagian."

"Excuse me?" the old man said.

"The group that believes Iceland was invaded by space aliens from a planet called Hobnag, remember?" Kristin replied. "They latched onto Saknussemm as their hero. Frankly, they are responsible for helping to destroy his reputation. No disrespect intended, sir, but the real Arne Saknussemm was a genius and a good man—a real human being who deserves his place in history, and I am proud to be his great-great-great-granddaughter."

Annsa said nothing for a long moment, and Max worried he'd had a heart attack. Finally he rasped, "What is your name, dear?"

"Kristin."

"Sweet Kristin . . ." A tiny droplet winked down the folds of the old man's cheeks. "I care not a whit for history, but it pleases me greatly that I make you proud. And that dear Jules's discovery made this meeting possible."

Kristin stared with utter bafflement into the old man's face. "The serum . . ."

"Yes." The ends of Saknussemm's lips creaked upward. "I accompanied Verne and his nephew on their initial voyage, as a guide. But when they left, I stayed. These beings, this environment—I found it much less dull than the world above. I thought I would die here, if not from the environment then from old age. None of us predicted the serum would do this to me." He held out his emaciated arms. "Although my body has aged, my soul will not leave it."

Choking back a sob, Kristin gently hugged the man she never thought she could meet. "That is so awesome," she said. "And tragic."

Alex's jaw had dropped open. "This is getting weirder and weirder."

"I just *adore* family reunions," Niemand said. "Now, why don't you all stay and have a party? My treat, send the bill to Niemand Enterprises, no expense spared. So if you'll give my daughter and me our backpacks, we will be on our merry way."

"No!" Alex and Max blurted at the same time.

"You may stay or you may leave," Saknussemm said, releasing Kristin from a long hug. "But I'm afraid it is necessary that we keep the serum here."

"We need it, sir," Max pleaded. "It saved my mom's

life and cured my friend Evelyn."

Saknussemm stared at him. "Are you sure you want that? Do you want them to be . . . like I am?"

Max fought away the thought. He didn't want to think about that at all. "I want them alive," he said. "And healthy. And we know you have some of your own serum here, because this hairball dude used it to save Brandon. So please, give it back."

"And teach us what you know," Alex added. "We have so many questions. How much of it does my aunt need? Is there a dosage? And why did Jules Verne bring the serum here?"

"In his note he mentioned something about propagating it," Max said. "In a large body of salinated water, I think."

Saknussemm reached over and put his hand on Max's. Even though it felt like frozen crab claws, and Saknussemm's eyes were solid white, Max didn't flinch. "Do you trust me, my boy?" the old man said.

"Trust," Niemand said, "is not his strong suit."

"I did not ask you," Saknussemm snapped.

Max swallowed. Looking at Niemand made him smell ammonia. Somehow that always happened when he knew someone was trying to fool him.

But the smell vanished when he looked back at Arne Saknussemm.

He nodded. “Yes, sir.”

“Then listen closely,” Saknussemm said. “What you should do now is go back to your family and pray for the best.”

38

A moment of stunned silence was all Niemand needed.

Leaping across the table, he bolted into the next room. The flying-monkey guards shrieked. Caught by surprise, they fell into each other in a tangle of wings and arms. Before Max could react, Niemand was racing back, pulling something from a backpack with the black Niemand Enterprises logo on it.

"Stand away from the wall! Now!" His voice snapped against the stone walls, cold and threatening, and no one dared disobey.

As they all leaped back, Niemand threw a small black pellet that missed Max by inches, hitting the wall where they'd just cleared. It exploded into fragments and black dust.

Not missing a step, he plowed right through, with Bitsy close behind.

"They have the serum!" Alex shouted.

"He almost exploded my ear!" Max yelled.

Alex covered her face and ran through the cloud. Max followed close on her heels, inhaling a mouthful of dust.

"Right behind you!" Brandon called out, as Max dropped to his knees coughing. "Here, drink some of this water. I swiped it from Bitsy."

Max guzzled from a cool plastic bottle, blinking against the black soot. Brandon was pulling him forward, shouting for Kristin over his shoulder.

"What about Saknussemm?" came Kristin's voice.

Max stopped and turned. She was still near the hut, staring at the destruction.

Brandon pushed Max forward. "Go—follow Alex. We'll split into twosomes. Kristin is going to need some convincing. Don't worry, we'll catch up."

Spitting out as much dust as he could, Max sped into the jungle. For a moment he thought he'd lost Alex, but he spotted her parka moving far ahead among the bushes. The thick, humid air was turning the soot on his face into a black soup that dripped into his eyes, stinging them again. *"I'm here!"* Max called out. *"Keep going!"*

Small animals moved in the underbrush, startled by the commotion. He ignored them as best he could, taking care not to twist his ankles on arching roots and stray rocks.

When he caught up to Alex, she was panting and hunched over. "I . . . I lost them," she said.

"You didn't, don't worry." Max glanced around for any movement. He looked up in the trees and across the tops of bushes. "Lucky for us it's an island. They can't get far."

"How do we know that, Max?" Alex said. "We never saw the other side. It could be an isthmus or a peninsula. Or if it is an island, maybe it's miles long. Miles of Gumby bushes and mutant animals. Maybe Niemand is being eaten by a lion crossed with an alligator, or some crazy thing—and maybe we will be too."

Now Brandon was barging through the underbrush, breathing hard. Behind him, Kristin was sniffling, wiping her eyes.

"Oh no," Alex said. "Is Saknussemm . . . ?"

Kristin shrugged. "I don't know," she said softly.

"So sorry," Alex said.

"What about Skunky and Brit-girl?" Brandon asked.

"They got away," Alex said.

"They know a different path back," Max said. "For

all we know, they could be back inside the volcano wall and—"

A muffled boom shook the ground, and then another. Max fell silent.

"Where'd that come from?" Brandon asked.

"Feels like an earthquake," Max said.

"Earthquakes don't sound like thunder," Kristin said.

Max spotted a broad, beaver-like animal silently hurrying through the trees. For a moment its footfalls tap-tap-tapped on something solid before it vanished from sight.

"Did you hear that?" Max asked.

"Hear what?" Alex said.

"The beaver—whatever it was—its paws hit something solid," Max said.

He headed farther into the woods, in the direction of the tapping sound. But this part of the jungle was exactly like every other one, and for some reason it scared him. He began thinking about Hansel and Gretel, and how he had cried and kicked when his mom told him the story, because it was just wrong and dumb for Hansel to leave bread crumbs. Bread crumbs were food, and food could be eaten, and that was the night when Max first sensed the gas-stove smell in his nose, before he even knew the word *mercaptan*, before he realized that he smelled it every time he was anxious. Like he was smelling it right this moment.

Fact: They were lost. Fact: They hadn't left bread crumbs or any kind of crumbs. Or even twine like the Minotaur in the labyrinth, which was another sad story. As Max began to moan, the others came running. "Max, we're here," Alex said. "What just happened?"

Booom.

Clank.

Max went still. That *clank* was new. It came from somewhere on the forest floor. Nearby.

Everyone's eyes went toward it.

"Nothing," Max whispered. "Until that."

An upside-down U shape was sticking straight up out of the undergrowth. It wouldn't have been noticeable without the noise from underneath. Max moved closer. He could tell it wasn't a plant, but something metallic. He squatted down and tried to brush away the moss and sand around it, but it all stayed put, as if glued.

"Looks like a handle," Brandon said, as he wrapped his fingers around it and pulled.

"Be careful!" Alex said.

A section of the forest floor lifted up, as round as a

manhole cover and twice as large. Brandon maneuvered the disk until the entire hole was clear, and he let the lid thump to the ground.

From below came the rushing sound of water and a murmuring of familiar voices with English accents.

A crude set of stairs, carved into the stone, led downward. With a smile, Max stepped onto them.

"Guess who's coming for dinner?" he yelled into the darkness.

39

NEAR the base of the stairs, Niemand was banging with a hammer on a solid metallic door embedded in the lava wall. Bitsy sat near him on the stone floor, consulting a stack of papers. They barely looked up as Max, Alex, Kristin, and Brandon loomed over them.

"Don't just stand there like the bathroom queue at Harrods," he shouted, over the noise of a small waterfall. *"Help us."*

They were all on a ridge, overlooking an underground grotto with vertical walls that stretched farther than he could see. The ceiling glowed with eerie green moss light, but the lagoon below was a deep, clear blue. Neon-bright fish wriggled slightly beneath the surface, disappearing into the froth beneath the waterfall, which began just below the rock ceiling and cascaded into the pool below.

But Max's eye was drawn to a giant boulder just beyond the waterfall, wedged against the wall and carved into the face of a wise, smiling man. "Is that sculpture who I think it is?" Max asked.

"It looks like my great-great-great-grandfather as a much younger man." Kristin choked back a tear and turned to Niemand. "He had made his peace with whatever happened here. And you murdered him."

"So sorry," Niemand replied. "That was the smallest targeted explosive we manufacture, far less powerful than a grenade. Not much one can do about shoddy construction, I suppose. Ah well, look at it this way. The old man had a good, long ride. We should all be so lucky."

Kristin let out a scream and ran for Niemand. But she stopped when Bitsy lifted out a palmful of black pellets—the same ones that had taken down the hut. "These hurt," she said.

As Kristin stepped back, her fists were clenched. "Now then," Niemand said cheerily, "I know you're eager to learn why we're here and how you can help. Because like it or not, you are working for me now."

Alex let out a laugh.

"Amusing?" Niemand replied. "Then go. Turn around and go. All is forgiven, no questions asked. I take it you have an alternative way home. Bitsy and I will miss your charming company."

Max looked at Alex. All four of them shifted uncomfortably.

Niemand smiled. "Well then, welcome to the Gastonian Grotto—catchy name, eh? Discovered by the Vernes, uncle and nephew. Although the island is surrounded by the green sea, this water is connected to a different source. It penetrates deeper into the Earth."

"This was what Verne wanted," Max said. "A way to get the serum distributed to the world."

"Verne should have died after Gaston shot him," Bitsy explained, "but for the serum. For the latter part of his life, Verne committed himself to making more of it. He wanted this universal cure for sickness to be available to the world."

"But Verne limped for the rest of his life after he was shot," Max said. "And Gaston was committed to an institution."

"The limp was a pretense," Bitsy said. "If Verne walked effortlessly, people would want to know why. It would arouse suspicion before he could succeed in his mission. He also struggled with great guilt. It seemed he had used all the serum on his leg, leaving none for his dear, demented nephew. His research led him to seek out Saknussemm. After many visits to the so-called center of the Earth, they discovered that the serum, when added to water of a certain salinity, would propagate. So they planned to pour it into the vast green sea, thinking it connected under the continents and would carry the healing to the whole world."

"The thing was," Bitsy said, "the great sea was a closed system. It connects to nothing. So Verne refrained from doing anything with it."

"So the sea down here is just . . . water?" Alex asked.

Bitsy nodded. "Saknussemm claims it is entirely free of the serum."

"Life was dangerous for Verne in this place, with so many of these evolutionary mutations prancing around," Niemand went on. "Cavemen and flying monkeys and such. Naturally there were fights. Some of the serum got into the hands of these creatures. Many of them possessed rudimentary intelligence, thank goodness. Saknussemm believes they still use some of it to benefit their sick."

"They do," Alex said. "They gave it to Brandon."

"Bully for Brandon," Niemand said. "Well, needless to say, they began to discover the side effects. The serum slowed the body's aging mechanism—it destroyed the marker that signals the end of life. In curing disease, the curious side effect was eternal life. Which, as you can see, is a curse so hideous that Saknussemm decided to hide here forever. Verne and Saknussemm grew reluctant to propagate the serum."

"Even after, at long last, they *did* find the channel to the great connecting sea," Bitsy added. "The passage that would indeed take the serum into the world's water system. And it is here."

"Here in this grotto?" Max said.

Bitsy nodded. "But there was one slight problem. *That.*" She pointed across the lagoon toward the carved boulder. "It was a shapeless rock back then. According to the notes left in the Hetzel documents, the rock shuts off the passage downward into the great connecting water source. The channel is bone-dry. Somehow the rock has stayed put despite eons of volcanic explosions, shifting plates, the actions of geysers all around, the forming of an underground sea."

Niemand turned toward the metal door. "Behind this is a healthy stash of good, old-fashioned trinitrotoluene. Also known as TNT. It was gathered over time, stored in this locker. And, of course, it was never used. Until now."

Kristin looked at him with disgust. "That's your plan—to turn people into living skeletons?"

"To *heal* people," Niemand scoffed. "The way Max's dear mother was healed. It's the twenty-first century, dear girl. My scientists will have this serum analyzed on a molecular level in no time. They will make the necessary adjustments. People will discover the disastrous side effect of the serum. They will demand a way to control it—and I will have the answer. I can see a customization of life span. Want to live ninety years, a hundred fifty? Your choice! So you see, children, we cannot let hesitation block progress. Climate is changing. Our days on the Earth are numbered. We need twenty-first-century solutions."

"Work is already underway for alternate environments," Bitsy added brightly. "Beautiful enclosed underwater Niemand Cities. We believe all of humanity will be clamoring to live in them."

"Think of the possibilities," Niemand said. "Contests for entry, sponsorships, tiered membership fees! At platinum level, our premiere offer, choose your length of life!"

"That," Brandon said, "is the most idiotic thing I have ever heard."

"And who would rule over this empire?" Alex asked. "King Spencer?"

"It does have a ring, I must admit," Niemand said.

Niemand drew back with his hammer and smacked the door again, hard. It clanged hollowly, and he let out a gasp of pain. "Gaaaaah, they knew how to make them then," he said, shaking out the pain from his hand.

"Papa, we can destroy the rock with our own explosives," Bitsy said.

Niemand gave a dubious glance toward the sculpted rock. "Our little stash doesn't carry much firepower."

"We have enough," Bitsy said. "We'll plant them strategically. It should weaken the rock. If it doesn't work, *then* we try to get the TNT."

"You are nothing if not practical, my dear," Niemand grunted. He raised an eyebrow at Max, Alex, Brandon, and Kristin. "You four work on the door, just in case. And don't even think of trying to stop us."

"We're not working for you," Brandon said.

As Brandon moved toward him, Niemand pulled a small gun from his pocket. "This is an open-carry grotto. Now do as I say, or this time you'll really be dead."

Niemand tossed one of his pellets toward the door, underhanded. It landed about four feet in front of it and exploded. Max jumped, nearly dropping over the ledge. For a moment the grotto was filled with smoke. From inside the door, Max could hear something fall.

But when the air cleared, the door looked exactly the same, except for a small, black dent.

"Are you nuts?" Brandon said.

"Papa," Bitsy said. "There's TNT inside!"

Niemand smiled. "I am a ballistics expert, my dear. That was enough power to shock, not damage a door like that. But as I'm sure you can imagine, small as they may seem, our explosives still will have a very bad effect on any human being who decides not to be a team member."

"Snaefellsjökull is a seismically unstable area, Mr. Niemand," Kristin said. "Using that, that . . . whatever it is, would not be wise."

Grumbling, Niemand took his daughter's hand. Max watched them scurry to the other side of the grotto, climbing over rocks and scrub brush to get to the sculpted rock. *"Get to work!"* Niemand shouted.

Max turned. He could see Alex, Brandon, and Kristin staring at the door's handle, which Max had been hiding from Niemand's sight. It had bent from the impact of the explosives. But there was no keyhole underneath it, only a deeply indented pattern:

"Lásabrjótur," Kristin whispered, clutching the talisman that hung around her neck.

Max nodded. "The lock breaker, right?" he whispered back. "It allows the bearer to open any lock without needing a key."

"Should we open it?" Brandon asked.

"Absolutely not," Alex replied. "Throw the talisman away, Kristin. We can't let Niemand get at these explosives."

Kristin nodded. They all looked over their shoulders toward the Niemands. Carefully Kristin lifted the chain from her neck.

"Use it," a low, guttural voice hissed.

She stopped cold. "Brandon? That's not funny."

"I didn't say anything," Brandon replied.

Max shook his head and looked at Alex. Her face was

a great big *no* too. Together they turned toward the door. "Is someone . . . ?" Alex said

"Use it now!" the raspy voice continued from behind the door. "Come, come, stop wasting time. There's not much oxygen in here. I don't know how much longer I have . . ."

The four kids exchanged a glance. Brandon gulped hard. "Should we do it?"

"Are you kidding?" Kristin said. "It sounds like a trap."

"We're already in a trap," Alex pointed out.

"Please hurry . . ." the voice groaned.

"Who are you?" Max asked, but there was no response. "We have to help him!"

"Let's do it," Alex agreed. "Really, what do we have to lose . . ."

Shaking, Kristin took the talisman from around her neck, inserted it into the plate, and twisted it hard.

The lock clicked, and the door swung open.

40

THE light from the chamber did not penetrate deeply into the room.

All Max could see was a stack of rotted wooden crates, some of them still faintly labeled TNT. The placed smelled of mold, mildew, dead animals, and something vaguely rotten and sweet.

"H-H-Hello?" Max called out.

"Yesss . . ." a voice hissed from the darkness.

Surprised, Max screamed, turned, and bolted for the door with Alex and Kristin behind him—only to run straight into Niemand, who was already at the entryway. A grin stretched across his face as he leveled his gun at them. "Not so fast," he said. "I have good news."

They all stopped short. "Um . . ." was all Max could manage.

"Looks like our little stash of explosives may be sufficient for the job at hand, after all," Niemand continued. "We have a few more minutes of work to do. Of course, Bitsy and I will have to return to the surface for a moment. Wouldn't want to suffocate while the shards and dust clouds fill the room."

"S-S-Somebody . . ." Alex gulped. "A person. Is in there. Behind us."

"Oh?" Niemand walked toward them, forcing them back into the room. "I hear those Neanderthals like to explore."

"We did what you wanted," Max said. "Now let us go."

"Nonsense, one good turn deserves another," Niemand said. "I wouldn't want any of you to suffer from smoke inhalation either. What a convenient shelter this is. Better safe than sorry!"

And with a quick step backward, he slammed the door shut, trapping the four explorers inside.

"No!" Max shouted, banging against the inside of the door.

Brandon struggled to pull the latch, but it wouldn't move. *"Let us out!"* Alex screamed.

An answer came from deep inside the room. "Do not

worry. You have the talissssman."

All four of them stopped moving, as if every nerve in their bodies had been twanged and then pinched shut.

"Who are you?" Max said.

"Where are you?" Alex asked.

"Jjrrreeep," Kristin squeaked, too frightened to form a word.

"We do not have much time," the voice replied.

The sound was reedy and small, more breath than voice.

"Saknussemm?" Brandon said. "Did you sneak down here?"

Max could hear a rustling of fabric in the darkness . . . a click. Then a beam of light shot across the room. Alex was holding a flashlight in her hand, scanning the walls. Stacks of wooden crates created shadows, and cobwebs hung from the domed stone roof like forgotten piñatas from some long-ago party.

Except one of the piñatas moved. It wasn't a cobweb at all.

Alex focused the beam on the wispy shape of a man. His skin was papery-thin like Arne Saknussemm's, but he seemed shorter, with a wiry cluster of white whiskers that hung from his chin clear down to his chest. A ripped tunic hung open over his chest, and the outline of a tiny shriveled heart beat beneath the surface of the nearly transparent skin. He was more mummy than man, but his eyes were wide open and his pupils were a sickly amber color. A pair of lips like old rubber bands began to twitch. "You . . . are not . . . afraid?" he whispered.

"N-N-N—" Alex stammered.

"I am," Brandon said.

"Your names?" the ghostly man asked.

"A-A-Alexandra," Alex said.

"Kristin."

"Brandon."

But Max was staring closely at the mummy-man's face. The cheekbones were high, the white hair on the chin thick and unruly.

Max felt like he'd met him before.

"D-D-Do you want last names too?" he asked. "I'm Max Tilt, and my cousin's full name is Alexandra Verne."

Max saw a twitch in the mummy-man's face. His forehead squinched, and a piece of it flaked off like old cellophane tape. "Alexandra," he rasped, cocking his head at Alex. "Ssssuch a beautiful name."

"Sir . . ." Alex said in a tiny voice, "those people are trying to blow up this lagoon. We don't know who you are, but—"

"My condition has made me unrecognizable, I know,"

the man whispered. "But I can ssssee, even across the generationsss, that you are a Verne."

Alex brought her hand to the side of her face, as if to keep it from exploding. "Oh . . . no . . . no . . ."

"Pleased to meet you. I've spent much time in this grotto, but I am not used to vissssitors. I thought I could duck out of sight into this closet, but voilà, you found me." The mummy-man thrust forward a skeletal hand. "You may call me Jules—Jules Verne."

41

"**PICK.** Me. Up. Off. The. Floor," Alex whispered.

Max's head felt like it would rocket off his neck and into space.

It was him. Max had known it. It was impossible and totally exhilarating. "OK, I got who you were," Max said to the talking corpse. "But you died. In France. There's a grave and everything."

"And in front of it, a statue of a body bursssting out of the ground," Verne replied with a rattling sound that Max guessed was a laugh. "Sssubtle hint about what had happened to me, *n'est-ce pas?* I was already in Iceland when they lowered the empty casket."

"That's another thing," Alex said. "You're speaking English to us."

"Jules Verne was French," Brandon said. "Even I know that."

"Saknussemm and I brought many books to our new home," Verne said. "We are both rather fluent in German, Greek, Urdu, Hindi, Zulu, Russian, Ssssspanish, Basque, and most of the Scandinavian languages. We hoped, sssomeday, to return. But it was not to happen."

Max stared at the old man. In his mind, he superimposed the face of the portrait from his family's living room. It fit him like a mask. "Your clues were awesome," he said. "Especially Levi Hek. Not to mention *The Lost Treasures*. And because of you, my mom's life was saved. And also my friend Evelyn."

"Ah, thank you, how exciting is the work of Louis Braille!" he said. "And *mon Dieu*, *The Lost Treasures*! I trust you found the chest and were duly rewarded? And that inflation has not made the contents worthless?"

Alex smiled. "We did really, really well, thank you. That guy out there with the white streak in his hair, Spencer Niemand? He tried to stop us. He's descended from your old nemesis Captain Nemo. He's putting explosives into cracks in the sculpture of Kristin's great-great-great-grandfather—your pal, Arne Saknussemm. To release the serum into the world's water supply and then claim credit for curing the world of disease. It's part of a crazy plan that involves underwater cities and political power—"

"That electric lamp," Verne said, creaking forward to the stacks of crates. "Do you have more?"

Max and Kristin each pulled flashlights out of their backpacks.

"Voilà." Verne gestured to the stack nearest the door. "You must move these asssside. But leave the last box. Quickly. *Vite!* Don't worry. They are . . . how do you say? Duds. We neutralized the explossssives years ago. When we decided to kill our plan. And banish ourselves to the underworld."

Brandon was first to move into action. He lifted three crates and moved them to a corner of the room.

As Alex grabbed onto a crate, she smiled at Verne. "That was brave of you, and selfless."

"Saknussemm was the one who convinced me to kill the project," Verne said. "He was right. I would not wish thissss on anyone. Nor on a ssssociety that must deal with a population that lingersss forever. Out of gratitude to my colleague, I carved that boulder into his likenesssss."

Max, Kristin, and Alex cleared out the crates as he spoke, until there was one left. "You told us to leave the last," Brandon said.

"Yes." Verne's head creaked up and down in a nod.

"I never thought I'd sssay this, but it is time for the endgame."

Max and Alex both stared silently, curiously, at the old man. "Endgame?" Max said. "That sounds scary."

Verne gestured to the remaining box. "Open that," he said. "It contains a fail-safe. I have not felt the need to use it. Perhaps I have been too sssscared."

Cautiously Alex and Max leaned over the box and pulled off the lid. Inside, lying diagonally, was a thick metal pipe with a pump handle. "What the heck—?" Max said.

"Lift it out," Verne said. "And then kick the crate aside, please."

As Brandon held onto the pipe, Alex moved the crate with her foot. Embedded in the stone floor underneath were three circles of metal, one inside the other. Max knelt and ran his fingers over the cool surface. The outer circle was only about three or four inches in diameter. He was able to squeeze his hand in the center and dig out a layer of cobwebs. Under it was a hole that went deep into the ground.

"It's a kind of pipe," Max said.

"A gassssket," Verne said. "Please insert the pipe into it. And turn clockwise."

Brandon lifted the pipe over the metal rings and set

it down. It fit perfectly. He twisted it into place with a deep click.

"What is this thing?" Max asked.

"A detonator," Verne said.

"Wait," Max shot back. "I thought the whole point was *not* to blow up the boulder."

"You must trust me," Verne said. "Use the talisman. Open the door."

With quivering hands, Kristin inserted the talisman into a slot on the inside of the door and swung it open slowly. Across the lagoon, the sculpted rock was studded with small black explosives. Niemand and Bitsy were dumping the vial of serum into the water below.

"My children, Saknussemm and I anticipated that ssssomeone would do this. People like Niemand always find a way," Verne said softly. "Luckily, in 1947 we found fissures below this lagoon—long lava tubes that empty straight downward into the depths of the volcano. We have placed explosives—real ones—that will rip it right open. Anything that goes down there will be lost into the molten depths of the Earth forever."

"You want us to do that?" Alex asked.

"It will destroy the serum," Verne said. "But listen to me. The water is full of serum molecules now. I am certain your scientists have great capabilities. Take some.

Let them study it further. You will have twenty seconds from the time you pull the lever. Unfortunately these fissures also run along a very unsssstable fault line, and you will need to go fast."

"But—but what about you?" Alex said.

"I have had more than my share of time," Verne said. "Listen closely. After pulling the lever, you must go immediately. There will be a twenty-sssecond lag before the explosion. Fourteen minutes and twenty-three sssssseconds later, you must be exactly one and a third kilometers to the northwessst. Repeat that to me."

"Wait . . . *what*?" Max replied.

"Twenty seconds before explosion. Fourteen minutes and twenty-three seconds later, exactly one and a third kilometers to the northwest," Alex said.

"Brava," Verne whispered. "Take my love with you, and Godspeed. Pull!"

Brandon was clutching the lever. He looked at Max and Alex, hesitating. "Ready?"

In response, the room's door flew open and Spencer Niemand stormed in, vial still in hand. Bitsy was close behind him. "Papa?" she said. "We're not finished."

"But they will be," Niemand said. "What in heaven's name do you think you're doing?"

42

AS Verne stepped forward out of the shadows, the white stripe in Niemand's hair seemed to grow before Max's eyes. "What . . . on . . . earth . . . ?"

The mummy-man pulled back his lips, and a tooth fell out. He reached two bony hands toward Niemand's neck. "Sssssso good to sssssee you, Ssssspencer."

"Papa!" Bitsy shrieked.

"Now, Brandon!" Max shouted.

Brandon yanked the lever down.

Alex was the first out of the room, followed by Kristin and Brandon. As they ran for the hatch, Max snatched the vial from Niemand's hand. He raced out and quickly slid-walked down to the lagoon and scooped water into the vial. When it was full, he stoppered it and headed back up.

Alex appeared at the top. "Hurry!"

"I got serum!" Max shouted.

"You've got eleven seconds!" Alex reached down and yanked him up. He scrambled out of the grotto through the giant manhole cover, where Kristin and Brandon were waiting.

Kristin was looking intently at her GPS device. "Let's get out of here before . . ."

From behind them, a bone-shuddering *GA-BOOOOM* echoed against the rock dome. The ground juddered, and Max nearly lost his balance.

A scream welled up from inside the manhole cover. As a plume of smoke rose upward, Max turned away.

He didn't want to see.

Kristin led them through the woods, expertly leaping over bushes, roots, and scurrying animals. Max struggled to keep pace. He could hear rumblings in the distance. Screeches overhead. The domed sky filled with winged creatures of all sizes, flying every which way. Like panicked animals in advance of some natural disaster.

He had no sense of time. It was easy to lose sight of the others. His shirt was soaked with sweat, which meant they'd been running a long while. *"How much time do we have?"* he called ahead.

"Four minutes!" Alex yelled back.

Max's calves ached, and bugs were swarming around his face. As he slapped one, his foot caught in a root, and he went down with a cry.

"Climb on, buddy," Brandon said, taking Max onto his back while barely breaking stride.

"Are you guys there?" came Kristin's voice from up ahead of them. *"I don't see you!"*

"Here!" Brandon shouted. *"Following your voice!"*

"Two minutes thirty-three!" Alex was shouting.

With each bounce, Max felt the pain in his calves. And when Brandon stopped short, he thought he'd fall off.

Kristin was standing in a clearing, still staring at the device. "We're here," she said.

"Twenty-seven seconds left," Alex said. "Now what?"

Max rose and fell on the big guy's breaths for a couple of seconds, before Brandon finally let him down to the ground.

"Thanks," Max said. "I'm sorry I said all those nasty things about you. You're not as bad as I thought."

Brandon smiled. "Arrrgh."

They were standing at the edge of a big, ugly, white circle in the crust of the Earth. The center of it was filled with some kind of bubbling liquid that looked to Max like milk. "Are you sure we're in the right place?" he asked.

Kristin nodded. "The question is, why are we supposed to be here?"

"Fifteen seconds," Alex said.

Max felt a strong breeze, much colder than any air he'd felt since he'd been down here. He glanced up. Above them was a wide vertical shaft rising through the rock as if it had been dug by machine. And at the top, a blinking black sky winked at them.

"Ten," Alex said. "Nine . . . eight . . ."

"What the—?" Max said.

"My question exactly," Kristin said.

"What is happening?" Brandon demanded. "Does anybody know anything?"

". . . four . . . three . . . two . . ."

The ground jolted beneath them like an underground bomb test. All four fell to the ground. *"Curl yourself into a ball, now!"* Kristin said. *"We're on top of a—"*

Max didn't hear the last word, but he didn't need to. He brought his knees to his chin as the bubbling circle exploded.

He lurched upward so violently he thought he'd lost a leg. Like a giant monstrous fist had broken through the Earth beneath him. In that instant, he thought about black holes, about how they could suck in a star so fast that it would become negative matter. In a black hole you couldn't even think of screaming. Or seeing. Or hearing.

But he wasn't in a black hole because he was hearing a roar. A whooshing noise. The sound of breaking waves from a hundred stormy seas.

He flew upward above the crust of the Earth on a column of water, high and fast, zooming into a cold black skyscape of stars.

43

"A freak of nature . . ."

"How did they get down there . . . ?"

"Not one broken bone . . ."

"The temperature . . ."

Max registered the voices before his eyes opened.

When they finally did, he was staring into the sagging face of Dr. Gunther Zax-Ericksson, framed by a clear night sky. "Haw!" Zax-Ericksson called out from a cushy, padded wheelchair. "The youngest one is awake!"

Max blinked and looked around. He was in the middle of a flat plain, slick with water. Cool water. Water that felt so refreshing that he leaned down and licked it from a rock.

A small group of uniformed people surrounded him.

Behind them was a ring of vehicles with blinking lights. Emergency medical staff. "Alex?" he called out. "Where is my cousin?"

About fifteen feet away, a mass of unruly black hair rose from within another cluster of people. Alex burst through them and ran to Max, nearly tackling him to the ground. *"You're alive you're alive you're aliiiive!"* she screamed.

"Are you trying to kill me?" he asked.

As the medics swooped in to check Max's vital signs, Alex turned to Dr. Zax-Ericksson. "And . . . Kristin—?" she said.

"Already in the ambulance," the old man said. "Ten fingers, ten toes, ten thousand instructions to the medical staff. She is just fine, thank goodness. The big fellow is in there too. Brendan?"

"Brandon," Alex said.

"Of course you know his name," said Zax-Ericksson with a wide grin. "I saw you kiss the lucky fellow."

"Ewww, there goes my frisky mood," Max said.

"And how are you feeling, dear?" Zax-Ericksson asked.

"A little waterlogged, but perfect," Alex said.

From behind her, a medic said, "We need you in the ambulance too, for follow-up."

"Let the girl talk to her cousin for five minutes," Dr. Zax-Ericksson said. "They just survived a historic event.

I'm a doctor. They'll be under my guidance."

As the medics scooted away, Zax-Ericksson leaned forward. "I didn't tell them I was a doctor of philosophy. Haaa! Ah well, the medical staff are saying that no human being has ever ridden up from the depths of a volcano on a geyser. You could have easily died. It is frankly a miracle you all survived."

"And Niemand and Bitsy?" Max asked, turning to Dr. Zax-Ericksson. "Has anyone found signs of other people?"

"Sadly, no, I didn't realize there were more people in there. I must emphasize there was major seismic action this evening. Scientists report evidence of several collapses inside the volcano. Not to mention a shift of the tectonic plate that registered 6.1 on the Richter scale." Zax-Ericksson shook his head with a hearty chuckle. "And here you all are, popping up like trapeze artists with barely a bruise. Inconceivable!"

Alex shook her head in disbelief. "I'm thinking the same thing. Did that really just happen?"

The events of the last day rushed into Max's brain. So many of them made no logical sense, and he knew it would take a long time to put the pieces together. "He knew . . . Verne. He'd been hearing those geysers go off every day for almost two centuries. He knew their schedule and their location. He was a fact nerd."

"And he sacrificed himself to keep the world from being consumed by a genetic nightmare," Alex said.

Max reached into his pocket, hoping not to feel the shards of a broken vial. But there it was. Completely stoppered and intact.

Nightmare.

He thought of his mom's face, her cheeks so red and healthy after she'd been sick. He pictured Evelyn, who may even be walking on her own now.

In his mind, they were transforming into mummy-people. Like Verne and Saknussemm. "What are we going to do?" he asked.

"What Verne told us," Alex said. "We find the best scientists in the world. We let them analyze this. We hope they find a way to solve the side effects."

Max nodded. "*Hope.* Yeah."

"Did you say . . . *Verne* told you?" Dr. Zax-Ericksson said. "As in . . . Jules?"

Alex shot Max a look. He shrugged. "We have to tell someone if we want to get this into the right hands," he said, turning to Zax-Ericksson. "Alex will explain, sir. I want to talk to my mom and dad."

Max called out to the EMTs: *"May I borrow someone's phone? If you incur roaming charges, I will reimburse you."*

A baffled-looking medic handed Max a phone, and Max handed the vial to a baffled-looking Zax-Ericksson. "This is a serum," she said. "In order to get it, we met a few mutant creatures, collapsed a tunnel, and negotiated with Jules Verne and Arne Saknussemm. . . ."

Zax-Ericksson's response was more a series of amazed clucks than real words.

As Alex continued, Max smiled. He tapped out his country code and phone number. After it rang four times, his dad picked up. "Yeah?"

Max knew that tone. Dad had seen this random cell number and hadn't recognized it. He was assuming it was some kind of phone scam. And Dad was an expert at stringing along scammers, just for fun. By the end he would be pretending to throw up, or inviting the scammer over for a dinner of roast salamander stew, or talking in a completely incomprehensible accent. He would do this kind of stunt whenever Max was in the room, and by the end Max would be rolling on the floor laughing.

Max missed that so much. He ached with how much he missed it.

At the moment, with a million things racing through his brain, tripping over themselves to be first through his mouth, Max instead said, "This is the Visa account services calling to inform you of an opportunity to lower your interest rates on credit cards."

It was what they all said. Max waited for a Dad response. But instead he heard a moment of silence and then, "Max?"

Max was disappointed. But not really.

Actually, not at all.

"Hi, Dad," he said. "I want to come home now. I think Alex does too."

He could tell his dad was crying. He was calling Mom to the phone too. "Max, we were so worried about you!" she said.

She was crying too.

"It's kind of a long story," Max said. "And we kind of got what we were looking for. I think you're going to be OK, Mom. Evelyn too. At least for now. And maybe forever." He looked up into the faces of the EMTs. Dr. Zax-Ericksson was wiping something from his eye. Snaefellsjökull loomed to his left, looking exactly as it had when they first visited. It was as if nothing at all had happened and no one had been trapped inside. As if an entire ecosystem that seemed to be from another planet simply didn't exist. As if the bodies of Arne Saknussemm and Jules Verne were actually in their graves the way everyone assumed they were.

In the clear, crisp night it was easy to imagine that

Mom had never gotten sick and Alex had never come to his house, that Max and Alex had never been kidnapped, never found a treasure in Greenland, never traveled around the world to collect the ingredients of an ancient concoction only to have it stolen from under their noses and found again.

"I—I feel wonderful right now, Max," his mom said. "And I'll feel even better when you're home."

Max grinned. "I'm smelling mint, Mom. I haven't smelled mint since I left home."

"Well, that's good," his mom said. "That means you're happy."

He nodded. And then he laughed because nodding to someone on the phone was ridiculous, but sometimes you just forgot. And doing dumb things when you're in a good mood makes you laugh, instead of getting angry at yourself.

Max liked the feeling. He wanted to hold onto that feeling for a long time. He took a deep breath and heard Alex trying to explain the detonator mechanism to Dr. Zax-Ericksson.

"Mom, I want to be a kid again, is that OK?" Max said. "Just stay home and make robots and talk to Evelyn and explore with Smriti and perfect my cupcake recipe and not fly on a jet for a while or deal with detonator mechanisms. Because I'm already thirteen, and there's not much time."

"I think we can do that, Max," his mom said.

"But first, tell me about those new interest rates!" Dad said. "I'm sure you hear this a lot, but I just dumped my old interest rates in the toilet by mistake."

"Use a plunger," Max said.

It was fun to hear Mom and Dad laugh. He couldn't wait to see them again. He felt he could feel their smiles through the phone.

It was funny how you could do that.

EPILOGUE

ALEX was the worst driver Max knew. She drove too fast and was too distracted, and she talked too much. But on a cold afternoon in March, a couple of months after they'd returned home from Iceland, her new car screeched to a stop in front of Max's school so suddenly that her tires left thick black tracks.

She had never done that.

"*Awwwwwesome!*" yelled Dugan Dempsey. He was one of the Fearsome Foursome, so called because they used to make fun of Max before Max became rich and famous.

Max could hear music blasting from inside her car. Some loud rock anthem he didn't know. The whole vehicle was bouncing up and down in rhythm because Alex was inside, screaming the song and dancing on her butt.

That made Max laugh. He was glad to laugh, because Evelyn had not been in robotics that day and that had put him in a bad mood.

"You're happy," Max said, sliding into the passenger seat.

"Eeeeeee!" Alex squealed, holding out her phone screen to him. "They said yes! The Morgan Group. One of the best literary agents in New York!"

"Wait," Max said, squinting at an email message. "You wrote a book? Called *The Lost Treasures*?"

"A proposal," Alex said. "And four chapters. I based it on our adventures. With names changed. They want me to write more. They think they can sell it. They'll help me. Can you believe this, Max? This has been my dream! *Woooooo-HOOOO!*"

"That's awesome," Max said.

Alex snuck a kiss onto his cheek so fast, he didn't have time to lurch away. "I thought this year would be lost, Max. I thought taking care of you would be a sacrifice. A way to make some money. To prepare for my real life. But what we've done, Max—oh my goodness, I have material for years. And I have you. Who would have thought I could meet a cousin I never knew I could love so much? It's you and me, buddy—family forever!"

She stuck out a fist, and Max bumped it. "Can we go now?"

Alex's face fell. "Was it something I said?"

"No, I'm happy you're happy," Max replied. "But I'm not happy that Evelyn wasn't in class, that's all. Whenever she misses, she's supposed to tell me. We promised we'd tell each other. But she didn't."

"Maybe she just forgot," Alex said, putting the car in Drive. "She's busy."

"She always lets me know," Max said. "It's something we worked out. And can you turn the music down?"

Alex drove through the streets of Savile, humming to the softened tunes on her radio. As they pulled up to the Tilts' house, Max's mom and dad were both waiting at the foot of the walkway. Smriti was with them.

"Evelyn wasn't in robotics," Max said as he stepped out of the door. "And why are you all smiling?"

Smiles were fine, but Max was not used to three of them for no reason at all. He wasn't used to being greeted on the sidewalk of his house either. This was starting to seem odd to him.

"They've sequenced it," Mom said, the words nearly getting stuck in her throat with excitement. "They've sequenced the serum. At that lab at MIT. They've never seen anything like it, they said. They joked about winning a Nobel."

Max's mood lifted about thirteen quantum levels. "*Whaaat?* That's amazing."

"It doesn't mean they know how to control it," Dad said. "They're still a long way from that. They have to do some lab tests, and some clinical tests with Mom. It may take years. But they think they're on the right track."

Behind him, Alex cranked up the music in the car. She left it on while he jumped out. Smriti started dancing with her. Mom and Dad were moving with Mom and Dad dance moves. They all linked arms and headed into the house.

Max laughed. It felt good to have music when you were walking into your own house. Especially when there was so much news.

As they stepped inside, Max's heart slumped. Standing inside the front door was Mrs. Lopez, Evelyn's mom. Max liked her, but he didn't like seeing her without Evelyn. Ever since Evelyn got sick, she and her mom did everything together. They had to.

"Hello, Max," she said.

"What's wrong?" Max asked. "What happened to

Evelyn? Why wasn't she in robotics?"

"She . . . she had to prepare for something," Mrs. Lopez said.

Max's mom took him by the arm and led him into the living room. Streamers had been strewn over the walls, and a glittery disco ball hung from the ceiling. "What the—?" Max said.

From inside the house, Evelyn entered the room. She walked slowly. Her walker was gone, no wheelchair was in sight, and neither arm was balanced on crutches. As she entered the room, she spun around slowly. "Hey, Max, what's up?"

Max felt his mouth dropping open. For the first time in a long time, he had no idea what to say.

Someone had activated the Sonos system—Alex probably. It was playing some boring rock music—Dad's probably. Dad and Mom were off in one corner, doing some crazy jitterbug thing. Alex and Smriti were trading hip-hop moves. Mrs. Lopez was clapping hands and smiling at her daughter.

"Want to dance?" Evelyn said. "I mean, I know you hate to, but . . ."

As she moved to the rhythm, free and happy, Max just looked at everyone and smiled.

Then he closed his eyes and began to move too, and he didn't care how he looked or what anyone thought.

"Just this one time," he said. He had never, ever felt better.

And that was a fact.

CRAVING MORE ADVENTURE?

TAKE A SNEAK PEEK AT
PETER LERANGIS'S NEW SERIES,

NOW

When Corey Fletcher was five, he saw a woman on the C train take out her teeth and argue with them. At age seven, he ran out of his house on West Ninety-Fifth Street in New York City and nearly collided with a man walking a pig.

By thirteen Corey had seen a naked wedding by the Hudson River, an elephant lumbering up Amsterdam Avenue, an actor falling off a Broadway stage onto a trombone player, and a singing group that burped entire tunes in harmony.

Corey didn't seek out strange things. They just came to him.

But nothing was stranger than the vision he saw six years ago outside his window. It disturbed him so much he told no one, not even his grandfather.

And he told his grandfather *everything*.

Up until about a year ago, the old man had lived with Corey's family. His name was Konstantino Vlechos, which no one could pronounce. To the world he was known as Gus Fletcher, or just Odd Gus. He was the only one who believed all Corey's stories. People said Corey had an active imagination, but Corey didn't think so. He didn't imagine any more or less than other people. He just kept his eyes open. And he had a good eye.

He knew this because way back when he told his grandfather about the woman and her teeth, the old man said, "Corey, you have an Ed Gooey."

It took Corey only a few seconds to realize that the letters of "Ed Gooey" spelled out "good eye." Odd Gus liked anagrams. He could mix the letters of words in his head and make up new words on the spot.

"Both eyes are good, Papou," he replied proudly, which cracked the old man up.

"Bravo, *paithi mou!*"

Papou is Greek for "grandfather." Which sounds a lot nicer than Odd Gus. He was a New Yorker through and through, but he liked to use Greek expressions like *paithi mou*, which means "my child." And *bravo*, which means "yay."

Corey loved his mom, dad, and sister, Zenobia. But if you asked him in secret, he'd say he loved Papou best. Odd Gus—I mean, Papou—liked crossword puzzles, word games, and the New York Mets, in that order. But he *loved* hearing Corey's stories.

Well, he *did* love them, before he disappeared one year ago.

Which brings us to the story that Corey never told.

One night when Corey was seven, Papou was reading aloud from *A Wrinkle in Time.* His voice always put Corey to sleep, even when the book was amazing.

Corey's eyes were half-shut when he saw a shadow outside his window. Behind Papou's shoulder.

The Fletchers lived in a sunken, ground-floor apartment in a four-story building. So they were used to people passing by the front windows. Not so much the back, where Corey's bedroom was.

In the soft drone of Papou's voice, Corey was seeing tesseracts dancing in his head. He knew those weren't real, so he didn't think the shadow was real either.

Even when it leaned forward and pressed its nose to the glass.

It was someone Corey had never seen, someone much older than he was. But he knew who it was. He recognized the face.

It was his own.

He did not scream, although he wanted to. Instead, he lay in bed silently for hours and finally fell asleep. Papou hadn't seemed to notice. Which meant, Corey thought, that it might not have really happened. So he never said a word about it to anyone.

If he had, this whole story might have been different.

Or maybe not.

Corey, like everyone said, had an active imagination.

ONE YEAR AGO

On the last day Corey saw his grandfather, the old man paid a late-night visit. He chose not to wake the boy. Corey looked like an angel in his sleep. His feet already stuck out from the end of the bed at age twelve. Papou smiled sadly. Twelve years of foot growth and laughter and pizza and hide-and-seek and crazy discussions. Twelve years that his dear wife, Maria, had never known.

He gritted his teeth. He couldn't think about her now.

Over the years he'd pummeled his grief into a withered lump buried deep in his heart. He'd trained himself not to think about that sunny September day in 2001, when a jet plane that sounded like the end of the world stole those years from Maria.

At least he'd had those years. He would miss them now.

As Papou carefully wrote a note, the pen dropped from his hand and clattered to the bedroom floor. He was tired, but his grandson was tireder, if there was such a word. The noise didn't wake Corey. Not a bit.

His face etched with sadness, Papou watched the boy as he mumbled in his sleep—garbled words mostly, but Papou could make out one clear sentence: "Is that you, Oliver?"

Oliver?

It had been a couple of years since they'd played Oliver and Buster Squires, Gentlemen of the Distant Past from the Town of Twit. They would crack each other up so much that Corey's mom would scold them both. By now, Papou thought Corey had grown out of that game.

Not a chance.

Papou leaned close. "Indeed, Buster," he whispered, "but we must have a good night's sleep, in order to retain the quality of our sweet body odor."

Corey smiled and let out a giggle. As his lips settled downward, he began to snore. Papou ran his fingers lightly through his grandson's dense thicket of hair. During the daylight it danced with every shade from amber to chocolate, but in the darkness it was jet-black. He knew that his grandson hated that hair now, but Corey would grow to love it someday.

Papou did not like thinking about someday. Only today. And today, his time had come.

Time was one thing Papou understood. People said time stopped for no man. It was an arrow. It marched on. It would always tell. But that was nonsense. None of those things was true.

Papou had learned this the hard way.

He kneeled and picked up the pen he'd dropped. His fingers weren't what they used to be. Before long he wouldn't be able to write at all. Placing the pen back on Corey's desk, he glanced at the note he'd written:

Dear Corey,
You look so peaceful, I don't want to wake you. Sorry, but I was called away to Canada—an emergency with one of my close friends from college. I may stay for a while. So sorry I couldn't say a proper farewell. I left you something to remember me by.

Wear it every day. Think of me. And time will fly.

XOXOX,
Papou

He carefully folded the letter and placed it into a big padded envelope he'd brought into the room, wedging it next to his genuine Civil War–era belt, which Corey had always admired. The one with the brass buffalo-head buckle stamped Oct 31, 1862.

Leaning over his grandson, he brushed the boy's forehead with a kiss. "*S'agapo, paithi mou,*" he whispered. *I love you, my child.*

He could neither stay anymore nor say any more. If he had to face Corey and tell him directly, if he had to see the look on the boy's face, it would crush him. Leaving silently was already too painful. He backed away through the door, so as not to let the boy's sweet face from his sight until the last possible moment.

Shutting the door behind him, he quietly left.

Corey turned in his sleep toward the window. In the dim city light, a small tear glistened on his forehead, from where it had dropped.

By morning the tear would be gone.

And so would the man who had left it.

3

THE PRESENT

As Corey stepped outside on a foggy Halloween morning, he was not surprised to find a horse, a buggy, and a plastic pack full of blood.

For a week, his whole block had been transformed into a set for the movie *Victorian Zombies of Olde Manhattan*. The street really did look olde. Gas lamps were installed at the curbs, plastic cobblestones were laid over the blacktop road, and all the neighbors had had to move their cars out of sight. Last night Corey had snuck a peek out his window at a noisy shoot-out scene with horses, carriages, and people in old-timey costumes. Lots of fake blood had sprayed from the actors as they pretended to drop dead. It was beyond awesome.

Now Corey knew how they did the spurting-blood

part—square plastic packs of red goo! Genius.

He strode to the blood pack, which was lying on the sidewalk. Without any traffic on the block, he could hear his own footsteps. He smelled horse manure. The whole scene made him feel like a kid in the late 1800s. Standing straight, he called out over his shoulder to Zenobia, who was climbing up the steps from their apartment, hunched over her phone: "What a glorious morning, dear sister—but, hark, what lies on yonder pavement? It suggests blood, in color and in thickness!"

"Ew," Zenobia grunted. "One of the stunt people must have dropped it. And stop pretending you're in the past. It's so nerdy. They didn't talk like that, anyway."

"How dost thou knoweth this?" Corey looked up and down the block and smiled. "Admit it, this whole thing—this movie set—it's awesome! Doesn't it change you inside? Make you feel like you've stepped into another time?"

"Pssht," Zenobia replied, which was her way of saying no, when no wasn't strong enough. "I auditioned to be an extra. But they took Emma Gruber from Number Thirty-six instead. She even got her SAG card. She's fakey, and so is this set."

"And a SAG card is . . . ?" Corey asked.

Zenobia rolled her eyes. "It means you're a professional movie actor."

"I sag. Can I get one?" Corey was thirteen and barely one hundred pounds. If you counted his stupendous nest of hair (thanks to his Greek American dad and Puerto Rican mom), he was already more than six feet tall. So in truth, he *was* in the habit of sagging when he talked to his shorter friends.

But Zenobia was not dignifying his question, so he bent over to pick up the blood pack from a pile of swirling red and yellow leaves. Next to the dropped pack were a dropped fake cigarette, a dropped New York City MetroCard, and a dropped silver-chain necklace with a large oval-shaped locket, all of which (except the cigarette) he slipped into his pocket while Zenobia was looking at her phone.

Corey held up the fake-blood packet, which was labeled Property of Gotham Cinema Solutions. "How do you think it works—do they just squeeze it and . . . *goosh?*"

Zenobia sighed with great drama. For days she had been composing a symphony based on her epic poem, *The WestSidiad*, mostly during her subway rides to

Stuyvesant High School. With her red cat-eye glasses, close-cropped hair, and black-on-black wardrobe, she never seemed exactly cheery, but interruptions by Corey made her downright mad. "Well, duh, the actors can't be squeezing those things by themselves on camera, right? So the packs must be hooked up to some kind of wireless detonator. When the shot rings out, someone presses a button on a device, and—"

"*Goosh!*" Corey exclaimed.

"You said that already," Zenobia snapped. "Work on your vocabulary."

"Splursh?" Corey offered.

Zenobia groaned. "Did the hospital switch my real brother with you at birth?"

"Ha ha. Not funny."

"I'm serious. You don't look like Mom or Dad."

"I look exactly like Papou," Corey said. Which was true. "Plus, he liked to pretend to be in the past. Remember our alter egos?"

"Otto and Bimbo Something?"

"Oliver and Buster Squires, Gentlemen of the Distant Past from the Town of Twit."

"Right. He made you wear a monocle." Zenobia smiled faintly. "That was back before you became Nerd on a Stick. When you were cute. And he was alive."

"I'm still cute," Corey said. "And he's still alive."

"Corey, let's not start this again."

"Well, that's what I believe," Corey said defiantly.

"Welcome to the Never-Ending Fantasy World of Corey Fletcher." Zenobia turned silently and began walking up the street toward the subway. Corey saw only the back of her head, but he could tell she was sneering.

That was when he had his first really bad idea of the day.

He examined the blood pack. It seemed pretty clean. He spat on it, rubbed it on his shirt for good measure, then put it in his mouth. Tucking it into his left cheek, he followed Zenobia up the street. "Hey, Zenobe! Hit me. Seriously, just slap me in the face. Lightly."

She pulled out one of her earbuds and said over her shoulder, "First, that thing was on the sidewalk, so you probably have a communicable disease. Second, if you think you're going to bite down and spray me with fake blood, save it for your middle school friends. And, oh, by the way, your school is in the opposite direction."

Corey felt himself sag again. He stopped, watching her walk toward Central Park West. Then, in a perfect imitation of Papou's Greek-accented voice, he said, "Don't take any wooden neeckels!"

Zenobia ignored him.

Traffic whizzed by in both directions on Central Park West, but police barricades blocked the end of Ninety-Fifth Street, so none of the vehicles could turn in to the movie set. As Zenobia veered left toward the subway stop, Corey could hear the soft clopping of a horse behind him.

He turned.

A couple of trainers were leading a horse with a lustrous brown coat and tufts of white ankle hair up the block. They had come from the direction of the trailers parked around the corner, and they were giving the horse exercise, brushing it gently. With no cars parked at the curb, the hoof steps echoed crisply against the fronts of the four-story brownstone apartment buildings. Corey smiled. In the morning sun, the buildings glowed and the windows cast deep shadows. Columns, flat fronts, massive stoops or none, brick walls or stone—they were like people shoulder to shoulder, with different faces and personalities. Even though he saw them every day, Corey had never really noticed how unusual and unalike they were.

His phone chimed, breaking the spell. This would be Leila Sharp, his best friend, who always texted at this time. Fishing out the phone, he quickly answered.

meet at my house 2 walk 2 school?

u mean like we do EVERY SINGLE MORNING lol???

hahaha. b nice.

nice is my middle name. corey nice fletcher.

don't b late. ;)

Leila liked to be early for everything. But George Washington Carver Middle School didn't start for another fifteen minutes and it was only on the next block, which meant maybe a four-minute walk.

So Corey had time. And when he had time, his mind kicked into gear.